JOSHUA'S DREAM

BY THE SAME AUTHOR

Poems

The Blue Vale: Poems from Mallaig and Beyond
ISBN: 0-595-28913-4
Songs for Gillian: a Collection of Love Poetry
ISBN: 0-595-37851-X

Novels

Edge Of The Glen
(Under the pseudonym, Clifford Geddes)
ISBN: 0-595-23621-9

Troubled By Love
(Under the pseudonym, Piers Blake)
ISBN: 978-1-907294-53-2

Blogs

Calendar of Capture: A West Country Blog
ISBN: 978-1-78003-302-0

JOSHUA'S DREAM

MICHAEL LAMB

Matador
Unit E2 Airfield Business Park,
Harrison Road, Market Harborough,
Leicestershire. LE16 7UL
Tel: 0116 2792299
Email: books@troubador.co.uk
Web: www.troubador.co.uk/matador
Twitter: @matadorbooks

ISBN 978 1803132 686

British Library Cataloguing in Publication Data.
A catalogue record for this book is available from the British Library.

Printed and bound in Great Britain by 4edge Limited
Typeset in 11pt Minion pro by Troubador Publishing Ltd, Leicester, UK

Matador is an imprint of Troubador Publishing Ltd

In Memoriam
Peter Anthony MacPherson
(1971–2012)

A Note For The Curious Reader

This is the account of a terrestrial called Joshua who journeys in a continuum of time and space different to our own. In exploring a world comprising several lands and various times, he necessarily participates in experiences both paradoxical and challenging. During his travels he is addressed by particular persons who contest and debate his spiritual beliefs, else entertain different cultural or ethical ideas. Some of these discoursers are merely named, others are expanded upon to highlight their role within the plot itself.

Instanced in the second category is the occasional figure of Jacob. A curious reader may wonder whether scriptural allusions to Jacob and to Joshua may be significant, realising perhaps that the cognomen of Moses' disciple is allied to the appellative of Jesus – so, indicatory perhaps of a similar salvific, reconciliatory meaning; or, congruent with that, also investigate the legendary tale of Gen 32: 22–32, the mystical narrative recounting the patriarchal battle with an uncanny presence beheld as an angelic wrestler. To those familiar with the Judaeo-Christian tradition, such references may be difficult to resist. Again, an analogous outlook may be conjectured in relation to the characters, Tom and Pedram.

Nonetheless, the author wishes to make it clear that no kind of straightforward identification is intended. Indeed, the story in the round may be adjudged to take place *surreally* – independently of our familiar world: one enacted, that is, in a similar yet unknown sphere constituted within a multiverse. In such an imagined realm the protagonist on his journey may feel at times traumatically transported, peculiarly and illicitly abducted. Even the reader, perhaps, may not escape a kindred process, confronting conspicuous instances of diction regarded as arcane or archaic – discernibly disorientating, albeit serving as a metaphor for the instability implicit in man's migratory and competitive temperament.

If there be a primary or persistent motif to carry forward the progress of this tale, it will lie in the quandary as to whether or not an existence for the individual *beyond the moment of demise* remains a legitimate hope. Does entertaining this concept disclose a thinker's disinclination to adopt an adult mind, or, is it a recourse which our race ignores at its peril or likely diminishment? The imagined history of the pilgrim no more resolves such dilemmas than does it seek to be dogmatic rather than suggestive.

Michael Lamb
Bradninch
January, 2022

The Characters

Joshua: *The Man Who Might Be*

Solomon: *The Militant Atheist*

Rachel: *The Modern Feminist*

Jacob: *The Faithful Fighter*

The Awkins Of Celebros: including, The First Brother or *The Friendly Challenger, The Truly Silent One:* Ann-Gel and Zeltar

Pedram: *The Blunderer*

Tom: *The Cautious One*

Othias: *The Secular Atheist*

'L': *The Lady With The Long Neck*

Captain Bill/William: *The Curious Conniver*

Mothers to Elmer and to Joy: *Bubble* and *Squeak*

Store Promoter

Hairless Harry

Clive, Frances, Chelsea and Rory

Murdo: *The Old Soldier*

The Devil's Advocate

Twelve Religious Malcontents

Twelve Anarchists

Alberic: *The Holy One*

Rafael: *The Man Who Makes Pictures*

Hank: *The Man Who Watches*

An Unknown Youth

Male with Placard

Beautifully Named: *The Good Mother*

Peter Anthony: *Artsman Of The Croft*

A Modern Young Man

A Girl and Her Mother

Ebenezer: *The Helpful Verger*

The Gravedigger

The Twelve: Tobias, Morwenna, Sebastian, Martha and Mary, Joseph and Stephen, Morag, Clifford and Elspeth, Sophie and Gerard

The Staff: Matron, Thora, Rodney, and an Unfamiliar Attendant

THE SEQUENCE

THE TELLING

Part the First: *in which a philosophical Joshua talks to* The Militant Atheist, *dances with* The Modern Feminist, *and is obliged to flee from a black hound.*

> *Drifts of gold,*
> *Trails of topaz,*
> *Saffron with tan*
> *Desert with dun:*
>
> *All now succumb*
> *To an ashen*
> *Fall – drained become*
> *Of colours all:*
>
> *Lose liminal*
> *Lustre to night's*
> *Pall. Thence to*
> *Heaven's lucent rule.*

(An introductory *Fragment* to *The Final Vision*, ascribed to Yannis, epicist and seer of Patmos, first century.)

Alone wanderer, fathoming the path ahead, tires at last of his diurnal trudge and plods lumberingly to a sudden halt. Contentedly, he directs his gaze to the far-flung vaulted skies, a pitch-blue world abrim and ablaze with a myriad of stars. Countless be the distant suns he sees: glinting like jewels, glistening within gyres – tokens of a measureless beyond, of the enigmatic unknown.

The itinerant in his quest but partly comprehends the reality that time's parameters flex, the lineaments of space change and shift. What he observes is not what it seems. Ancient fires blazon their yore into the brightness of today's world: their light of old piercing the present.

Whence by a spell the solitary trekker is held: seized by stellar, spiralling displays; by luminous nebular networks of moons and comets, meteors and planets. Of the last, his tribal lineage has its genesis in one denominated – in the parlance of its dwellers – *Terra Firma*. Though conceding his roots within it, his questioning and awe-struck eyes look far and wide in wonder and curiosity. Numbering that aggregate, scintillating in the blue-black above, an erudite mathematician must presume a gargantuan sum. Moreover, discerning the commencement of consciousness, the years heralding its origin and ensuing advance must assuredly be considerable – a multiple in truth of billions, the sheer enormity of its span too humbling to comprehend.

His family, it is small, his town provincial. Time and again, however, his companions and followers see within his intelligence the hallmarks of wisdom. Notable besides is his critical readiness to exemplify empathy as well as his recognition of the signal role of paradox in the making-sense of experience; thereafter, moreover, with the formulation of dogma: allowing that opposites at times complement as well as oppose – prime integrants, as it were, greater or tangential of the total truth, surpassing both compromise and a middle way.

Evaluated commonly, however – viewed historically within an unfolding of millennia – a predicant, even if celebrated, comprises but a gossamer-thread, a wisp of grass in an acre of green; amidst a squall of rain, a mere drib or drop. Hap the hour, evidentially, spirit expires, flesh decays. Then, too, olden bones splinter, fissure; break. Else, perchance, close to the pyre, remnant-ash bestrews runaway wind or the river's wave. Sentient-self removed becomes. Selfhood, where could it persist? Unto which exotic entity might it be re-aligned? Else crucial cord of memory be yet maintained? Mustn't it hereafter become undone: fostering novel engagement, realising an alternate dimension?

Albeit the hour is quiet, yet, in the lull of the silence there is sound, amid the stillness there is action. Audible, noises here a riotous, desperate beast savaging a competitor in the brutal endeavour of existence: a ravening animal in a decisive scuffle over loin and rib – extirpating another; battling essentially and merely to live. What's more, similarly terrestrial by nature, perforce he too travails to endure, endeavour against the odds to *make it*. Procreate. Profit. Pass on down. Realise conscientiously a creative urge: mayhap, paint upon a wall, pluck a string, sing a song. Even so, labouring done, still the purportedly random scythe cuts, strips, lays bare and void. Perceptibly, love itself as good as gone. Therefore, again, barely a footfall outwith the heft and thud of multiple variants of animated life.

What then, said-beholder queries, could obtain *out there* within the silver-studded sphere, aloft and beyond? Enhancement? Commination?

Association? Surreally, indeed, a few were warning that alien reifications of terrestrial sentience could also be found. Statistically credible, opined respected, sagacious men. Equally, surely all would die? Again, among such beings, myriads might share in heinous and noxious deeds, initiate pain purely for delight. Kindred psychopathy occurs among his own, he is constrained (dispiritingly) to admit. Over and over, so much weakness; so much poison. A figurative snake writhing and arching in the conscious mind.

Admittedly saddened, he nonetheless permits the distant, supernal parade – exhibiting its blazing, cold-white fires – to mitigate despondency, now uplifting his arms in obeisance to the wonderment, glittering and pavilioned above. To that nocturnal grandiloquence (a quietude almost crepitant) the hallower commences his heartfelt prayer.

'*Heavenly Father, our Source and Trusted End, may you be revered above all that is. May what you desire attain its fruition; assuredly in times to come, as well as in this era besides. Have mercy upon us in our neediness, meeting our weakness and wrongdoing with compassion and forbearance. Assess us in truth as we strive to become. Help us to decry the unkind: endeavouring neither to call forth evil upon others, nor to be troubled by the allure of its dominion.*'

As he lowers his arms, the tiring supplicant – soteriologically, perspicaciously identified as Joshua – forges faithfully to the latest inklings of light betokening the dawn: ineludibly benumbed by the rawness of the hour, still, the rigours of the inhospitable terrain continue evidentially. The committed walker picks up his pace. Of a sudden – surely, withal, as though from nowhere – a vehement behest detains him, adjuring him to desist, verily in the tramp and stomp, the tread of his tracks.

'Listen, you there, ease up a bit! I've a query, compelling to broach.'

Coming to a halt, turning quickly, he descries a spectral personage coming hastily towards him. A chilling quality encompasses the moment. Most daunting then does it feel to trust a person not known: verily, as the stranger solidifies in the liminal domain between light and dark.

Howbeit, this sharer of shadow and sand transpires to be a big specimen of bearded bonhomie. Anxiety seems out of place.

'On the other hand' – the inquiring individual observes, incongruously, letting up on his stride – 'dialogue properly a while should wait. Follow me to where I'm camped. Acknowledging the morn's chill, with laggardly light, I think let's an hour cease our fast afore enduring the sun. Confront not the day harbouring an empty stomach!'

Close to some nearby ridge, anon the itinerant settles cross-legged in a marquee-of-a-shelter, appreciative of the humble fire at its heart; as, too, the pronounced aroma of dark coffee pleasurably assailing his nostrils, provoking his appetite. Summarily, a modest receptacle is handed him of the aromatic, suitably-warming potation diminishing the remnants of the cold, inspiriting positivity within. Descrying the celerity with which his benefactor devours a fistful of bread, he too desists not-at-all in assuaging his hunger.

A veritable sense of relief befalls both. Finally, the courteous host challenges Joshua, asking him without demur: 'Advise me, what were you doing when I saw you?'

'Doing? I'd finished praying, whereupon I'd begun again my journey, only at once then to hear your call to cease my advance. Shouldn't you divulge your name? Who are you?'

'Me?' answered the interlocutor. 'People refer to me as, *The Militant Atheist*, which is who and what I am. Believe, yes I did, that you'd most likely been praying. Palavering before the skies: soliciting them, a trifle bizarrely, as being heavenly *and* terrestrial. Predictably, I consider you to be wrong. No more does God exist, objectively-speaking, than does a material Heaven exist: albeit, copious heavenly forms there be; an alluring instance of which you'll no doubt concur has evolved uncommonly well, being beauteously endowed. Even so, she is currently asleep! *Scilicet* – you'll have to wait to see her!'

A grin of gaiety broke the host's features into a series of wrinkles. A stentorious guffaw emanated from his toothy mouth.

'Decidedly,' endorsed Joshua, 'if a person sees in Heaven some zone beyond the stars, analogous to *Terra Firma* albeit with a nimiety of home-comforts continually on tap – mayhap a paradigm of which parallels the woman you commend. To whom I intend, by the by, no discourtesy. Should Heaven, even so, really have to be equated with an especial locale, infinitely removed, outwith our continuum and antagonistic to the hypothesis of optimum selection? Mayn't it be some dimension sympathetic to an evolving nature, howbeit beyond its thrall?'

'*Mirabile dictu*! You uphold the theory of evolution! Forbye, have a sense of humour! Excellent! Even so, clarify this peculiar *dimension*.'

'Divers learned men of the orient,' the dialectician began, 'acknowledge that our universe is made up of many worlds, many withal as yet neither sighted nor known. Genera obtain and variations in biological life which, again, our species fails properly to discern or as yet comprehend.

Demonstrably, this macrocosm incorporates and demonstrates mystery and paradox. What's more, our observations and deductions, they are, of their nature, perforce received. We decidedly inhabit a cosmic process our species did not invent – rather, a gargantuan system exists in which we realise we have being and consciousness. Egregiously, when we fail to give to this matter enough paramountcy, we eschew legitimacy, think awry, inexorably go astray. Say any of us should've stood – without sight, faculty of recall, sentience or wit – veritably at the very genesis of time, apprehending just a nihility of potential, would we ourselves consciously have brought to birth of all of this?' Joshua waved his arm expansively, incorporating thereby the circularity of the tent, but, by implication, the surround of the globe and beyond-ness too. 'Who knows what attendant, consequent marvels there may be?'

'Indeed, indeed,' nodded the other. 'There are countless occasions for astonishment.'

The desert-host rendered afresh his gallipot of liquid to the flamy heat, commenting, 'Besides, I perceive naught to reveal how any Superior Being, obtaining eccentrically, should be regarded as terrestrial – irregardless of *fatherly*.'

Perceptibly, there here materialised, shrouded within a parting fold tucked within the tall canvas wall, a noticeable rustle. A slim and nubile girl stepped forth, clothed provocatively in diaphanous veils, intriguingly banded beneath with two cinctures of silvery material.

'Ah! Well there you are, oh daughter of mine! All the while listening! I'd before assumed you to be asleep!' Turning to his guest, *The Militant Atheist* declared, laughingly, 'Young man, here she is. Think you not, as well, she is undeniably lovely? This is – for all my paternal bias – the aforesaid *supramundane* form to which I alluded. Recognise, nonetheless, she is not my woman but my offspring!'

Joshua was inclined to agree that the unusually lithe creature, coming over to him in a lissom, lilting gait, preferring to lean close to the crook of his leg, was most decidedly of exquisite loveliness. Even so, opening her mouth to venture criticism her eyes were afire and her tone was harsh.

'Well suppose my father is as he defines, I myself, equivalently, am *The Modern Feminist*. How is it you surmise there to be a *Grand Being* alike male and patriarchal, who – as far as we know – comprehends equivalent faults and abuses to those portrayed in our indigenous fatherhood?' Demanding so, she inflicted a covert squinny in the direction of the older man. 'Suppose indeed there be a God, with a capital *g*, cannot *she* be a female, a mother, a matriarch?'

Lonesome theist, the apostle was silent – perturbed by the outrage exhibited by such a beautiful woman. Joshua studied her for several seconds, then endeavoured his reply.

'Perforce, our theologians employ anthro-pomorphisms, the easier to enunciate upon God – though generally viewed as man rather than woman – picturing the deity akin to ourselves. In sooth, such language is metaphorical. To desist from this linguistic register, however, would be to disallow any numinous colloquy, inhibiting thereby the desire to achieve intimacy with an entity beyond our terrestrial kind. Consonant with this, let us say that the *Ineffable Being* – thought of as within terrestrial form, devotees being termed children; sons and daughters, even of God – would best be perceived in terms of some empathetic, parental figure. Even so, I'm confronted by yourself as to the gender of the metaphor. Phrase it this way: the extramundane Father relates and behaves dissimilarly to any tyrannical opponent or cruel dictator – the beneficent aspect of his nature finally prevailing, withal his forgiveness forever applicable, his sempiternal love expansive as the ocean is vast. Assuredly, I might just as well say of him that he is a most *Motherly Father*. Equally, there are disciples who tell of a Lady of Grace. Such pious followers speak of a maiden whose name translates, *beloved*; a highly-favoured woman called Miriam, in some way supposed to have been "lifted up" (or again, *assumed*) phenomenally – even unto the orbit of the moon and the twelve suns – whom copious souls still cherish for being a charitable access to the Divine Mind.'

Here, the wild wraith of woman kissed her companion on his knee, conceding a smile.

'Admittedly, you evince a certain wisdom. Natheless, teachings maintaining her ongoing virginity I vigorously contest. Those who tell of Miriam oft-times iterate that she never truly loved. Precisely, that she never exhibited full intimacy; i.e., committing to a man in a variety of ways, including sexual.'

'Aha, daughter of mine, certainly you are in mischievous mood!'

Unsurprisingly, it was *The Militant Atheist* who had interrupted. He scowled at his all-too grown-up, plain-spoken girl.

And she – she leapt to her feet, tore away a veil, forbye without further ado blatantly began to dance; verily, her stripped belly absorbing the light of the flames betraying her skin a gilden hue, bestowing a moist glow to her intoxicating mold, moving itself like a flame, this way that way – undulating up, down, oscillating her swaying hips, here there.

Curling thereat brusquely aside from the pilgrim (already dismayed at being teased, taunted, even denied) the wily creature skipped to the corner of a handsome chest (all-crafted in battered metal) that lured to its façade the burnishing of the ever-present fire. Over this bolted, antique trunk, elegantly stood an ivory-edged mirror within which now o'er-flew the fiery likeness of the feminist protestor; whilst the latter (beholding herself fleetingly keeking back) wildly laughed a crazy, joyous laugh, tossing her head in blithesome, exuberant fashion.

Spryly hereupon she reeled about, anon upon her feet tip-toe – agilely-arched across the ripplets of sand – luringly to hold forth to Joshua each hand in a signal of invitation.

'Come!' she cried. 'You will dance with me!'

Before he'd had time to decide, the analytical guest found his wrist gripped, then his figure compelled to rise, the heft of him up, now his hands constrained, his body haled-hard to hers in a spinning motion that wound round and round, gloriously, all-athwart the living gold at the shelter's heart.

The bronzed girl then led the pair (the air itself charged and shimmering) through a wild curve, traversing the shining coffer with fulgent and ample mirror set thereon. Peculiarly, whilst rollicking with the other about the duplicate domain, disquietingly her neophyte athwart the screen was not to be seen. Nowhere, nowhere, nowhere therein.

Immediately the host – espying his guest, surreally nowhere at all within the flickering replicas beheld in the refulgent screen – to his feet uprose, forbye of a sudden seizing, then yanking at a free, ravelling chain visibly conjoined to an animal, heavily-breathing, all hunched in readiness outwith the layered cushions and rugs, amassed in a pile before the canvas escape. Hurriedly was then there uplifted from the dim shadows a pure abomination-of-a-beast, sheer-sabled (even as a night-sky without stars) massive and mighty of jowl. Catching at a cudgel thereat, *The Militant Atheist* roared at the half-seduced wide-eyed man.

'Be gone, be gone, whoever you are. You bedevil my hospitality with your unholy art.' To his daughter he yelled, 'Rachel, Rachel (*forfeiting her name*) oh can you not behold, look – mirroring there be not to the incomer you've lured via the glamour of your dance. Let him go, let him go! At once!'

No sooner had the girl's father spoken than a flurry of air, a zephyr-like breeze occasioned a flimsy wallop about the fly of the sizeable, tented abode. Straightaway, the outcast lunged, tittupped towards it, sprinting from the girl and her father – with the coal-black hound angrily-growling from the taut chain's end, the itinerant now hieing as fast as he could.

Natheless, he failed to bestir himself nimbly enough. Anon, anon was he hearkening, audibly, to the padding of those canine feet upon the sand, while direfully sentient to the abominable pant and pant of doggish breath. Closer. Closer. The sun, too, it was beating upon his back. The runagate's habit clung in sweat to his skin. His lungs tore as though they would burst.

So he stopped. And turned. And stood, perfectly calm. His inner poise was entire, his worriment at an end; his discomposure gone. He eyed the rippling muscles, the flesh of flanks and underbelly too, the animal's open jaws, the limbs that quivered as the creature reared – reared above its prey to fall, fall heavily upon him in his unbearable calm.

Then all was black, an instant unfathomable void of black.

Part the Second: *in which Joshua discovers a partially sighted man, becomes abducted by aliens, and endures complex mind-invasion and prejudicial debate.*

Yet, the one who turned to confront the mystery of oblivion awoke to existence, alive again. However, Joshua now felt insecure and hotter than hitherto, his visage overlaid by an unfamiliar beard, and his hair ragged and withal bothersomely long. Moreover, though evidently immersed earlier in a profound repose, he remained thoroughly fatigued: a weariness of existence was pressing upon him. He realised within his mind that consciously he was philosophising upon exceptional dimensions: because, when earlier he had twirled, swung, hopped with the young woman, Rachel – such was the name the atheist had bellowed at his daughter – he'd surmised that he was (to phrase it thus) in another realm: a novel domain of near delirium; of inner intimations of rapturous intimacy, pleasuring as if in a womb of bliss; a milieu in which ecstasy be safe, albeit given to alteration or cessation. Mightn't there, therefore, be spheres, worlds, dimensions surpassing the known?

Similarly, a poser came to him uttered out loud: 'Does the lion and the robin, the starfish and the long-legs realise the drift of time always the same?' And yet, and yet, quietly again, he became wary of inferring principle from analogy – some comparability of this with that. Viable as such a coupling could at first appear, nevertheless, *this* was not *that*, and *that* was not *this*. True, a consonance there could be, singular or no: albeit not enough to be denoted an unalloyed parallel, as withal the favoured contiguity would not then be required. His very mind was, admittedly, by now nigh effete; his focus blurred, close to envelopment by convoluted rumination. So he smiled. Notwithstanding, almost immediately he looked stern. The steadily-sinking star was dipping to the horizon.

Then it was that he fell. To be exact, a bristly shank – jutting from a partly-obscured crop-of-rock – toppled him, forthwith tumbling him toward the almost-certainty of swearing an oath – which nonetheless he avoided, seeing straightway another desert-soul sitting up, both legs out, evidencing a canny wise about him of not inconsiderable glee.

'I do beg your pardon, stranger,' the latter wryly confessed. 'Although – and, as a matter of fact – it is really you who should be begging mine! My ability to see the world has become greatly curtailed; so – questionable in truth it may appear – you may as well be some arboreous terrestrial ambulating within the drearisome gloom! My name is *Jacob*. Stay with me, please, whilst I proffer a rationale for the unsought accolade I've obtained – yes indeed, *The Faithful Fighter!*'

Joshua leant against the conspiratorial rock, attacked of a sudden by an involuntary cough, caused by a violent gust of arid air driving now a flurry of grain from a sand-crested billow. Then he spat vigorously. As did the sedentary one beside him. The former then observed (*being predictably again entirely alert*):

'May we ignore who's at fault? My name is Joshua. Concerning whether or not you are dedicated – and to whom – I cannot say. Even so, your visible comportment is not that of an active fighter.'

'Ah well, advise me, Joshua, all in all, how *do* I appear?'

The keen-sighted pilgrim at once regretted his forthright remark. He wanted now, however, to honour this nomad-of-the-void with an openly candid reply.

'You may be compared, at least in your appearance, to a middle-aged person positively revelling in thick grey hair and a stupendous, anarchic beard, one beflecked with ebony; whilst boasting besides the sharp-furrowed mien of a man that's travailed and toiled, weathered copious years barely shielded beneath the glare of the sun. Briefly, Jacob, you could own to having a *lived-in* appearance, together with a complexion rather rivelled – perchance indicatory of calamity or hazard.'

'That bad, eh, and not yet twenty-five!' roared *The Faithful Fighter*, emitting then a boisterous cackle and going on to approve: 'Decidedly, what you observe fits the picture well enough. Anyhow, I've ideal reason to appear as I do, more or less having survived three years cooped-up and half-starved in a forsaken pound. There I was (and more than once) tortured by sadistic guards who abused me – who struck, spat, and jeered – who drank too much – urinating on their victim and laughing to boot. I endured months – who knows how many – cribbed below ground in utter darkness. One night, unexpectedly, I felt an immense explosion. All about me the earth trembled, whilst then, beyond the powdery rubble and suffocating dust, rescuing, searching hands dove down determinedly to haul me back to life – or, whatever of my life remained. Nigh paradoxically, I was (albeit in a loathly way) *baptised*: even, peradventure, *blest*. You see, I had actually been able to finger, properly touch, there in that interning tomb, sundered skulls and skeletonised left-overs of earlier prisoners, yes, their very bones – their bits and tatters of shredded clothing. Men had dwindled and died in that stinking pit. Most like, too, those same bricken, rubbly surrounds were bloodied by nail-less fingers. Furthermore, I myself – notwithstanding being also a dissident – was the possessor of knowledge my rancorous inquisitors might've utilised to their tactical advantage.'

'Genuinely, Jacob, I grieve to hear of such horrors; regardless of how we have chanced but now, each upon the other – and you (brazenly!) properly thrown me to the floor of this desert-heap!' Now-sympathetic, Joshua countenanced an ironic grin. Gradually, he inquired: 'Did they – withal, I ask respectfully – bully, beat and badger you so as to disclose particulars that could've effected detriment to your cousins or compatriots?'

'Yes, Joshua,' responded the acutely-myopic survivor. 'Incidental details, I'd have preferred not to have admitted, in the end I divulged. Besides, oft-times I lied, perverting the truth. Never, howbeit, in all that while did I spurn or betray my belief in God – even supposing my captors worked hard to make me lose hope or mind or heart, typically insisting how no-one would know if I were to expire, else be bothered at all, or bethink themselves of my life in years to come. Egregiously, there in that boarded hollow – and to forbear from gross self-pity and feebleness of mind – did I have recourse to harassing the Almighty. Yes, verily, I sounded off my protest; argued; bawled like a child: veritably, even as though our ruthful and revered divinity be of a propensity as I must derive no mercy from, rather, was of a kind I'd confusedly to lash-out against.'

'I am confident,' advised the philosopher: 'God comprehended your wilderment and despair.'

'I suppose that's right – I mean, to use that word – *despair*. No more could I sustain my hope for an ultimate release or regimen less severe. I believed in God; albeit the salve of this godhead hampered my proficiency to fathom or find serenity thereby. Moreover, I disputed whether the Almighty was all-mighty at all: yes, in sooth, whether this omnipotent entity be somehow impeded by a clay heart, ignored a restraint on proper liberty. Admittedly, I survived. Even so, the cost was high.'

'You are, veritably, a *Faithful Fighter*. Evidently, a taxonomy of reasons obtain, paradoxically, to preclude the *Divine Benignity* from debarring misery and calamity in our fragile lives. Undeniably, any *Initiator* that quickens my being ought not to be indifferent to our terrestrial travail. I infer, primarily, that our God, whilst other than yourself, genuinely languished and endured in that grave, invisibly, alongside of you. In you, fundamentally, at the very core.'

The listener nodded: 'That perspective, it engenders a certain appeal, perhaps hope, harbouring most like a wellspring of compassion. We've survived alike – God and I. *In extremis*, I'd cerebrated if it could've been the very idea of God with which I wrestled more than this ruined world. Now, of course I'd better let-up – well, just a little! Let's entreat, however, that neither you nor I be tried or put to the test beyond our endurance. If we so brook or bear more, endeavour then we must to maintain our hope in *Love Manifest* to implement purposeful recompense.'

Hereupon, the analyst's ability properly to keep up tailed off. Signally, he was conscious now of a traveller's holdall, visibly pendant below his right shoulder. Finding as well its opening flap, he unfolded same and alighted upon what (benumbingly) he knew would be there: a large pomegranate, some figs, and an ampulla of water. Withdrawing from a side-pocket an edged and silver bodkin, thereupon he stove in two the multi-seeded fruit – albeit having first passed-over his water-flagon to quench the other's thirst.

'There's fruit, besides. Assuredly, Jacob, it behoves us to take care of ourselves. Undeniably, I'm feeling thirsty beyond measure.'

'Joshua, some day I shall honour you similarly. Thank you.'

Jacob planted his teeth into the shell's pulpy interior, having already returned to his new acquaintance the weight of water minus a modest draught imbibed.

Shortly, and out of polite interest, he remarked, 'Where are you making for, Joshua?'

'Coincidentally, I'm trying myself to decide. I think for the coast.'

'Fear not,' asserted the other. 'You are journeying in the right direction. My own route is different. Anyhow, I need to warn you: avoid the unwonted abode of lights – the circular abode, of pink and yellow and singularly-white lights – the panoply of which ere today a lonesome herder of camels disclosed he'd seen but a few ridges widdershins of where he then camped.'

'Surprising indeed,' noted Joshua. 'For sure, I'll keep my eyes open – albeit (with sorrow besides) to better effect than your own. Wholeheartedly, I wish you well. I pray indeed that the *Merciful God* be minded and empowered towards you to be more mildly disposed, verily as we venture our separate ways. Pray, take good care *Faithful Fighter*!'

A solicitous Joshua then rose to his feet, wrapping in his arms the almost-blind man, who, stotting a little, stoically steadied himself to continue his exigent, meandering peregrination. The seer of the two, similarly inspirited, here assumed afresh his overdue footfall, readily aiming for an approachable reach of coastline, surrendering his gaze to a point far-removed, all about which liveningly bestirred a mild wind indicative of a wide-open sea, of waves for miles, of an ocean of fish and craft, and a towering sky with sea-birds soaring and diving. A locale full of promise, brimming with salt and savour.

Increasingly now, as he tramped doggedly across a nigh-vertical dune, a feeling welled-up of emotional disjuncture, palpable as it were of some actual loss. Even though, alas, he'd not delighted in Jacob's company for very long; still, there remained enough about the demeanour discernibly displayed, along with the brief history also revealed, that'd anon engendered within his heart a heavier mood – in his mind a ruminative unease. Again, he was being asked to cerebrate upon the direful, loathsome tactics by which various individuals had necessarily to suffer. Typically, again and again and again.

Forbye, he'd once listened (seemingly) to a narrative about a dissident missionary gruesomely nailed to two beams of wood, limbs of a tree deliberately crossed-over, as an upturned anchor, so curiously contrived had they been. The pensile body had still lived and breathed, clamoured a while, until piteously a quiet had befallen declaratory of death. Following burial, the corpse was posited surreally to have belonged to a person so good – so righteous and true in his judgement of others – amen, that should God ever take upon God's self a true terrestrial-form, it'd indeed be in just such a similarly-sapient and beneficent apostle. Some deep apprehension of injustice, therefore, shortly acquired significant hold. Goodness, sagacity, openness: all'd proved insufficient to escape the overt barbarity, the evident cruelty. What's more, myriads in time challenged whether so terrible an outcome could conclusively obtain. Vitally, could God – notwithstanding the reason – condone such an end? If forsooth there be a God. Further, if properly there be, mustn't that deiform *Presence* be vulnerable as well as powerful? Even as he'd adduced earlier before Jacob: should not the *Merciful God*, in suffering in parallel, have been animate in the preacher who'd been lifted, outstretched? Again, like God would've endured too with those in the hole who had died. And, similarly, as God must've suffered – surely been at one, truly with his friend?

Finally, he'd then recalled how the maverick-elevated (his arms upraised, without) was later descried through the revelatory-lens of self-offering: a unique witness surrendered to make his people worthier in God's eyes. His amenability to God had been understood as a vehicle for divine being and benignity. Thereafter, the ersatz, sacrificial-lamb had been recognised in images of the spring-lamb; the lamb of innovative life; the lamb at play upon green pastures, joyfully gambolling, else recumbent and calm under an oasis-shade. But, to be sure, the Lamb of God.

Thus there came to be expressed a tenet, later to be preached: *Dolorously suffers God within the pain and wrongdoing of our terrestrial kind.*

So Joshua concluded, with feet, calves, body aching – confronting the rick, the tensity of the footslogger.

At the top of a particularly high crest of ashen sand (to be attained for his singular venture to continue) the messenger abated his progress awhile to take in a curiosity – a phantastry beckoning beneath the luminous sapphire of night's fall: an abode it was, a circular abode of lights; some pink, some yellow, some white – its fullness vibrant and orbicular, giving off a peculiar leakage of misplaced or crooked energy, adumbrating a life unnerving and better left behind. Only, the peregrinator – he must go forward.

Howbeit, miserably, of a sudden he was knocked to the ground. Enfeebled, the pilgrim sank his head between his knees, energy spent, respiration abruptly cut-short. Incongruously, now he noticed that the lobe to his left ear was mysteriously gone; again, how between wrist and elbow, his dextral arm was badly scarred. The terrestrial shuddered. His destiny, natheless, should not be ignored. Then, even as he confronted the burthen of his calling, a radial shaft spread forth from the abode sending a dazzling glare so vast – forwarded so far – that it clearly o'er-lapped his curviform figure. Perceptibly, said place evinced an ultra-worldly air; one alien, yet more proximate than far. And, as the curled line of light consumed the length of Joshua's folded form, it straightaway upraised him internally to its heart, its coloured, shimmering corpus.

Nothing but a breeze remained to disturb the sandy summit that lay below the violet-ebony sky, an empyrean locale wherein spangled the first bright star, alone, lost it might have been in that vast etheric-ocean of star-seed materialising diminutively, albeit materialising markedly, bestowing on the brightest another variant of solitariness and uniqueness of being. A star above. An emptiness below, where once Joshua had dwelt.

* * * * * *

The subsumed philosopher was himself now accumbent at an annular table wholly contrived (or so it appeared) of polished glass. He was, to boot, restively-sitting in the surreal, elite society of five creatures of alien origin. These last exhibited enough of the typical and everyday to facilitate a man's sanity, albeit sufficient of the unfamiliar to prompt alarm. Their smartish green-and-white arrowed uniforms were ultimately of less interest than the fact that none of them had any hair of any kind; and, withal, their globular organs for seeing were placed farther apart than what is familiar, besides seeming notably broader, arching more noticeably over the prominent roofs of their cheeks: wider, even if not communicating an impression of elongation, in that both were positioned higher whilst involving the quality of being larger overall. The tightness of what they wore served to evidence gender, apart from peculiarities in composure as well as behaviour.

Of these personages, one, a male, pronounced in a sing-song voice, declaring of them all: 'We are the *Awkins* of *Celebros*. My popular honorific is, *The Friendly Challenger*.'

The same individual continued. 'Contrary to what your new friend has been implying, we have no quarrel with you, your species, or indeed your planet's organisms as a whole. We mean you no harm. Which brings me to my first point. How does that incline you to feel: expressly, given your sense of accord and association with the terrestrial you were earlier addressing? Really, his thoughts about us, the crew here, indeed the race as a whole are totally incorrect. And, if all in all they can be so unreliable, well, possibly his ontology, his grasp of direction in life, and his reliance on a Transcending Entity, assuredly may be unfounded too. I must ask (for the sake of the argument, and in deference to us) that you actually avow this fact: which is to say, we intend you no harm, no hurt.'

The terrestrial stayed silent. His challenger continued.

'Oh, I'm aware you are weighing up, how, whilst we may not wish for you anything unfavourable, we may not, contrariwise, intend for you anything agreeable. Discernibly, an intelligible trepidation. After all, one ought to concur that an ideal or optimum time might exist for receiving specific data with respect to life, its drawbacks, its checks and restraints.'

Straightaway a female *Awkin* spoke up. 'Don't be alarmed; albeit, yes, we're capable of reading your thoughts. Moreover, likely-enough there will betide an era when your discrete, indigenous planetary-kind (through the same token) will be proficient enough to read and interpret understanding in all of its citizens. Devices you terrestrials refer to as *computers* ought, ultimately, to be able to comprehend links to the neural interconnections inside of the brain. As a corollary, all recorded facts will (with a properly trained mindset) be open to summoning, but, so too – sufficient time allowed – spontaneous thoughts and deliberation. In truth, unbeknown to you, your up-to-date cerebrum was subjected to a total scanning upon admission, when, too, our own cerebral template was temporarily introduced to your brain, a subtle intervention triggering no damage. Forgive us, please; forasmuch as we cannot now recommend any reciprocity. The advantages are all one way. Our way. We believe it is for the best.'

'Thank you, Ann-Gel,' spoke *The Friendly Challenger*. 'You see, even within alien mores, any hiatus in rapport may be picked up and dealt with by another. Although, don't infer that it is chiefly the female who does so! Howbeit, returning to my point: of course you'll be curious to know, directly, what's motivated us to bring you here. Primarily, it's to facilitate pursuing you apropos certain ideas arising from your concept of God; the innumerous ways they manipulate your popular outlook upon life – or, to be more particular, a perceived *afterlife*. We jettisoned such delusions four centuries ago. Now we are excited to know if you terrestrials shall follow suit. Natheless, you yourself appear to insist upon being irretrievably stubborn. You have, for all that, your peers in this respect: markedly, even now that purblind, bearded-one with whom you were discoursing.'

The cogitator chose then to ask a question. 'Is it all right for me to imbibe what is in this glass receptacle? (*Before him stood a goblet of an unusual potable.*) Rarely do we drink libations of such colour – not this electric, iridescent blue. Please advise me if I may do so with safety.'

'Of course, of course. Doubtless it will remind you of a somewhat superior honey – in this case, employing specially-farmed particular bees – further and sublimely flavoured with damson essence, giving to it a distinctive tang. Thus, it is not only mellifluent to consume, since it is also effective in quenching thirst.'

'You are right; it is indeed delicious,' volunteered the guest, sipping with relish from the lucent if modest chalice. 'Withal, I've an idea even the dullard, gullible Jacob would appreciate it.'

'Oh, come now, Joshua, you exaggerate; I did not depict him so! Irregardless, I can see how we may appear a trifle condescending, even presumptuous, in envisaging terrestrials the way we do. Nonetheless, bear with us, as I'm proposing to broach but three questions, all associated with the striking supposition of an *afterlife*. In essence, they are connected to the uncertainties of number, time, and process.'

Joshua squirmed, imagining he'd maybe not perform very well, despite the serious nature of the topic.

'Initially, I need to show you something. Now, Ann-Gel, would you on my behalf please supervise the screen, since it's impolite to invade our visitor's mind with more *Awkin* technology than is required.'

As Ann-Gel picked up a thin device from the round table, her womanliness was elegantly and sensually given shape within the tugging and stretching of her official garment. Joshua experienced then some abashment, being cognisant fully how he had regard for her feminine winsomeness as well as how such an ancillary detail would not at all be overlooked by his hosts. Notwithstanding, he considered it expedient to afford them his ongoing trust – after all, he supposed he had little choice. The alluring creature pointed the instrument at a sizeable screen (disposed about a glass-furnished top) affixed alongside a technical backdrop with several buttons on either side; buttons which, conceivably, were rarely required, granted simple intention itself could effectuate with active and substantive potency.

In the eye of this curiosity a small black dot drew the observer's attention. This grew as the seconds passed, opening larger and larger, suffusing the monitor to the degree that it was virtually blank. Virtually. But not quite. There was movement within the blackness. In due course, various forms could be made out. These spectral contours took on the appearance of inhabitants, possibly of the *Awkin* world (albeit vested in brown) and marching by the thousands into a serried configuration of conflict and war. The not inconspicuous display comprised a combat-area full of slaughter and carnage: one replete with bodies now felled, ripped and split – forbye, even of blood exuding, slopping in pools – with mouths roundly aghast with a ghostly but evocative silence; remnant-flesh being blasted and scraped, in extremis devoured or pulverised – unto the letter, to dust itself.

The visitor stood up. 'Enough! What is your question?'

'Sit down, Joshua, sit down. Direful to witness, yes. Even so, I'd surely to let you view such harrowing images to be sure you'd weigh-up my questions properly. If life-lived isn't pictured in the raw, then the hard rub of it fails to strike home. Typically, we let ourselves off the hook, yielding to the familiar and the parochial. Instance yourself: finding you are in an environment of a few hundred – percase a thousand-and-a-score inside of the promoted season – suddenly confronted with a citizen dying, how inspiriting to offer solace in declaring an innovatory existence. Mightn't such a continuation be permitted? Mindful of the trillions of stars, a meagre thousand deceased to inherit life again – even; well, a myriad more: half a million – really should seem timely and reasonable. Unsurprisingly, as a corollary, the gullible regress towards a state of comfortable presumption, ignorant of any analyst or guru directed to challenge such a scenario.'

The Friendly Challenger sighed, smiled, and recommenced.

'But, within the archive here-broadcast has been documented a war-scenario that saw the death of 50,000 men-at-arms in one day. Further, kindred past malefactions could be summoned from across time's continuum in innumerable different cultures, not to say divers levels of racial and evolutionary progress. Still, no; never mind any or all of them!'

The insistent *Awkin* here chortled out loud, as if such a possibility was redundant and absurd: the matter it entertained should be self-evident, requiring no further vindication. With alacrity he continued: 'What then of all the others? What of all the residents of your planetary world across all the ages that have ever been, else still in sooth to come? What, moreover, of all the other variant, co-existing life-forms? Ultimately, Joshua, you're surely not discounting from your reckoning the entirety of every other animal that's outwith your specific species? As though (forsooth) every indigene is so obnoxious compared to yourselves that they must, willy-nilly, expire at their death in a terminus unknown to you as *Terrestrials* – you who are privileged, singularly, to constitute a *chosen people* (to borrow the phrase): and, as well, that all the parenting and daring and struggles and heroic deeds and humorous charms of all of them, following the development of life on the globe, ought purely to be *snuffed out* – whereas, the peculiar set of *Terrestrials* are to endure? Really?'

After a pause to take breath, the disputant went on: 'Therefore, my concern is a basic one. Where, oh my sincere but gullible friend, have you it in mind to harbour all of those *souls* (alas, for want of a more precise word; and, when does one ever hear it judiciously defined?) – as I say – *souls*? What planet or realm would you have them inhabit – in their billions and trillions – never mind to what end? Anyhow, let's stay with the numbers. Is it really a credible picture – even to you?'

The one impugned let his shoulders fall. Swiftly though he drew himself up. To indicate poise was not to be guilty of hubris: rather, to signal tenacity in the face of opposition. He considered he'd need to espouse truth and good faith – else all was lost.

'As your argument stands, I believe I must concur with your dubiety. Such a depiction of an afterlife seems inconceivable. Indubitably, it strikes the rational mind as preposterous. Please, you may as well go on to your second conundrum.'

'Mayhap, the temptation now,' the other continued, 'is to build up ammunition going forward in the debate, totally conceding in the interim. Fair enough, I'll proceed to the next stage; namely, the duration and consequences of time – oh, permit me by the way to utter a rejection of any conceits or fantastic conjectures harbouring no meaning in this context; such as, *timelessness*: an erroneous locution contrived only to afford numerous, ill-founded alternatives. Reality indicates that terrestrials have existence within time, it being the intrinsic *modus* by which creatures accomplish what they do, serving as the milieu within which our ontic-being is framed. We ought, then, to forego any such nonsense; any such philosophical trumpery. To the point then: shall this so-called *afterlife* be for a generation, a thousand years, a million, a million-million, a trillion-trillion? And, what on *Terra Firma* – why, even on *Celebros!* – will all the zillions of unique, rejuvenated-beings effectively do during all the ages and epochs to come? Augment-exponentially the propagation of their progeny? Surely, when you reflect, you can discern such an idea to be wild in the extreme. Disquieting, assuredly, for thinkers even to contemplate.'

Hereupon, the availing Ann-Gel leant across the glassen table so as to refill the elegant goblet with a potation of the refreshing, blue beverage. Offering a grin to her guest she intimated quietly (albeit, ebbing of vocal volume would scarce alter covertness): 'You know, you do but delay the issue.'

'Ah!' opined another *Awkin*, so far silent. 'Now he intends to postulate a doctrine of *reincarnation*. Percipient, seemingly, since it does alleviate the full shock of the numbers' problem. An individual may be granted the opportunity to exist (severally) as one of a great many vegetal, animal, terrestrial, or other orbital species afore reaching the tedium of the never-ending *afterlife*. Also, beyond doubt, it dulls the unrest over attendant boredom by legitimising all sorts of experiential innovation to be endured, enjoyed, or whatever. Yet, as Ann-Gel rightly says, it does but delay the inevitable. An awfully long time!'

'Thank you, Zeltar. I believe we see, similarly. Presumably, dear friend, so do you?'

An answer seemed necessary, leastwise an observation or comment: irrespective of whether he might be drinking with a 'dear friend' – or no.

Curiously, it was at this point that the appellant for the Divine unexpectedly experienced a troubling, dreamlike sense of disassociation; as though he, whilst still conscious, be yet lacking critical *agency* in forming and articulating the argument. Rather, contrariwise, he'd assumed the title of a player in an opus of dramatic, elitist fiction, one where the eclectic register of a writer was being utilised so that the general meaning would be difficult for the lay or average reader to apprehend. Materially, no more was he sure that what he should say would be true, supposing-even that he honestly comprehended it to be true in pronouncing it. As opposed to cognising it to be true, albeit not feeling it to be so.

Similarly, Joshua had the unlikely impression – hitherto never encountered – that, regardless of his inclusion within an anomalous environment, he'd also secured (as if by an unhabituated mode of delivery) a unique vantage-point perceptibly further-forward of his prevailing lodgement in the time-scape of history. Notwithstanding these unsettling notions and perceptions, the alien visitor was prepared to endeavour his periphrastic reply.

'Hypothetically, let's assume I find Zeltar's reasoning (courtesy of Ann-Gel's discretion) to be deserving of legitimate attention. Nonetheless, reincarnation is a construct I have never fully favoured. Even though it be tactical to argue, how surely as a soul is shown reliably – and *affectively* – to affiliate with an earlier existence, just so then (most like) the impact of karma ought palpably to be felt and afterwards acted upon. That said, now even if bluntly: why on *Celebros* or *Terra Firma* must I endorse as veridical the frankly tendentious enunciated by others? Weightier, to be sure, would be an arresting memory to be called upon, connected with. Seriously, it could be, I think *would* be different. Typically, when there be a nucleus of those asseverating how they can effectively bring to bear such recollections, the ineluctable impression is that they are especially affiliated with just two or three karmic forebears who uncommonly transpire to be of rather imposing or extraordinary lineage. There is too much of the bizarre, the arcane, not enough of the ordinary or quotidian for me to feel secure about such an hypothesis. Equally, it's easier to hold a degree of sympathy for the tenor of this doctrine when it reveals a genuine moral seriousness, epitomised now and then in doctrinal formulation and religious belief. Necessarily, I'll by no means endorse any whose wealth or boredom, dubiety or curiosity, occasion an inequitable discovery of states of artificially-induced, supra-natural consciousness – never mind potentially-exploitative control. Where religion, by contrast, undertakes to implement ethical redress through conjuring with an afterlife – of either retribution or reward – well, veritably, I do consider its *gravitas* should compel our attention, perchance our admiration. Venturing personally, I'd suggest any sporadic or arbitrary experience of reincarnation will sooner or later fail to persuade or finally convert.'

Zeltar was about to interject. However, the visitor had his left hand upraised.

'No – if you will – permit me to finish. I apprehend the point made earlier concerning *numbers*, else, percase-correcter, *population* – plus the veridical extent of time (as well as just how it might be occupied) being simply deferred. Plainly, I'm able to see how in any common or prosaic view, the proposition of eternity – identified with time as having-no-end – appears outwith what is either rational or desirable. On the whole, it feels somewhat appalling. Howbeit, inventive methods of perception might obtain which invite greater appeal.'

Of a sudden, *The Friendly Challenger* was anxious to intervene.

'One is relieved to discover you're in sync with the argument! Forbye, I'll not put it down to what lies in the glass! Again, I'm stoical about your advocacy of the term, *population*, rather than mere *numbers* (foregoing at this hour my rationale), instead prioritising what I assume to be a variant of probationary trial or necessary disbenefit. I advert here to the *post-mortem* domain, denominated *The Domicile of Preparation* – itself a halfway-abode between *The Home of Goodness* and *The Hall of Fire* – wherethrough those deserving neither the bane of the one nor the blessing of the other shall progress for as long as their wrongdoing and perversity demands the penalty. Its critical position, of course, is void of appeal to citizens of *Celebros*. All the same, espousing your preferred paradigm, it's forgivable how you'd desire to go off-track, want to promulgate its incidental formulas and patterns of justice: researching, then likely transmuting various misdemeanours carried-out; pivotally, redeeming the deficiency and ruin of multiple, meaningless lives; whilst, inter alia, summoning – (not to add) ordaining-upon – the possible implication of your specific *genus* in the ever-and-anon designated, *terrestrial predicament,* or, additionally (assuming the locution to be correct) *original sin.'*

The teacher sighed, a profound and heartfelt sigh; satisfied how he'd earlier discriminated between these explications. Here, again, he felt he was being compelled to tell apart an apologue from a philosophy. (Only, had he – when all was said and done – had he really? Whilst the genres – did not each of them overlap?)

Irregardless of the flow of the argument, the importuned proponent surreally, albeit only for a while, got out of conjuring an appropriate riposte. Instead, his interlocutor grinned – an almost ironic simper – allowing thereby a glimpse of his narrow and lower-facial aspect, indicating withal superior lines drawn, sharply dinted, on his mighty forehead. His eyes, furthermore, appeared watery with merriment.

'Bethink yourself now, *markedly-Firm Terrestrial*, all here hold the wherewithal to detect the musings of your mind – discernibly when they are bestrewn with such fervid, wayward, manifest affect – easily capable of knowing the content of what you are going to propose. Demur not, then, if your interrogator insists he is sincere. All the same, regarding our discourse (oddish to aver) I've a whimsical reminiscence; *videlicet*, a number of remarkable head-to-heads of the basic-dimensional game of chess, competing with my brother when both he and I were toddlers! Just as I could see, but moments ago, the proposal evolving in your mind, likewise, many years ago was I able to apprehend how – boasting an infernal precocity! – one might penetrate the subtle intricacies of my brother's strategy or *modus operandi* – yes, he who'd in the future be spoken of as *The Unfriendly Conventionalist*.'

Of a sudden, one of the other crew, so far resolutely mute, chimed in: 'Allow me, First Brother, one second – your humour, it'll not be appreciated.'

Hereby informing Joshua, he went on with affected bonhomie to explain: 'Said locution, *The Unfriendly Conventionalist*, corresponds to a so-called nickname, which turns upon the use of irony or antinomy. You'll find upon *Celebros* verily no such thing, no-one to be reckoned as, *un-friendly*. We are typically set apart, assuredly, as being the opposite; as being *friendly*.'

'I see.'

Not entirely cheered by this testimonial, the newly-advised ponderer preferred to relax as before, setting aside every vestige of mistrust, side-stepping potential qualms by exhibiting full-hearted reliance upon the genuine wherefores and whys belonging to his quirky prosecutors.

'Declare to me, nonetheless, my line of argument.'

'You were,' the agreeable sibling replied, 'on the verge of warning me against interpreting *The Home of Goodness* and *The Hall of Fire* too literally – in other words, as if they be actual territories of terrestrial happiness, rehabilitative-labouring, or punishment for evermore. Supposing I've discerned you aright, well, now you are going to propose something about *dimensions:* opening our thinking to the strange para-normality of so-called *existential realms*, highlighting the proper requirement for an appropriate judgement, apprehended as aptly analogous to being *newly* and *self-critically* aware. Regardless, it is not the arena of dialectic selected for evidencing our axioms, for our theses to contend, our interpretive registers to conflict. May I proceed?'

A sudden nod was sufficient to prompt *The Friendly Challenger* to return to his prosecution.

'Actually, what pothers me most is how a cadre of those referred to as *devotional* reiterate that earnest souls experience a degree of control apropos the forfeit of actual *time* that is spent, lived, endured in the morally-oriented and expiatory home adjudicated as transitional – the reintegrating, *Domicile of Preparation* – irrespective of how you hypothesise about that *place*, naively setting forth in this jejune fashion in an idiom that legions of devotees appear wholly prepared to endorse. Argue, do you not, that the employment of petitionary prayer – as well as the gaining of so-called *indulgences* – will predispose the divine mind on behalf of others, securing as a corollary their commutation from an anticipated *condition-of-existence* – evidently you'd concoct some such formula – even more keenly and readily than would normally be presumed, realising serendipitously supernal *agape*, via divine blessing, for those souls-on-remand, giving them their reward of rapture and at-one-ment?'

'As you know,' confirmed the accused, 'I argue for adopting as much nuancing as material in evaluating complexes outstripping the facile, as indeed in managing our inadequate understanding. Anyhow, I do concur with you that there are myriads who supplicate, carry out good deeds, enact practices of devotion so as to relocate the not-fully prepared more summarily to their Maker, or Life-Giver, or God. Amen. Yes.'

'Yet,' began the other, pursuing his theory like a keenly-probing barrister, 'is not this view entirely childish? Does it not bespeak an extraordinary infantilism within the comprehension of (save-for-this) adult-minded terrestrials? Not to say injudiciously lodging them amid inexorable and lamentable double-binds. Imagine this scenario. Upon a little girl's suffering the loss of her grandfather, thereafter, every night (and prior to repose) she implores politely for his departed soul, iterating a handed-down formulaic pattern of words, repeated again and again within the pieties of devotional practice. By and by, the bereaved maiden is disquieted to ascertain that her uncle, too, has died; she intuits likewise that this person ought to be privileged in a kindred fashion. Forbye, presenting at her centre of liturgy, she's requested to intercede for a coterie of sickly citizens who've recently succumbed. Yielding to this desideratum, the obedient soul subsequently voyages on a seasonal holiday, thereby acquainting herself with congenial contacts of whom, two years later, she is apprised that among the aforesaid an adolescent is no longer alive. Naturally, it now feels wrong to ignore one so young, albeit she's guiltily-aware by now how this list of hers is becoming *just that* – a list, a catalogue. Discernibly again, whilst the years pass by, her roll-call increases recurrently. What is she to do? Purely forego mentioning each and every soul she chances to hear after their demise or departure? Potentially, such a denial though could detain (else retard) the still-tainted souls in the preparatory realm. Possibly, when she's decidedly jaded or ailing in her body, then empathetic succour would be afforded and minimal setback be endured. Again, sensibly, she'd be able to rationalise compeers within groups. That said, such a ploy might issue-forth in a dilution of the overall efficacy, occasioning a person to secure simply a percentage of the total provision indicated for final intromission – *mirabile dictu*! – to *The Home of Goodness*. What's more, the same prospect summons up again another difficulty: namely, doesn't the growing woman incur as well a certain liability to attend additional liturgical-practices – in sooth, generally to perform other pious and applicable deeds – even as would, assessed in the round, constitute due leverage for her kith and kin, along with myriads privileged within her providence as being *the most entitled*; so that, precluding none, all may have expedited the *terminus* to the terrible waiting, the emptiness and fissure demanded and ordained by the sacred decree of *The Domicile of Preparation*? What cumbrance to wreak upon anyone! What power, what responsibility! – What guilt!'

The terrestrial experienced again a notable weariness. Wildered as to the issue, not at all, howbeit he remained dubious as to the ideal point of departure, the formula divined as most felicitous to characterise the argument.

'Worry not' – it was Ann-Gel, quietly encouraging – 'as you feel able, as you feel able.'

'Surely intelligible, I consider it proper to begin by underscoring what you yourself intuited my understanding of *The Domicile of Preparation* would be: i.e., that it be befittingly perceived as a heart-felt inquiry into the unvarnished delineation of a character at the cessation of its incarnate existence; one in which it is tenable to realise the several ways in which the deceased individual, during life, be properly implicated in the suffering and distress of others – whether intentionally or unintentionally. Seriously to divine the weight, the full heft of one's history impinging: experiencing it powerfully, not just assaying it with a detached mind. Furthermore, conversancy with abundant honesty ought then to instil within the departed soul – in whatever world or domain the dependent finds reinstatement – a deeply felt humility, as well as a clemency wide and profound. Even so, how this sensibility will take place, never mind what duration of time will be required, both constitute quandaries I cannot resolve. That said, naught shall the affected forlorn, e'en in their sorrowing, validly realise by way of support or duly congruous relief. All itinerant spirits being reviewed-soothfully need to accede to the enjoined process, yes, wherefrom any accelerated release would insinuate a defeat of purpose. Reality must be confronted.'

'Happily, upon that,' exclaimed the issuer of a former caveat to the First Brother, 'we are all agreed! Reality must be confronted! However, upon *Celebros*, abiding by the veridical signifies the eschewing of all dogma and credenda upon life after death. Your own argument, nonetheless – within the rationale of the implied paradigm – fittingly presupposes a degree of judgement. Howbeit, shouldn't you concur that any repetition of prayer must hereafter be posited as ineffectual; not what hitherto it's been purported to be?'

Lesson adduced, knowingly, the predominant (withal also clearly athirst) scrutiniser – himself a politic listener, besides – openly procured for himself an allocation of the cerulean offering, pouring it from the pitcher's glassen lip with an air of undisguised concentration. Descrying about him his cohort seated, he insisted then in sombre tones:

'Initiating our mutual discourse earlier, we numbered topics for dialogue with our visitor to be limited to a total of three. Inquiring outwith the chosen concerns does seem – talking honestly – short of legitimate.' Openly eager to reassure Joshua – besides being newly sustained – the speaker held out a degree of comfort: 'When all is said and done, it's up to yourself as to the matter of providing additional information.'

Discernibly – *horribile dictu* – there was something about the specific configuration of the more persistent alien which dismayed and discommoded Joshua: for, the disputant's uncommon brow seemed inordinately sized; whilst his odd gaze – it disclosed an ogle of ferocious intensity. Anyhow, the cogitant perceived interiorly, how, all in all, any true elucidation should now include an endeavour to repel this foray against *interposition for the departed*; even if, *nolens volens*, he be drawn further and further into a most troublesome sphere of debate: *videlicet*, the sufficient reasoning for, even effectuality of, petitionary prayer. Again: where to begin?

'Seriously, it's difficult to know,' he acknowledged, 'how best to convey the dynamic of prayer; no less, how to apprehend the reality and purpose of God. As you perceive, I'm somewhat oblique vis-à-vis the method of setting forth the identity of God and, explicitly, what to pray for. God and prayer, nonetheless, denote realities I do uphold. Apropos the notion of *request*: impetration, if realised, ought not to place at risk gratuitously the welfare of anyone else, or, for that matter occasion any unwanted or ill-advised superintendence with respect to their lives. Suppose, cognisant of some probable or potential delay, the unquiet suppliant beseeches his God to ensure a conveyance will arrive on time. Cogitable factors for so doing may range from neurotic impatience through to a respectful desire to be punctual – supposing withal the trepidation may or may not feel timely or rational. Possibly, should the vehicle be descried a few minutes late, it will (in the event) forestall an accident, facilitate a meeting, engineer advantage or positive gain. Weird or wonderful it may sound, yet, to be truly altruistic sincerely appears prudent, avoiding thereby the semblance of any impediment to the beneficence of my God – chiefly forbye for my own convenience.'

'And now,' said Zeltar, 'you are going to give a more delicate, a more challenging example.'

'Assuredly,' replied Joshua. 'Suppose – for the argument's sake – that I be the lucky father to a grown-up daughter, even as she quests for her regular niche: researching employment, finding a home, securing a soulmate to love. Conceivably, I'd still be wrong should I wish to prognosticate over her preferred vocation, else conjecture on probable outcomes; or, likewise, concerning acquaintances she by and by goes on to make. It'd again surely be impertinent to opine upon particular lovers whom I might presume to think suitable – or, then again, not suitable – for her to arrive at a joyous and enduring mode of contentment. Yes, even to solicit she be excused of certain difficulties, or sufferings, or tragedies – why even that may be ill-judged. After all, one may not predict whether each could not ennoble her character in a benign way; permit her thereafter to become more sagacious or amicable – more proximate to God's nature and aim.'

Joshua paused: he seemed almost pained; liable to sadness. Despite this, he resisted the temptation to gledge at Ann-Gel – forthrightly resuming his account lest he betray his direfully-concealed vulnerability.

'Which is why I strive to make my prayer as simple as possible, honouring withal the modifier, typically appended to any respectful appeal, namely: *Thy Will* – or, *capacity which actualises the benign intent through the wholeness of time, space and beyond – Be Done.* Notwithstanding I myself ardently aspire to embody the divine spirit, demonstrate the divine meaning, always it befits me to be courteous before the Omniscient – accommodating in what I seek. And yet.'

'Yes, do go on.' So supported the female *Awkin*, typically promoting cheer – lest dismalness give way to bewilderment.

'Indeed: regardless of how I conceive of God – of this I'm sure. My demonstration must be suitably and benevolently incarnational; delineating a transcending reality that is, withal, personalised and immanent, that is (paradoxically) involved in the workaday, actual world; committed to the betterment of all its creatures and, assuredly, of indigenes exhibiting a responsive conscience – contributing benignly to the good of the whole. Ergo, I propose that there must be a full-hearted accord between ourselves and the *Influence* that makes us live and move and have our being: the *Influence* that alerts readiness should our being-alive seem pointless, ourselves pre-ordained to some sickening deprivation or inevitable or fearful end. This is a deity to whom all of us may relate, veritably, even as we are; for, necessarily, any other is an irrelevance. What is more, the *Efficacy* I describe – encouraging of personal evolution, integrity and honesty – shall evidence empathy for our weaknesses, our fallibility, our childishness: yes, for our silliness forbye and now-and-then inanity. By the same token, a justifiable lenity shall be exhibited vis-à-vis whatever precise phase attained, else but latterly approached: any timely purpose still being pursued, else contrariwise foregone. Imagine (to illustrate) that I await on or around some bleak solstice, alongside a halt, suffering hunger in my belly and worriment in my brain; then, my genuine orison that a vehicle be on time oughtn't justifiably to be viewed as morally misplaced or maladroit. Belike, for all that, I'd venture to demonstrate a disposition that is open-minded apropos the outcome. Critically, the trivialities of a particular life are unlikely to be determinative for the *Divine Life* as a whole.'

The Friendly Challenger clapped his hands. 'Good. I apprehend the tenor of what you are saying – supposing we subscribe to such discrepant premises. See here then if I'm now-able to take forward the argument as it bears upon devotional, *interposition for the departed*. A magnified deity will surely employ patience towards an ill-informed terrestrial liable only to a peculiar (as well as likely biased or ignoble) already-settled disposition of cherished detainees – such as for whom any clemency be particularly sought.'

'Yes indeed,' approved Joshua – once more prizing the baton to run with it himself. 'Additionally, the *Theos of Tolerance* will be totally cognisant of spiritual confusion; of accommodation and harrowing inevitably instigating adjurations to avail the late-lamented. Peradventure, a plenitude of prayer – together with a fair quantity amounting to such within the current debate – commonly will avail the still-extant supplicant a deal more than benefit those deceased managing the forensic of self-examination and necessary confession. So much allowed, though, nobody comprehends reliably how the exercise of prayer proves truly to be efficacious: particularly, whether it coheres with the same ordinance of time and space we imagine we inhabit ourselves; even, whether it entertains a retrospective reference, through which (may be said) some practice or computation solicited within the afterlife acquires purchase in the present-time, facilitating the eventual judgement-of-insight at the final reckoning. Or, quite straightforwardly, coherent with traditional guidance, mayhap even the frail and imploratory solicitations of the inconsistent and distracted believer may, just the same, solace and embolden a multiplicity of deceased venturing to actualise fortitude and veracity. Man (vacuously) may mock God: even so, I do not hold that a benevolent deity would ever be contumelious towards man. As far as we may conclude, therefore: intention, sound heart; some faith, hope, and love – these may enliven along conduits not accessible to our habit of reasoning, though betiding to be apposite for the *Source* and *Capital* of our timeless, over-vaulting universe. Amen, supposing even that they bedevil the assurance of the learned and cosmopolitan *Awkins of Celebros*!'

So determining, the asseverative Joshua came to a halt. A crew-member instanter clapped and called out, 'Bravo! Bravo!'

It was Zeltar – applauding the responsive visitor. 'Terrific, you've done your best! Shall we now then ascertain whether our Cardinal Brother is to reward you with some good news of his own, disregarding any unscientific and erroneously-postulated concepts: whilst endeavouring withal to refrain from the hazard of sounding superior – easily or not!'

A politic interlude at once ensued, serendipitously capacitating *The Friendly Challenger* to make solemn reply: which he did with cordiality and befitting graciousness.

'Assent hereupon to my expressing alike our relief and good opinion for the amiable way with which you've endeavoured the task imposed. Albeit no proper consent was granted you – and withal your being *assumed* into our ship! – still, for all that, you've been considerate enough to confront the issues as best you could. Even so, as to your disquisition, you've admitted inferably to the clear absurdity, preposterousness, and problematic make-up pertaining to all ill-conceived hypotheses founded upon a realistic *afterlife*. Pivotally, you've supported our claim that you've had to *retreat-to*, even then been required to espouse notions of *mystery, invisible domains* – some ultimate *trust* in the splendiferous essence that you are adjured to call *God* – so as to declare a phenomenon perceived by us as unbelievable, believable; as impossible, possible; and, as conjectural, a straightforward guiding light. Withal, my disclosures to you about us, by way of appreciative recognition, may elicit reactions of ambiguity and ambivalence. Be prepared!'

Joshua winced at what was coming, perceiving something resonant, alarmingly, of an eerie smirk more-or-less crawl across the lower countenance of the less agreeable *Awkin*. The itinerant now wanted to depart straightaway, only (the want scarcely realised) did forthwith nod to his urbane captor to set forth again his narrative.

'Alright, I'll attempt to give ear to your disclosure with an open mind.'

'Very well,' thanked the Cardinal Brother. 'I'm duly appreciative of such indulgence; for, decidedly I'd like now to set before you some knowledge about ourselves and our culture, delineating a positive-path likewise to be pursued by any of your own kind. To begin. Though – and withal possibly to your chagrin – you yourself have come upon your middle years, verily among ourselves there be not a man, or woman, who's not by now double your age. I myself am 225 years-old, Zeltar 193, and Ann-Gel, she is… No, no, assuredly, I am not going to say! (*Instanter, much mirth, allied to frivolously-delivered giggle.*) Our primary matter is this: specialist *Awkin* analysts have pioneered such capability in cloning and cistron-devised therapies such that no-one today envisions a cessation of wariment or affect before 300 years of age. Palpable pain *per se* is as good as unheard of; whilst, equally, an elaborate array of remedial aids exists, which – in line with our mind-control plus telepathic connectivity – guarantees that the modus operandi for our discontinuity is adhered to with a minimum of un-timeliness. It is possible to isolate the minute of the day at which to surcease further brain-agency, plus vital force, preserving in the undertaking plenary preparedness in tandem with equanimity for all concerned. It's genuinely believed by us to be a *pathology* if a seldom, vexatious individual be unwilling to accede to their inevitable end.'

At this, the speaker gave a slight cough. Before chuckling out loud.

'Dear friends, be not alarmed – I'm hearty for another three score years and fifteen! Suffer me then to enunciate to our guest, that, being able to confront the truth that *this is all there is* – as if that in itself were not enough! – ought not to raise any eyebrows amongst those of us who can (*more laughter*): forasmuch as our labours are orderly and civilised, our excitements of actual benefit, and our felicitous mindset oriented to the race as a whole. Besides, seven years hitherto, importantly, we succeeded in discontinuing competition and rivalry, outwith (that is to say) functional play, sport, and constructive games. Markedly withal, we are everywhere sustained via the augmenting artery of channelling-silently within our cognitive-processes together with audible iteration. Further, the predominancy of *Awkin* citizenry naturally undergo erotic rapture via the same fashion. Yes, dear friend, any female of our race is enabled to have reified her pleasurable ecstasy through another *Awkin* but cerebrating-lovingly, or, prevailing-upon both longingly and in unison. Furthermore, the average male upon *Celebros* welcomes (by and large) a not-dissimilar, freely-chosen protocol fostering the equivalent sensation. Still, effectuating these advances has taken our people several centuries. Assuming, however, that those endeavouring upon *Terra Firma* (phenomenally!) do not destroy themselves prematurely; withal, wondrously-avoid destruction by aliens of a different persuasion to our own; then, determinedly and stalwartly, their special lineage shall realise its own duly-acquired and rightful abode: *scilicet*, its innumerable denizens shall together realise, conclusively, how they endure with consequence and meaning; how, indeed, they co-exist in congruence and contentment; and, too, how they have a propitious number of foregoing decades to allow every expirant to fulfil, equably, an absolute and unavoidable demise.'

Sometime around the reference to erotic connection, the student of *Celebros* (its ways, habits, and protocols) began to feel more on edge – not hale or assured-enough forbye to bestow a gladsome wink-of-the-eye to the skin-tight cladded creature anxious for his needs. Instead, proffering an averment that he was grateful for, and awestruck by, *Awkinalite* exploit and praxis, he stated there and then how he was desirous above all to reconnect with his familiar terrain; amen, to plant his soles upon the well-tramped, undulant, gritty desert-floor of his regular world.

Ahead of the approval of his keeper, howbeit, did there then occur a disquieting episode surely likely to prompt reflection for many a long hour. Peculiarly, it chanced now that an *Awkin,* evidently to whom might have been accorded the title of, *The Truly Silent One,* signalled in the direction of the de-activated screen – the very one and same that'd recorded hideous, murderous events – clearly motioning towards the Cardinal Brother. Joshua himself noticed the signal, descrying thereafter the grand, lifeless monitor, numbering (from side to side) just five of the craft's crew gawking before him. Indeed, to be sure, nobody else. Still, however surreal, in the farthest corner could that be – amassing in the dark, opaque glass – a peculiarly and incongruently brutish dog, ebony-toned and massive, potentially just lying in wait?

The Friendly Challenger was quick to react. The alien's right hand straightaway went up to obviate any awkwardness that the apparently-dumb interlocutor might hereupon be about to demonstrate. Averting such a possibility, the former interlinked his arm with that of his quiet visitor, saying, 'You are indeed, Joshua, a remarkable terrestrial, discernibly more estimable than we could possibly have anticipated. Even so, it is wrong to detain you from your terrestrial path.'

The assuring sentiment uttered, Joshua – with but the slightest gledge-of-a-glance to the lissom and lovely Ann-Gel – stepped out. Stepped forward. Stepped down.

Stepped down the crescent-curve of the sloping dune of desert-sand.

What's more, soothfully did the soil of the sand straightaway feel good. As too, the balmy breeze blowing in his face, savouring of salt and ocean and odyssey ahead. For a moment he stopped. He gazed here and there, but, of cities or spacecraft he could descry not a jot, not a shade – merely the eloquent, eerie calm of the twilight dawn.

Moreover, for a brief delicious lull, the itinerant continuing his journey noticed interiorly a novel serenity; a breadth of emotion inspired by blissful, verging-on painful sensitivity, as well as evincing sureness and attendant repose. He queried anon, ruminatively, whether he had come under the spell of the female *Awkin*: figuring even that she had vouchsafed to him some powerful sensation through the medium of her mind – maybe not through and through as mentioned, but, withal in a limited and attenuated form; so, not entirely dissimilar. Then he laughed out loud. Surprisingly, he'd become conscious of a serendipitous memory: that of the most heavenly, but corporeal, Rachel; Rachel (progeny of *The Militant Atheist*) who'd defiantly hauled him by his hands, dragging him cold-footed to the circle of her dance; Rachel, again, who'd allured the considerer, who'd enticed him beguilingly with her beauty and her unexpected wildness.

He allowed this recollection to engender a perspective upon what he'd experienced. The uncommon physiognomy, congenial deportment, and dulcet intervention of Ann-Gel had, truth to tell, been reassuring, albeit also, peculiarly *tempting*; endowed undoubtedly with an especial lure. Now, shimmering across his mental processes, almost palpably, was the flow and brush of *The Modern Feminist* – even with her scramble of hair, her hair in a dangle (randomly), and, in the tambourin, nighly conspicuous as to kindle within him a hankering to outreach, forth, verily embosoming the gracile figure of her body close in his arms! Oh yes, let there be hair! Despite his own tousled outcrop, despite his itchy beard and unkempt head of it, oh yes – God keep us in hair: all the while, amen, for as long as we can! Removal from the extra-terrestrials suddenly and assuredly felt like a reprieve – for all that they'd appeared amicable, yes, even good-looking. More or less. Mostly, anyhow.

In such an idle reverie did Joshua wander and slope along the edge and elbow of the dune's rise and fall, before (alas familiarly) careering-over onto and across its grainy floor.

'Finest Heaven!' – wasn't quite what he found to say.

And then, 'Gracious me! It cannot, surely, cannot be you! You've a deal of a look, yet, moderately different. A mite older – if you'll forgive my saying.'

'Would it make any difference?' The question sounded at once rhetorical and jocular.

Joshua shifted his rear in the accepting sand, fixing the frame of his anatomy that he might admire more comfortably the amenable smile of his companion, Jacob – the aforesaid not dilatory in re-claiming the initiative.

'Ah well! How is it again (you may ask) that I happen to be here? Be advised, yet not alarmed, about yourself: under your right eye is a visible scar;

a corollary perhaps of a trial endured. Who may discern its origin, or myriad fortuities in the wake of our initial exchange?'

The bowled-over auditor was now more discomfited than ever. Gingerly, he touched his cheeks. Upon the first (namely dextral) he could make out hesitantly an inexplicable indentation, inferring it notwithstanding partly to be hidden by his beard.

'It's partly hidden by your beard,' added his friend, helpfully.

'Even so, I bethink myself of your warning,' noted the other, 'anterior to my setting off. Decidedly, I was to circumvent a weird, noteworthy, and discoidal-looking abode of pink and yellow and most arresting white lights!'

'Yes, you are correct. A ternion of traders, within a fugitive caravan, referred to it as such. Exercised be not, Joshua, if I remind you of a truism periodically expedient. *All is not as it seems.* We come and we go, we apprehend the route winding-ahead. We walk forwards. At times we go up, at times we drop down. But forwards and on. Here, there, an isolated terrestrial theorises he could stay that way – on and on to the actual end, the sheer cliff-edge of the very world. Natheless, even if this is how it betides in plain observation, typically our kind concur that this good globe of ours is rather like a large sphere, navigated by going round and round. Similarly, we behold the sun rise and the sun set; up and down each day she goes. Yet, assuredly it is us, our planet all the while which goes circuiting inexorably around the sun – the high molten star looking on, the fiery colossus bestowing warmth, drawing flame from our bits and strips of wood. All is not as it seems.'

'Confess to me then,' opposed the other, 'was the last day yesterday? And this day today? The upcoming still the morrow? Are they, feasibly, again not what they seem?'

'Who can say for sure? Who can say? All the same, countenance me now to confide in you: the deficient aspect of contour and frame I divined before – why, Joshua, even that has diminished. You yourself, understand, you're here but a big blur, a blur even so that's departed an abode positively coruscating with so much pink and yellow and white. I imagine you're suitably flattered!'

'Howbeit – you perceived my scar!'

'All is not as it seems. There are some who dream what is true. And there are others who find truth in their dreams.'

'And God? Wherefore likewise is God a dream? Or, we ourselves, are we percase the dream – even as dreamt by God?'

'Should I have to choose,' replied the good-as-blind ageing itinerant, 'I should say – the latter. Consider then if God woke up! God is beyond doubt – *That Which God Is* – and defines all being. We do not define God, but find ourselves by God defined. Meanwhile the semblances shift. Assuredly now though it is time to go: whilst, Joshua, your peculiar journey calls you towards the coast. One day afresh our paths may cross. I'd have it so. Methinks, though, I must desist from toppling-you-up! I assume twice is enough!'

'I wholeheartedly concur! May our paths overlap – withal your friend upstanding remain!'

Then Jacob avouched: 'This is the future, and this is the past, and this was, and will be, the present. Beyond. Over there.'

'Where?' rejoined the descrier, unfamiliar with such curious sagacity in one dispossessed of sight. 'Where?'

He turned, this way and that: then, realised to his chagrin that again he was alone, owning wide-ranging views long and far, the morn now bright and blue and inviting, but disconcertingly empty, and himself as a crane in the wilderness (so it seemed) solitary, clamouring, alone. Then, as his slowing feet were yielding, tumid and throbbing, his head in a flurry with the swelter and his whole heart thumping – full of amazement, he saw it. And so – not alone. Not anymore.

Part the Third: in which Joshua philosophises with Pedram and Tom ahead of voyaging to Zenith Island.

O nly just what could Joshua see?
What was to be seen was this: a naturally-created mariner's cove; an irregular voe of leviathan boulders cast as mighty ocean-Orca; a beach wrack-littered and stone-strewn; a flickering cyan-bright embrace of sand-and-sea. Likewise evident to the eye was the bobbing of gaily-decked brine-battered craft, careering and tittupping betwixt the jostling waves.

Scattered behind some young combers – studying now the strand beneath a choir of gulls discordantly caterwauling – there were zig-zagged some modest, plain-white dwellings, nighly unembellished, denoting an ostensive bias in favour of the original or rudimental (it might have been): albeit containing (who could say?) the less ancient besides, being networked and elaborated by contrivance and gadgetry of every devising – although secreted within.

Content to rest – hereupon to gaze upon the broad, fresh, watery view – the depleted traveller slid himself gradually into the concave hollowed-out indenture of a not-quite slippery whale-of-a-rock. There he found that he was thirstily gulping from a bottle of dark aerated liquid, dilatorily apprehending that he was eavesdropping on a pair of local fisherfolk, harking back (if truth be owned) to a wrestling head-to-head that the voluble wrangler, newly-slumped by the rollocks of a dinghy, had had the fortuity to observe.

'You may be called Pedram by most,' admitted the dissentient, only then continuing, 'howbeit, you do have the more familiar *honorific*, flattering though it hardly is, of – *The Blunderer*! Bear in mind, too, the revered tale of the singular wrestler: stubborn, proud stripling, withal trainer of the plaited and whiskery beard! In sooth, an antagonist you'd scarce (with any deftness or celerity) have subdued. Decidedly, I'd query whether you'd have managed it at all! Oh yes, gruelling were the harsh hours of the dark that he grappled and tussled-with the thrawn guise of the other, stubbornly refusing to let go. Alright, he went charging in. Yet, when the going got tough he toughed it out!'

At this *The Blunderer* laughed – with greater gusto perhaps than did he truly welcome the irony of the comment – yet, laughed nonetheless.

'I acknowledge, Tom – tiresome though it be! – how, yes, anent your tale it's I, not you, who comes over as *The Cautious One*. Even more so as you don't specify the opponent or his family's origin!'

'Although, as I've narrated before,' remonstrated his friend, 'it was the senior figure who was the one not divulging an actual name. Time after time the youth endeavoured, passional to ascertain, deriving mere taciturnity for his iterative questioning. The great bear-like shape, the shadow-wrapped adversary he fought, would not declare. The muscular stripling with the braids of hair nonetheless gainsaid submission or concession of release. It was a sight for sore eyes: though, not the whit less, every wide eye would be sore by the close. Twice indeed in the reckoning. To begin: whilst the lights of the *ethereal* fire and the *terrestrial* fire both blazed, both waned withal. Once the bright mien of the ensuing day surfaced slowly in the east, its incurved blazon revealed the duo a most *un-firm* and awesome sight. Observers would have been discomfited purely in the beholding. Secondly, the steely-clenched broil achieved its end in a manner evidently at fault. The elder as well as massier one duped the other. Seeing how he was not going to escape – not before the acclivitous bourn of the star would evidence them both – he grumbled and mouthed a dubious conjuring, at which orotund growl the hirsute combatant cried out aloud, stamped, back-stepped panic-stricken, with hands upraised unfurled about his head: some doing had befallen; a happening hardly behovely. Being not exactly blinded – not totally not strictly – he listed; stumbled – off-kilter and unsure – pawing at his eyes, morose as to his malady. Forthwith he betook himself to the still-visible, vicinal river, totteringly plashing the rippling element across his bearded face. He thereupon lunged, limp-limbed, into the rumbustious spate; wherein – vigour renewed – did he manage yet to swim stubbornly to the far-off side. Post-haste on exiting he turned on his heels, unquiet that he be now the quarry of some dogged pursuit. Mysteriously, irregardless, the otherworldly penumbra of the botherer had failed, concurrent with the crowing of the cockerel, betaking himself suddenly from mortal gaze. Yet, the now myopic Jacob manfully stood, wondrously no longer the assailant unknown of lineage obscure: rather, mirabile dictu, the bona fide victor of a terrible contest; the occurrent and clear-cut epiphany of which every bystander who'd watched would ne'er forget. All that looked on blinked – blinked their eyes, rubbing them, now o'er-glazed in wonderment with very effort of witness.'

'Well,' trumpeted Pedram, 'if only I, too, could have gazed upon it! 'Tis a rare story you tell!'

'I hope you don't mind,' interjected Joshua, 'only, I fear I've been listening-in on your yarn. You asseverate the nomen of the youth to be Jacob. Verily, I know someone who answers to that name. Indeed, I feel (surreally) as though we were discoursing but hours ago. All the same, he was fifty for sure.'

'It's a not-uncommon name, though, is it?' said Pedram, shrugging his shoulders.

'Yet, not exactly popular, to do it justice,' stated Tom. 'Withal, the event was copious years ago. Anyhow, do direct us, stranger, what do you call yourself? So far you have the advantage. How is it you are here?'

'Where I am called, there also I venture, albeit I know not the reason. Somehow, intuitively, perforce have I come to this locale, adjoining as it does the tidal strait incorporating an unfamiliar island. But, you may have heard of it. It's traditionally referred to as – Zenith Island. Oh, and my name – it is Joshua.'

'Well Joshua, of course, of course,' reassured the solid-looking rock-of-a-man who was also, for all that, *The Blunderer*. 'You may yet ferry to it from here – if a person be determined enough to favour the traditional vehicle, *The Black Petrel* – just visible yonder in the middle-distance.'

Joshua focused on where the man's right finger was pointing, picking out promptly a deep, pitch-toned fishing-vessel (notably some cut above the normal) currently secured a modest distance outwith the sheltered cove.

'Listen, I'll row you out if it'll help. The dinghy we own is that salt-infested one, beached next to those abandoned creels.'

'It'd be most helpful. Natheless, I fear today I'm unable to reimburse you for my passage.'

'Possibly,' prompted the other, 'and in lieu of payment, you'll let us know what you think vis-à-vis the nature of the world to come. Of course, any of us who are deprived now will be well-off then; whereas, any of us in the here-and-now surely who are comfortably off will lament their sufficiency upon departing this life. Even so, this mugwump-partner of mine yodels and yodels he's not so sure! No change there then! What do you think?'

'Whilst I take on board (no pun intended) where you're coming from,' answered the potentially indebted one – perturbed lest he forfeit Pedram's invitation to convey him to the ferry – 'howbeit, I can see why Tom, distinctively, may have a point.'

'It's alright, Josh, no need to fret – our behemoth will paddle you across whatever you say! Speak on! Speak on!'

'Okay, I will. Intrinsically, what's needed is to perceive afresh how the intricacies of judgement be optimally understood. Hence, it appears judicious to consider that all of us shall stand, more or less shamefacedly, confronting truthfully just who we are – what we have become. Basically, therefore, there will be imposed a supplemental consciousness of what it is *categorically like* to be somebody else: like any and each (either dead or alive) to whom – by whatever means – we have exhibited an unfair bias. Deservedly, it may transpire that the so-called *good* shall appear nearer than they are prone to assume to the so-called *bad*.'

'How so?' bellowed *The Blunderer* – and, it might be remarked, to cagey-Tom's considerable amusement.

'I think there will have to be, for each and every one, an unaccustomed honesty: whereby, educing this example, the solemn or reverent soul – exercising characteristically a most caring but careful existence – is made to engage with the paradoxical idea that he (or she) has simply *played safe*, veritably eschewing as a liability everyday trials and troubles as much as was practicable: instinctively preferring to rely upon the calm and predictable. Not comprehending suitably the chaos and tumult of life. Forswearing desire appears then to betoken securely-existing in a cowardly way, actualising inquietude in the proper stead of involvement and taking risks. Correspondingly, the esurient soul, wed to all sorts of perilous forays and adventures, transgressing oft-times during the endeavour – committing multiple errors and faults along the way – might (intrinsically) emerge as having shown audacity and enterprise. Similarly, the impecunious may discern how piquantly the rich have been lured; whilst they, per contra, in the wake of a doleful pauperdom stayed fixedly parochial, wholly absorbed in an ill-natured envy. Even so, they again – had their lot have been different – by the same token could've recklessly behaved, thereupon being reckoned likewise as deserving of reproof. Nonetheless – no less signally – this isn't to aver contrariwise that the puissant and privileged will (most assuredly not) escape the requisite application of rightful justice. They shall thole the consequences of their cold-heartedness, perceiving what they carried out to the detriment of the downtrodden and disadvantaged, similarly beleaguered by an awareness of disregarded incapacitation: realising the peculiar weight and disquiet of suffering not adequately in others recognised and alleviated.'

Giving ear to this, glumly, Pedram looked surprised – veritably, in his soul, down-cast.

'Joshua, what I've endeavoured to do is what I've considered to be meet and correct. Conceivably, everyone intends – as a generality – to do the same? Obviously, that's what you're saying?'

'To aver the truth – not entirely. Customarily, the insouciant majority behave largely as they wish; such as when they eschew remorse or connive at the penalty: seldom, however, will they instigate what they identify as malicious or perverse. By and large, terrestrials are neither especially good nor particularly bad, inclining to behave from an ethical viewpoint, should they espouse one, generally but now and then. Albeit, by contrast, I'd propound that to realise a spiritual identity is to adopt a morally-incentivised life, centred upon serious decision-making. Palpably, you do attempt, Pedram, to do the right thing; exceeding thereby the myriads who (at a glance) simply don't care very much. I'd assert, nonetheless, that – paramount withal – were you to wander awhile (so to speak) in the shoes of other people, you'd by and by heed how even the basic and clear-cut is apt to appear inherently less so when beheld in the round. Besides, I'd postulate that an especial openness be entailed to apprehend it in that regard, as well as (and again) the prerequisites of compassion, humility, a transmutation of one's desires – or not. Pivotally – would one have acted differently? Theoretically, perhaps. Even so, I'm inclined to add – not necessarily. Not necessarily.'

'Both as daft, misdoubting, forbye convoluted as each other!' blurted out the *Blunderer*. 'Doubtless the two of you should get on rather well!'

At this, the altogether-less-agitated (though surely more equitable) companion forthwith lifted himself from his occasional seat-of-wood (a spartan support on the edge of an ancient, scarcely-seaworthy boat) declaring, 'Things aren't always what they seem!'

'Think I can deduce what's coming!' exclaimed his friend. 'An avowal of how our immutable world is neither truly *firm* nor actually *flat*: but, really much more akin to an enormous ball; verily, one which (since mobile) wheels and gyrates gallivanting around the sun. I *know*, I *know!*'

A considerer of such matters but hours ago, Joshua here might've volunteered his own approof. However, temporarily, he became in the event utterly distracted, being now greatly surprised: for, he perceived hereupon *The Cautious One* (his soles upon the sand) to be in truth a diminutive figure when set against the majority. His theorising-propensity, all the same, was not a reflection of his physical stature. He went on to propose a discerning resolution.

'Barely: for, decidedly, I hadn't been going to iterate any such thing! Really – either from personal experience, else withal the viewpoint of intuitive-logic – I was going to maintain it's felicitous on the whole to appraise the floor beneath our feet as flat, albeit at times with undulation; and, ourselves upon *Terra Firma* – in passive mode, at least, amen not the-while in-motion going round and about, so much as steadfast or at a standstill. An astronomer, apprehending all through the prism of his more specialised worldview, possibly would be disposed to research in a locution such as you describe. Anyhow, apropos of ourselves – being inside a more mundane, everyday sphere – the judgement could be equivocal, irrespective of which perspective happens to be regarded as more *objective*.'

'Diaphanous as wet sand!' So said one of the three, adding: 'It's beginning to sound, within this hammering brain of mine, like so much mumbo-jumbo!' Pedram put a big claw to his head and scratched.

'Or,' wondered Joshua, 'may we not purport at times that the semblances seem more veridical than reality? Howbeit, when conducting our lives via the template of the habitual, and abiding by its governing rules, one shouldn't interfere with the foundations of congruence. Axiomatically, it's doltish to dive off your boat into the sea anterior to trying, unaided, below water to breathe!'

'Oh,' retorted Tom, 'it'd surely make no difference to our friend here, though, yes, it might intermeddle with the rolling and the drag of the tide! Natheless, being serious again: some registers of phenomena exist that it behoves us to discriminate. I am thinking of those we codify as bodily – mental – spiritual.'

The Blunderer here pleaded, explicitly mayhaps predictably: 'Even so, most real for me – whilst you gibber and twattle-away the day – belike is the astronomical chasm I can feel in my gut! I'm starving! Listen, how about we pull in our spare net; see if anything's there. What's more, we've fresh bread – supposing it's no longer warm.'

Harmoniously, the fishermen went about dragging-in a sunken drift of net, all-slumped amid the suck and the swill of the bay's embrace.

Little and large, mused Joshua. The polarity had barely occurred when the saunterer's mind was diverted by an astonishment of considerable proportion: *scilicet*, how the generous net itself was proving incredibly onerous to draw.

Ere long, astonishing to relate, a splendid stir with chaos of silvery, leaping life was visible. Tom and Pedram strove with determination, and, fairly soon, enjoyed success. Garnered about them on the sand and rocks of the shore lay fish flicking and gasping and writhing. Of a sudden, deep-voiced, one of the labourers called out.

'Gracious, Joshua! What's up? Espied a ghost or something? Come on – any food there in that bag of yours? Here, we've four barley-loaves – anything to add?'

Jolted into a response, Joshua realised then – albeit to his wonderment – how actually he'd acquired withal a loaf of his own!

'Now we've five,' declared the visitor, glancing up: although, descrying anon how all the quantities of sea-creatures heretofore flailing within the throes of choking had inexplicably vanished. Joshua saw two individuals (of lopsided height and girth) of whom the less robust had swinging from his hand just two fish.

'Forsooth not a feast!' grinned *The Cautious One*. 'But, it'll do!'

The three coevals separated then to collect bits of driftwood and whatever kindling they could find. By and by, between the rocks, a couthy and familiar warmth sprang-up from the jags of heat as the flares of gold jostled and flaunted. 'Twixt the quivering currents above there cooked, well-sizzling, the provender, skilfully skewered to the fabricated spit. But one orbicular loaf was broken to divide: howbeit, over the un-sundered share protest there was none: after all, the appreciative recipient was able to serve up (from under the lip of a rock) a glaucous-coloured and nicely-shaped bottle of reddish wine.

Materially – an abundance certainly not. Natheless, such gentle humour and quipping of the triad – accumbent beside the vapour and flame and crackling wood – palpably made the modest fare seem ample: the appreciable camaraderie limited whatever possible void remained. A certain itinerant even had the boldness to investigate how *The Blunderer* had come by his nickname.

'You mean, to be sure – *title!*' the man boomed. 'Simply, the epithet points to the prowess with which I make mistakes. Beguiled I hardly am – you'll doubtless concur – into *thinking* before acting. Typically, I go, well, charging in. Plainly, it's advisable to keep a reliable comrade at hand capable of rounding off my temperament. Verily, I mean (to be sure) our *Cautious* nibbler – ah! here, if you don't want all of that – alas: too late! What's more, I've a genius sometimes for mislaying things: which is why it's shrewdest for those reliant on keys for the doors of their houses, methods of conveyance, secured troves of treasure, veritably to keep such bobs to themselves! Guard them fiercely! My pockets, they have holes!'

So appreciated the stout-hearted fisherman, sure and trusted stalwart: one in whom verily there was no guile; who exemplified a rapport with the outcast and marginalised, as well as valuing honesty over and above falsehood. Desisting from error, then, denoted little when set against fixing an assertive shoulder to a sometimes-chaotic, Wheel of Life. Within him was an integrity, profound and heart-felt, inclining sanguinity to the wary or weary of soul; emboldening the pilgrimer to abide at his side, blithely; assuredly, as far as yon rolling barque, denominated *The Black Petrel*, withal reliably even unto the subsequent stage of the ineludible odyssey.

Even so, by now the lucency of the day was almost gone, inclining all three to conclude their lingering. Ambling withal lazily towards a dinghy, clearly blenched by the elements, the shortest of the ternion declined.

'Apologies – I've to go to the suppliers before sunset. Consider, in any case: dear old Pedram isn't going to covet this extra heft of yours-truly to tighten his muscles! Anyhow, Josh, I'm grateful for the hours we've shared. Haply, you'll look us up in the future – why not? Yes, endeavour to call by. Apropos the observation from our soulmate upon keys – not without a kernel of truth – in sooth, he's always had his negligence rectified in the end. On occasion, at a high cost to himself. Take care, my friend, take care.'

Iterating thus, the intuitive Tom put an amicable fist to the biceps of the peregrinator, pivoted finely, then post-haste trod-hard towards the angular disposition of homes distinguishable about the far perimeter of the rugged cove.

Seafarer and landlubber, meanwhile, scrambled into the worn-looking craft. *The Blunderer* handed Joshua a wooden pail.

'Perchance, if you prefer not doing it in the sea – perchance, for baling out!'

Dispensing this admonishment, the candid Pedram pulled hard upon the oars: threat the prow dividing the waters, the bow evidencing a wake of churning sea. The traveller, relaxing, noted then the scabrous hands of his formidable pilot, marking how the tug of net and ropes had scoured and chafed the skin to a sheen.

Seemingly, but minutes later, the passage was complete, with transfer of passenger being secured via a ladder (loose-hanging) formed of rope and of wood. So did the vessel acquire its peculiar freightage of intelligent cargo. A squinny rearward confirmed how already *The Blunderer* was labouring to return – an appreciable grin upturned upon his resolute visage, as well as a blithesome cry-of-farewell echoing thereafter from his mouth. A squabble of gulls, screaming and keening sought to drown out the bellow of his voice. Without success.

A potentially beguiling dusk – with watery sun adrift in the quietly rippling liquid – was well-nigh ruined by a suffusion of mist; of wraiths of hiemal vapour folding about the sturdy timber-and-metal carrier as it plied its dogged way towards Zenith Island. So decidedly was this the case, the predicted destination may've been thought to have been bypassed entirely, passengers carried further and further into the unfathomable night and hiddenness of ocean beyond. Notwithstanding, through the dreary-dank air (that had most of the boat's crew coughing-and-cursing) hereupon started into sight a spectre of gloom deeper than the haar that wove about them, betokening a reality more substantive and – with the march of the hour – emerging yet more solid, nigher and nigher, till a halloo of a sudden (from the hardening mirage) elicited a hurl of a line, so averring afore seconds had passed this same ghostly outback to be habitable land.

One man nervously edged his way down the gangplank. Conscious of his companions far away, predictably the visitor was boldened not at all in perceiving what emerged nearby as an eldritch blaze; namely, a weird fulgency – flame-like in its mimicking of a myriad blown lamps of yellow looming – disclosing an avenue away from *The Black Petrel* onward, to some locus for which a subliminal voice unknown had drawn him, lured him, a will o' the wisp commanding him to another world, a dimension he must, perforce, embark upon, should e'er he possess the benison of progress beyond.

Part the Fourth: *in which Joshua questions a former friend, only next to be cast out, confronting surreally thereafter* The Lady With The Long Neck.

There was not a star in sight. Only the dreich, caliginous vision of lanterns, albeit lanterns akin to domes lit up from within. As Joshua rounded a ridge of sand and marram, he could make out (through an aperture in the billowy miasma) a sizeable settlement of uniform architecture, enigmatic to descry in this mirk-ish airt, pertaining more itself to a half-world rather than the basis for society or befitting habitation. Even so, the break in the fog-bank made the place lose sufficient opacity for the searcher to get a truer sense that this same mist-beset skerry had an edificial disposition chiefly of comparable structures, illuminative at night, whilst resided in by those he'd decidedly now to encounter.

He marched up to the door of the first dome; then, in an affectation of boldness rapped upon the shining panel. This was opened by a tall, thinnish man retaining wisps of snowy-white in his fast-receding hair, albeit sporting a significant moustache of nigh-on mercurial grey. He looked genuinely surprised.

'Joshua!' he announced. 'Come in. Whatever brings you here? And why upon an evening such as this!'

'Oth – Oth – Othias,' blabbered the traveller. 'I had no idea. I've been somehow, inexplicably, led here. God knows, myself I'm at a loss.'

'Ah well, plus ça change! Still, still dost thou prate-upon miracle and mystification; yes, even now adverting to your God; paradoxically adhering to invisible presences. Bethink you yet, I'm brighter and cannier than you faith-heads: I'm *The Secular Atheist*. Led! Ha! Man, you've led yourself! Natheless, you and I are old friends. I'd like to hear your news. Forbye, you'll be coveting a billet for the while, else, I could prescribe an occasional bed you might prefer to share! Even so, a caller from the mainland such as yourself would be open to rejection. Enter the lounge, then. Grab yourself a seat.'

The outsider shuffled (in a slink) to where his host had advised, beheld therein an armchair, went over and dropped exhausted into it. Almost at once, he spotted that there was no door: rather, he was looking straight into an open bedroom via a traditional surround curiously devoid of hinges and restricted access. Upstanding once more, he squinnied here and there, discovering that in truth there were five spaces all in all, tending towards a centre, above which hung (however incongruously) a slender chandelier, begetting radiance as well as contributing something decorative to the sterile and nondescript ambience existing in the main.

But alas, he was wrong. Of the five rooms one did have a door: unnoticed till now, since earlier flung wide. And, almost immediately, Othias closed it!

'Ideally, Joshua, we are here to participate in what one might categorise as an experiment. All of us are volunteers, wholly accepting of the arrangement. Therefore, refrain from mounting your usual high horse! Our domes, identified already – albeit only in the drizzle – betide to be uniform, evidencing five rooms given over, respectively, to eating, relaxing, working, sleeping – and last, but not least, sexually-oriented activity. It is the last one which has a door – and, needless to assert, there's a degree of sleeping there, too. The constructions are of *Awkinalite* fabric—'

'Pardon!' interjected the visitor.

'You heard! Come on now: when all is said and done, we've to allow that a lot of the advances hitherto taken as our own, even reckoned at times to be *old hat*, are, historically not our own, being formerly dispensed in exchange for materials or information – else (from time to time) subjects – handed over to an alien species. Positively nobody denies that anymore! Going on, the fabric optimises protection from all violent elements without just as it promotes all the existing heat within.'

'*Subjects*?' Joshua gasped, unable to entertain the reality he had already suffered.

'Yes. Abducted, transported against their will, and then – a person might say – *engaged-with*. Man, get real. We're not living in the dark ages now!'

'Well, there's certainly plenty of light,' retorted the other, attempting to instil a note of levity into the proceedings.

'I take it you're referring to the chandelier – I mean other than the routinely well-lit outward-front which each Zenithular Pod individually has, regardless of the Island taken as a whole. Of course, the juxtaposition of rooms without doors (together with spherical illumination) does suggest surveillance. Although, I would say that – wouldn't I? On this outpost, you see, it's also my job! Just the same, I don't mean spying on people everyplace and at all times, forasmuch as the chamber conducive to sex is at least supposed – but, I do emphasise *supposed*! – supposed to be excluded (*at which dubious revelation the mustachioed host exhibited a rather distressing smirk*) even as the others in the suite, as well as the hub itself, remain all the while open to my over-view.'

'*Your* over-view, Othias?'

'Yes, Joshua, mine. To asseverate openly, one's progressed a good deal since we knew each other in days gone by, volunteering for this particular role at the very start of the pilot, displaying already a philosophical and temperamental predisposition for the requisite monitoring of our island's inhabitants – totally intended, needless to say, for the actual good of the community. Discernibly, you yourself shouldn't have been entitled to disembark at our sanctuary, not if the day-to-day norm had been applied. Dwellers here are disbelievers in God, loyal adherents to a *non-theistic* diagnosis regarding the cosmos, markedly intent upon upholding a correct or veridically-grounded life concluding – for ever and for good! – in the *terminus ad quem* of death.'

'And the *terminus ex quo*?' queried the believer.

'There ain't! As you well know. Know that I do not brook, do not condone any twaddle involving numinous reality, to profess nothing of existence ongoing: in short, primitive (or developed!) tenets about an afterlife. Upholding that line of belief, here on this island, constitutes today a contemporary crime. Yes, Joshua, a crime! Why, but yesterday I beheld an item on the monitor, one I use in the working-area, advising me as to the possibility of a violation. A woman, withal somewhat delicious – dubbed locally as, *The Lady With The Long Neck* – absolutely sexy: well, the very same was heard-unawares articulating dispatches behind her work-station which took in specific and singular elements, the nuances of which I was encouraged to look into. I explored this, uncovering how at one time she'd frankly sworn how, in reminiscing upon her cherished parents – each now deceased – she was inspirited by an image, now and then tolerated by her imagination, of the elderly pair happily on high *dancing* in the sky. That's right, dancing! Waltzing and stepping forth dextrously in some caper or foxtrot or parallel gait.'

'A whimsy – a fancy; pure fantasy.' Thus observed the listener.

'If only. Just the same: how can one be wholly sure? No, no, I've been instructed – that's to declare, duly validated by my office here on Zenith Island (I mean, the experiment that it represents) – to explicate how there can be no caprice, no chimerical dream of an expired couple *up there*, sensibly dancing in the heavens in a whirligig of stars. Each has died and separated into ash, or otherwise dried out to bone! Why verily this hour itself I was ready to drop by, even at the credulous woman's residence, to rescind her private allocation of erotic film. Howbeit, whether she'd welcome my good self in (instead!) who can say? Albeit, I wouldn't refuse – no doubt about that! Oh, and by the by, the gloaming hours of eight to twelve are those of fleshly-doings between the denizens of the domes. Then one is licensed to call in at a dome, as well as to enter – assuming one is welcomed – in every sense. Typically, our wanderers here are male: few of the women ardently go stravaiging-about during the witching period. Regardless, with the passing of time their number might evolve and duly be logged and looked-into by a sub-analyst. Apropos what she's signalled or done, *The Lady With The Long Neck*, well, for sure, she herself must be – huh, I nearly said *punished* – a mite strong, possibly – anyhow, taught the error of her betrayal – shall we put it like that? So, for nine or ten torturous weeks, no erotogenic or compelling diversions!'

Once more Othias' moustache seemed to stretch and twitch. Then he took up his account, unbidden though it was.

'Our lives here have been well thought-out and logically calibrated. No-one may elect to live with anyone else. We are awoken by an alarm around eight o'clock. Between then and eleven we are advised to attend to our day-to-day demands of eating, drinking, regular personal care, exercises and the like. From then until one we continue in our customised working-area: that is to say, at our principal information-widescreen, expediting whatever tasks, else designs, we've been called upon to complete. Necessarily, my own focus centres on recordings of sundry activities I've been allocated to examine. It is open to deduction, possibly surmise, what other personnel might be attending to during this time. Even so, detecting this female member unclosing her revelation – afterwards presented to me – indicates an effective level of co-operation and reliable liaison.'

'And the rest of the afternoon?' queried Joshua. 'More of the same?'

'Yes, including a conference between four and five, during the hour of which we investigate any input imparted by our fraternal or sororal comrades: their questions, their discoveries, their admonitions and so forth. The schedule is rigorously supervised, benefiting from a protocol as to how many minutes each participant is allowed to receive. So much allowed, it remains the case that precipitate drawbacks can occur in the material broadcast. Should then, for example, any buffering befall, I'd guess there's a reference transmitted which is intended for a specialist coterie or designated individual. Regarding *The Lady With The Long Neck*, opportunely, even as I was being signalled, the rest of the monitors would have lapsed into opaque mode. For all that, I am beginning to bore you!'

'No, no, no, no; do continue.'

'All right then, I will! Allocated three hours to wind down, inhabitants of Zenith may call by at some fellow-islander's dome. A single excursion per evening is allowed; pre-arranged – in principle, anyhow – howbeit not an identical partnership across the same week. The main door should be opened, whilst visual contact be made: likewise, a decision is approved as to the desired outcome; albeit, should the dweller be unwilling to flirt, else favour a cessation, then that is that. The other dweller must return immediately to his, or her (sometimes), Pod. As this is likely to occur from time to time, we also enjoy some alternative recreation.'

'Alternative recreation?' The phrase was uttered as a question, although, just as easily, it could've been an exclamation.

'This is where the pornography comes in. In the room given over to stuff of a sexual nature – and, leaving aside all other exercise-gear, contrastive devices, and an ingenious and not insubstantial bed – there is installed a largish rectangular screen the size of an entire wall. Onto this a broad selection of erotica, both earned and carefully chosen, is programmed and run. Secured as before, through dint of labour, are two distinct models contrived entirely from a newly-devised substance: rather rubbery in make-up, very nice to feel, very pleasurable to have next to the skin. Yours truly (in passing) possesses three of these: a very attractive *triuxorite* enjoying the kind of mien and pliable corpus viewed commonly to stimulate, as well as begetting some variety of experience (forbye nerve-sensation) befitting the preference any operative at the time identifies.'

'Withal, this facility,' inquired the visitor, 'what does it offer the *women* of Zenith? What do they have? The mind certainly boggles!'

'Say only that they possess a convenient variety of *objets d'art*, a marketable range neatly tailored to meet their several requirements.' Othias chuckled knowingly, before continuing.

'Really, their choice is theirs, it's all exclusively *their* world – assuredly not mine! It's up to the women to work it out! Concerning myself, I'm extra-fortunate as to how my preferences are addressed. My being in control you see is well deserved, seeing how I fabricated a novel method of mannequin-reproduction. It's based on procuring images of an object and thereafter printing a three-dimensional replica turned out in the substance already mentioned. Consequently, one's solely to generate images of a female to fabricate a life-size model of the chosen lady. One has a duplicate of the woman adored – even if her earnest consent has been withheld – as soon as she's been outwitted or cajoled into proffering her essential likeness! As a corollary, usual spells in the sex-room may, time to time, be solitary – but, lacking satisfaction? Never!'

Joshua's face registered not esteem but alarm, incredulity, a hint of disgust. He had alighted surreally upon a disordered and dystopian world.

'Listen, my friend,' emphasised the satisfied speaker. 'Isn't it clear how the sexual may comprise the direful as well as the pleasurable? Realising an outlet, that is. And, withal, in an assured manner so as to leave us genial, wholly ready to get on with our lives. What we've developed for this asylum comprises a distinctive template for taking responsibility. Yes, taking responsibility for our sexual urges: and, importantly, without getting into failed relationships; religious or secular covenants; impracticable but legally-binding agreements; abusive sexual practices; as well as the voracious vortex of shenanigans and illogicality that bedevils so much of humanity – irregardless of any variant species beyond. Really, it's all exceedingly civilised. What's more, everyone's free to get on with their work, equable because not fretful in the face of domination or destructive resentment. Settlers exist on an equal footing, enjoying a proven formula for governing the irksome randomness of terrestrial chemistry and humdrum encounter.'

'Tell me,' countered Joshua, 'what about perversions, else the grooming of children?'

'Really, I'm not sure I know what you mean, not when it comes to *perversions*; since, whatever folk genuinely suspire for remains the business of none but themselves. Surely, as long as participants are not harmed, exactly what concern is it to anyone else? As to children, there are none – none whatever on Zenith Island. Although – heaven forfend, I all but declared then *dear God!* – there are plenty elsewhere! Look, our outpost constitutes an experiment: albeit of a kind that is non-mandatory, reasonable, properly appreciated.'

'You see,' alleged the un-satisfied listener: 'devilishly tempting for sure – once a heightening of feeling befalls – to yield to the default position. Yes, suppose the redundant banana-skin impels an atheist to the floor – else other, sudden vagary surprises – how in fact do they refrain from unwittingly calling upon their God?'

'There you go again. Powerless to resist your theological-referencing, your pitiable rapacity for scoring a point!'

'Really, Othias, did I score a point then?'

'Oh dear, I'm not wishing to argue. I was going to inquire, Joshua, how your own – how shall I phrase it? – erotic-condition is coming along. You're not looking as young as you used to. Happen you've not glanced in a mirror recently?'

Joshua ignored the question about the mirror, choosing instead a different tack.

'I hear well your formula of an "erotic-condition" to replace an engagement in love. Have you then, Othias, forsaken all hope of that?'

'What most people define under the denomination of *love* is either a predisposition to parent a child, else (if one may phrase it thus) a purely lustful desire. Both have their place. Each may be potent. Even so, it's judicious not to confuse or conflate the two. What's regularly spoken of as *first love* ought to be discerned as a synonym of misapprehension about blissful-bonding, a state associated with infancy, a pleasing diversion outwith the worries of the here-and-now. All the same, we soon grow out of it! Worries remain, feelings change. Re-acquaintance with the everyday world is bilked but temporarily: save, that is, one chances to have reliable and on-going (not to say opportune) happenstances of encountering personnel of a plainly amorous nature – peradventure, via felicitous renown or sizeable resources – thereby equipping oneself to be poised for the predictable disregard for an erstwhile-admired woman in the face of unavoidable monotony. Plainly advise me: whatever, Joshua, befell you and Rachel?'

'Rachel!' exclaimed Joshua. 'However do you know about her?'

'From *The Militant Atheist*, of course.'

'All the same, I don't see.'

'Surely you're curious as to how the Pods and their inhabitants are serviced and maintained? Consider – practically-speaking – how we've got to be catered for, our essential supplies brought in; else, on an occasion, ensure a certain individual dome or screen be properly *tweaked* for some fault or glitch or the like. Thus did it befall at the outset – whilst our collective was being established – that an employee was dispatched to the *Zenith*-project: an engaging hireling conspicuously evidencing an appetite for hitherto-untried food not to add unexpected interest in scholarly semantics and convoluted debate. Verily, all of which you'll avow I cherished most highly myself. In the event, the structure and duties for the day became looser for us both and we discoursed often. He (as it happens) exerted a considerable influence over yours truly: directing my opinions, presenting proposals within the cold light of reason and sober reality. Yes, dear old Solomon. Alas, no longer do I hear reports of his whereabouts, wellbeing, or occupation. Anyhow in the event, one evening – since a severe gale had blown up – he desired to absquatulate back to his lodgings yonder upon the far side and boarded the *Weird Sloop* (alas, the sole craft available) that he might effect a passage to the same cove whence you yourself earlier voyaged. Plainly I warned him it fell short of common sense. Even so, distraught for the safety of his beloved dog, he insisted. Accordingly, preferring to do without a fuss – as well as by then having sought to put him off – I okayed his desire. Withal, troubling though it be, following that I never saw him again. His daughter, Rachel, though – she in due course engaged the regular ferry over to Zenith in order to investigate. Oh, a lovely creature to be sure. Sadly, I'd neither camera nor replicating-material to hand!'

Joshua instinctively bloodied his tongue. Then pushed his friend to go on.

'Never mind. Just how come I got a mention?'

'Two reasons. Fundamentally, your forever banging on about God. Secondly, surprising to relate, it appeared you'd found a golden seam (by default) in enticing the delectable Rachel. Indeed, a triumph by all accounts. According to her father, any rigorous feminist stance moderated thereafter. She herself iterated that those precious years of a shared life, an amicable overlapping, epitomised her very object and desideration – oh the pity of it – veritably, if only they could've continued! Startlingly, you went off in a huff and never returned!'

Suddenly, the demented Joshua had abandoned his chair, withal woodenly was stomping up and down; and, pardonably, looking decidedly annoyed. Then he turned upon Othias.

'Whatever do you mean, *enticing* – and then, *precious years*? Years! Hours, at most! Encountered her, yes I did. Even so, purely to talk – well, yes, briefly withal to dance! Never mind, all at once I was obliged to abscond. And, by none other than your beloved friend, *The Militant Atheist*! Occurrents betiding thereafter slide into a mental blur. I was chased. There was a great jet-black dog. I passed-out, supposing I imagine correctly. Really, I don't know. I'm unable to remember!'

'Obviously,' endorsed Othias, 'each has alighted upon awkward times, whilst neither of us is getting younger! Sincerely, though, you mean to say you cannot properly bring to mind your lovingly *being-with-her*?'

'Yes,' his friend almost screamed. 'I'm iterating I'm unable to recall! God above, I've no such recollection!'

'Show restraint! Shun such talk!' asserted the other. 'Glaringly, you've still to comprehend how – whatever imbroglio you've got yourself embroiled in – no availment or assistance has been provided by any Paterfamilias of the Heavens. What is more, one labours to afford you much empathy – openly speaking – given that it was you who left the girl! Even so, apropos Solomon, happily I'm able to observe how – albeit I never saw him thereafter – how evidently he was ferried to safety by the master of *The Black Petrel*. For all that, trumpet not, *Thank Heavens*! Solely, instead, how fortune and coincidence may not the while prove to be *widdershins* for an individual. At times, they'll orient dextrally, the *sunwise* way – verily, as we ourselves would prefer!'

Joshua sat down.

Othias got up, proceeding to enter the chamber of dining. Despite being invisible to the eye, a noisy blattering could be heard resonant of cupboards opening, closing, and opening again, in concert with what might've been the parcelling-up of knick-knackery – conceivably into a carrier.

Assuredly, once Othias re-entered the Dome's R & R locale, discernibly the host held stiffly in the angular strain of his knuckle a turquoise plastic-wrap bulging with provisions, which he hereupon tucked into the everyday holder belonging to his friend. Immediately, he sat down, this time with a flop. Audibly sighed. Looked up to the curved ceiling. A second time sighed. Wearily, but with feeling, he began.

'Ideally, you'd want me to provide you with solace, to comfort you sensitively. You'd like me to advise you that everything is for a purpose: how really you did have a legitimate excuse for rejecting the presence of Solomon's only offspring. Or, even, insist that the very act of mental erasure may embody an inherent meaning, which, once known, appears purposeful and plain. Such consolation, however, I'm sadly unable to give. Conceivably, all matters will turn out better in the end. Apropos the issue of *The Modern Feminist*, all the same, I've to emphasise that such a likelihood is not great.'

Again a sigh. And from the other silence. With blank countenance.

The secular adviser went on. 'I cannot leave matters so. Actually, this is the sort of painful, unseasonable centre about which authentic decisions can and should be formed. Transparently, it's when existence is at its bleakest and sorrows do abound that citizens here will adhere to a well-proven, congruent path, abjuring the unworldly or sentimental or delusional. Possibly, Joshua, you've come here today bearing within your soul the subliminal ache of many incomplete, ruined, even tantalising memories. To these, here and now, I've added assertions potentially which could increase your burden, giving to it an additional twist and taunt. You are alone, my friend. Here, now, you need to face this truth, this common aim of realising – whilst being yourself – your own, individual, sexuality. Else whether, even now, you be prepared to wait (naively) for what you crave to be the possibility of love – which is itself, I suspect, but a variety of youthly idolatry.'

'Idolatry,' muttered the bemused believer in another world, then continuing. 'Should you refer to idolatry and idols, then, mustn't you as a corollary concede the likelihood of a non-idol, and – that being thus – do you not accept at least the conceivability of an idol's opposite – in other words, a deity?'

At this mention, Othias did something quite alarming. He leapt up out of his chair, seized Joshua by the length of his arm and rudely withal yanked him from his reclining position. He heaved him to the door, foisted the shoulder-sack into his hands, and declared:

'I'm rueful indeed. Even so, later you may thank me. Here, now, this is the time for choosing: standing on your own two feet. For being a man. Not the mere child of a childish projection. Joshua, abandon your God! AND be gone from my house! I may not force the first, but I can demand the second.'

And Othias, so saying – with pliant and wiry vigour – flung his quondam companion into the chill night air. And slammed the door.

Joshua's head was in a whirl. Not able to think straight, he gulped in some of the gloom, distorted with its amber-like, yellowy light. Of a sudden, he picked up his pace, first ambling, then ere long beginning a jog, loping anon even at a goodish run, inhaling the vesperal, vaporous atmosphere.

Yet, abruptly too, he halted, divining that – *mirabile dictu* – he felt himself to be markedly better. Yes, now that the furlongs attained availed him with their gathering darkness, and, that the vantablack of the unknown was, chimerically, emboldening him to let go of what was done and gone. To be loosed from the dome felt good: to be removed from his one-time ally and friend, whose weltanschauung over the years had hardened, becoming alien, strange, disquieting. Over seasons to come, maybe he'd consider this event from an alternate standpoint; yet, for the moment, raw emotion must be prioritised, utter relief being the dominant; borne of reprieve. He began again to run. As far as the shore, further to which and away from the pier was an islet, accessible across the stone of the ebb, towards which the outcast made successful headway; and, once there, beholding a corroded, olden mollusc-bound anchor, stoically did make of that a counterfeit-seat; reviving, recovering his assuagement; dreamily staring, ruminating long; simply inspiring the while, elementally, the ethereal wonder.

Before long clouds clung where heretofore the haar had wreathed its strange allurement: clouds higher up clustering, yielding eerily-wide views of the turbulent waters and occasional, jettisoned snippets of wave-tops, arrestingly white where buffed by the wind and the combing of the tide's settle and shift. Preferable, palpably, it was to revive out of doors. To respire the enlivening ozonic milieu of the canopying night.

Then anon a rustle, a sound like a hard crunch of heel hitting, reiterating, even in the still-wet sliding shingle of exposed beach. Unperturbed, the man got up, turned all about, arrayed his back to the sea to behold, barely yards from where he was, the far out willowy figure and frame of a woman wandering, elegant-like in a flowing, flimsy garment – its hemline gathered up, hitched fast for ease and facility of pace: enigmatic angel, sylphish and soulful amid the ebony silhouettes and exhilarating sky; fine in demeanour, her face as-whey, beauteous, cradled within a flow of hair falling, falling to her shoulders and barely lifted from her brow. Mayhaps a muse, haply a harbinger, perchance a nemesis: still, she could be – not a whit of any doubt, no none – none other than she, *The Lady With The Long Neck*. Equally, the other, the visitor-outcast, forbye he was entranced, riveted; ravished:

'Hail, pilgrim of the night – who art thou?' Questing thus did he whisper: realising breath itself, articulation withal of words, alas, no longer easy.

'I am *The Lady With The Long Neck*,' sounded then the figured reply; mesmerically intoned with a sweetishness, albeit uttered not-without-mirth or an edge of mockery.

'This I see,' conceded her admirer.

And so it was, this especial *Zenith*-creature, decidedly did she own (as it were) an elongation of her neck; an anomaly, conceivably, whereby there be added grace unto grace to her giveaway-guise of slimness, flow, and elegance. Howbeit, this lady, she was not young. As Joshua drew closer to espy a fairer, truer view, he divined (courtesy of the luminant, emerging moon) not purely the fringe of silver-black hair (daintily curtaining alike forehead and brow), else her winsome oval, gentle face beaming now, but, here beside, girdling her nobly-held neck, withal, a round accrual of lines that still the light cotton scarf could not quite disguise. Risible barely, surely it be, to aver this gentle nigher to fifty than in sooth himself. Peculiarly, the measure of his own lived years he intuited not; albeit Othias – leastwise he supposed – already may've progressed well into his forties. By the same token, wherefore, he also must be of that age. Irregardless, what was the relevance or significance of such? He yearned then to touch her. Even so, he refrained, reprising his question.

'Your name? Once more I ask.'

'Again I pronounce, I am *The Lady With The Long Neck*. Only, also I am lost, unsure of what I seek; whither I ought to go. Though greatly do I need, really what do I want? Clarify, oh do. Truly, soothfully, does that *make sense*?'

'Haply dost thou presume, else surmise (*posited admirer to beloved*) that the idyll for which you suspire appears ill-befitting: not conducible to the ordained, celestial dance. Although, isn't it the ravishment and spiritedness of love for which, throughout the years, you long – though ridded of its inevitable, its wearisome intimacies undergone within the inexorability of days? Disquieted you are by the loss of the heightened, fearing the operose, the burden of boredom. Own it to be thus, oh *Lady With The Long Neck*.'

'Straightforwardly,' the sinuous denizen inquired, 'tell me: *does* that make sense?'

'In this controlled and atomised world, perhaps. Wherefore, imagine another! Conjure a domain wherein a rhythm of life waxes and wanes in the regularity of love. Suppose, besides, you chanced both ebb and flow, sustained securely in a single embrace? Consider, what then?'

Withal, even as Joshua advised, so was he driven (in his ample affect) to reach out: in actuality to touch her (as if to join with her) fingering thereto, dotingly, her fringe apart, ardently smiling into her open blue eyes that sparkled with a kind of crazed twinkle, of an ecstasy past as well as, perchance – perhaps, to come. And he urged her now:

'Hie away with me this lunar night. Hereupon, I'll revere you and love you in a life that is shared. Fain shall we pass our hours, appreciatively, for the givenness of the other. Come away with me. Come.'

'No, no, alas. I am unable to leave, unable hence to return. Hope there is none of a world outwith, no hope for life beyond. God was the tale of a ruined wizard, furnished by fable and failure, ne'er the facilitating *pneuma*, oh no, befitting us citizens here. Appreciate: I am a woman, body and soul, awake in the current domain. I must stay here.'

'And your parents?' challenged the man.

Wonderingly, his eyes searched aloft towards the sundered cloudscape, the crescent moon, the brilliant crepitant stars laughing (all-but, thus did it seem) laughing in the galactic blue of the world-wielding heavens. 'Do they not dance above us?'

The woman looked vexed. 'How is it thou hast knowledge of that? A conceit, it fell from my lips, a trivial remark – made off the cuff, only in jest.'

'Only in jest?'

'Entirely, why yes. Foolish it was, yet I brooded so. Aye, e'en out loud. Ere long will I – must I – thole the forfeit for my unfounded wish.'

'Be free, therefore,' responded the itinerant. 'Come away. You and I away. Let us betake ourselves from this place and its dreadful domes, experience joy in our destiny ahead. Come away with me. Come!'

Of a sudden, the woman appeared frail, she shivered, became distracted, turned to left, to right, back again to Joshua. She smiled, awkwardly, and murmured, strangely: 'Observe you with my eyes, yes, I am able. Discern within my heart, even so, alas, I cannot.'

Then the slimness of being that she was went about, veritably, within the blankness of black (whence she had come) airily hieing unto the bedimmed, amberous-irradiance of the many domes. Visible yet it was to the other, as he gazed – verily, as she pivoted about – how the thin buckles of her sandals did sparkle and flash, each like silvern crosses.

All at once, Joshua exclaimed: 'Oh, *Lady With The Long Neck*, present me at last with your name?'

Greatly to his surprise, she stopped, as if dead in her steps. And turned, and leant low, while some tetrad of marks she scored within the sand of the bent-filled dunes, those that now cleft straight her path from the wynd to the pier. Then, turning again, she lifted her shift, filmy and billowing in the stirring breeze – and fled. Away. Away. Away.

Joshua faltered not at all in going right to the spot, though not able to detain the wind in the sand from its swirl and chaos, its swither. So the same precious exchange, dwindled it had to a mere letter alone. Squinnying, he leant to the one-fold character: 'L'.

What precisely, he questioned, uneasily to his soul, did this poor logogram denote: taunting, tantalising, an obliquity quite? Mayhaps a dalliance; else longing unrequited? Hence, for *love* or for *lust*? Else, an ordinary appellation – plainly, simply – of *loveliness*.

The woman, she had departed, yielding the man forlorn wholly to his thoughts.

The man, he knew not the hour when this siren, this beldam fatale would arrive at her Pod: whether it be prior to the predatory Othias. He agonised, too: might she in truth allow him in? He queried again: would his whilom friend have gone with camera beside?

Then Joshua fell to his knees upon a floor of sand, dropping forth in a fold verily of grief to weep. His heart had become like wax, melted within his breast. The heavens had poured him libation-like, balefully, towards the calyx of the earth.

Part the Fifth: *in which Joshua voyages aboard the* White Raven, *detecting several things of a rebarbative nature.*

Time passed. A creeping, crepuscular light brought back objects to a shadowy plane, disclosing them transubstantiated into their diurnal guise. A horn sounded. A large, sea-faring vessel had pulled in at the pier. Emblazoned on its flank were the two words, White Raven.

As though in a kind of subliminal world, yet surfacing as he must for the reckoning to come, Joshua rose badly-limbering to the day's harsh and bitter dawn, so quitting thereat the domain of the domes with their myriad denizens, staggering tardily yet forward to his destiny, the odyssey to come.

No ticket or fare, fortuitously, was sought. The captain desired from his subdued pilgrimer solely that he afforded him the measure of his discourse through the voyage ahead: anterior to which he must secure his place to rest and prepare – to wit, in due course, a roundel of convoluted rope.

Permeating the piquant air at this hour was a lingering, oleaginous pungency resonant with brine, bespeaking besides a veritable abundance of harvested fish. Clamouring and screeching, moreover, was the ubiquitous chunner and chunter of gulls: as, heavily, ponderously, did the rugged boat detach from the island-pier, the asylum of Zenith – howbeit, not utterly from the echoes of that isle's identity; its ill-fated peculiarity.

Then, whilst the floating vehicle voyaged to the spread of the beyond, the meditative adventurer recognised a booming voice, trumpeting familiarly. In the reaches, a little way off, a fishing boat plied and plashed in a passable swell or lift of wave. At the prow, evincing legerity, were two erect, unequal souls – one stalwart and powerful of voice, less so the other, muted by comparison. So it was, decidedly, upon that expanse of morn, the peregrinator heard anew the valedictory cry now gifted to uplift his soul, hearten him, impel him ever-onward during his quest to come: 'Fare forward, dear friend! Fare forward!' The tiny arms (as it appeared) of the fisher-folk swayed from side to side above their heads; so, fleet afresh of limb, at once their former charge upraised his hands forbye, affirming his appreciative sharing; whilst, even as he gestured so, equally sprung too brotherly tears, sudden and artless, within his eyes.

*　*　*　*　*　*

Perchance, synchronicity had somehow conjured a singular moniker to become correlate with the character of the captain: it being, *The Curious Conniver.* A variety of the older hands, nonetheless, chose to employ his praenomen, Bill. A shambolic fellow, he was done out in shabby chinos, chestnut-coloured, plus a threadbare ill-fitting peacoat of apricot hue. His hair was flaxen and closely-cropped, whilst, to cover up his lost eye – plus the tragedy it recalled – he wore a round black patch. Roguish, to put it mildly (heeded Joshua to himself) hearing a raucous command to go down below and right-royally tank-up there with goodly amounts of the man's personal honeyed-rum. Coincident with this, a sudden pelt of rain with fetch of wind washed the pasting of sand away from his legs.

Although the *White Raven* was a smart-enough frigate, its superintendent was definitely not. Veritably slumped within a round, wooden armchair, and positioned at an untidy table, Captain Bill gestured to his latest passenger to 'take a pew', indicating the long-backed settle along the side of the cabin. Joshua did as he was told, noting as he did so – and on the corner of the table nearest to him – a small, thick glass, as well as a corked bottle of liquid the colour of black treacle.

'Help yourself – that's what it's there for. I have!'

The Curious Conniver grinned, nicely prizing the dimpled tumbler he preferred – swigging it back with gusto. Without waiting, he refilled it. 'Go on!'

Joshua was yearning to be beside his companions from the cove, appreciating modest gulps of precious wine, ruby-red and with predictable effect. Still, one had better act as advised. Deracinating the cork from the bottle he then, a tad gingerly, poured a generous measure ere he then began to sample little sips (nervously) so becoming seasoned agreeably to the potency and taste of this unfamiliar draught. Swallowing less than the total amount, the wary imbiber felt himself anon becoming more amenable. Tolerant, too, of his garrulous host's confident blethering.

'I like to keep a fairly tight ship here. If I'm not wrong, I reckon a God-fearing soul (same-as-yourself) would likely approve. If someone steps out of line or gets it wrong he's docked a point – else two; or three or four! And? What do points mean? Points mean punishment! Five points revoked by the close of the week and the man gets a flogging. Then again, if more, his rum-allowance is curtailed. Still more? Ah well, further ritual humiliation must be dealt him. Even so, implore me not to divulge its nature – better to turn a blind eye – howbeit, absolutely I'd figure it would not be very nice!'

Pronouncing thus, the captain roared and, glass to mouth – *down the hatch* – there went another half-tumbler of sugary tipple. Briefly then discomfited, he abruptly sat up – momentarily staring ahead – then evidenced a full-throated belch and crumpled back noisily into the now rickety chair.

Joshua slowed his imbibing – in an instant. Then queried, 'Suppose though the crew of the ship heeded their duties particularly well?'

'Should they do that, they'll not get punished! 'Tis easy really. Incentivisation through the use of stick without carrot!'

'Or,' intimated one more merciful, 'you could decide to supplement points from quotas forfeited through bad behaviour; keep a tally, yes, benignly permitting it to be a part of the determining, whenever they go astray or are ineluctably at fault.'

'Maybe that's why you as God-fearing guest remain but a transient appurtenance, whilst it is *moi*, myself, who must run this vessel! They've all to be toughened-up! Only, well, never mind that. You've spent a night on Zenith Island. I hear things about that place. Not all to my liking, either.'

'Nor to mine,' chipped in Joshua, predictably craving now to share some common ground.

'You see,' resumed the other, 'I like my women to be genuine women. I enjoy the affective *feel* of them, the smell of their perfume, their warmth. A sailor like me seeks adventure. Yearns oft to go a-roving in the troughs and the billows, cherishing the smack of the sea, withal excitedly entering the susceptive port! No, no: embrace sobriety a moment. Fain would I relish, even adore, verily worship a woman. Wouldn't it, my friend, befit you too! Also, mind yon trim specimen – herself you were pleading with, down near Zenith Islet.'

'Yes – possibly! How is it, even so, that you know of her? Surely, surely, you were too far off.' Joshua reached for the nectar in the bottle.

'With these,' replied the captain, handling an object from the surface of the table. 'Out and out snazzy; a felicitous instrument enabling a multitude of remote facets to be observed. I think belike they'll catch on. Maybe already have. Each regular scope is exceeded through the use of a tetrad of glassen lenses – two at each end – by which one may observe the distance ahead. See?'

The one found-out took the object offered and quickly stole a peek through the narrower end. There he saw a fuzzy, distorted vision of Bill's face and frame. 'You're saying that you made out both *myself* plus *The Lady*...'

'Good enough,' interrupted the captain. 'Adroitly beauteous she seemed, whilst you yourself assuredly keen. Irregardless, my drift is this. Seriously, you'd not be showing wariment apropos a god and to being good should you be able to lay your hands habitually on the like of yon. Really now would you? Primarily, folks that cannot indulge in reliable satisfaction have no choice but to airt their desires some other way – commonly, upwards. At whatever said *upwards* might awaken, else possibly betoken. The singular irony is that all their assurance – truly, their every *desire* – like it or not ends up settling on an invisible nothingness! Assuredly, that's what they worship! On the other hand, myriads who be not so pure of heart propose something realisable before which – under suitable symbolic guise – they proffer obeisance, visibly bowing down. A relic, some statue, aye, its guttering glim. Howbeit, as for me, I prefer a whole and wholesome woman! Yes, a reality I can get these tusks into!'

The argument was tempting: indubitably, concerning the current commander, alike its libidinous precursor and expected outcome. Even so, by now it had drawn to its inevitable close – regardless of a courteous suggestion from Bill's protégé: 'Still, mayn't one observe about this matter as of all? Sex was made for man – not man for sex. Intimacy espoused to truth comprises the chief pearl prized.'

'Here, here,' vented the exasperated skipper, 'there never was any making, don't you see? No matter, I've argued myself dry; withal, I favour tempting you with a bargain. Grant me your dosage in the bottle – I'll guerdon you then a share of this gadget! Behold the vista ahead, pace the deck, examine the scenery! Besides, we're not far now from the Three Farms' Peninsular, where I've to oversee a fresh drop-off. Natheless, for now – yeah, that's right – much obliged!'

Already Bill had the opening to his lips and was getting a voracious slug-slug of the potion down his throat. Joshua pulled wide the captain's door and escaped briskly to the purer air attainable above, anxious to be able to see what was what – to say nothing of clearing his head.

The honorary-deckhand, savouring again the air above – having hirpled at the start – still remembered he possessed the provender from Othias in his shoulder-bag. What's more, delving into this now he found a bundle of pasta, a boiled egg, a chunk of cheese, and a small container of milk. He'd intended, first of all, to toss them overboard – symbolically shaking-off the dust from his person. Anyhow, he considered it now more judicious to consume them. Heartily he ate and imbibed, devouring them, and no doubt feeling a little better for it. Subsequently, he utilised the gismo (now on loan) staring cautiously through its lenses – paired at each end: two large, two small – discerning how one way the landscape seemed more remote, whilst the other unusually near. Perceiving as well how the latter disclosed considerable detail, he was motivated to use it in just such a way. By this means then did he realise, absorbingly, a prolonged stare.

Soon enough wherefore he espied that a noticeable bulk of land was coming into sight; in reality, a promontory to which the *White Raven* approached closer and closer. A derisive *pensée* passed through the watcher's mind: videlicet, that now was the timely point at which Bill ought to let go of his tipple to apply at least one functioning eye to the task in hand. Soothfully, he suffered also then his imagination to contemplate the removal of the ocular mask, uncovering in so doing a socket, empty and eyeless, louring into some private madness. Natheless, sounder it was now to pay heed to the Three Farms' Peninsula, the very spur-of-land – a markedly-dismal bog-ridden *ness* – now signally luring them to its shores.

Suddenly, Joshua, newly affected by this enhanced capacity to descry, disturbingly made out a discomfiting scenario some modest quarter-mile from the sizeable pier then steadily beckoning. Alike feral and despoiled of clothes, a middle-aged man was running *nolens volens* across a stretch of mire. Occasionally, he would glance behind, even as he'd also brook, now and then (and wilderingly), a mud-covered hoof to thrust, lumberingly, into the squelching quag. Startlingly, two things then occurred. An explosive report was heard and a brisk order given: 'Time to return the thingumabob!'

It was *The Curious Conniver* announcing the end of his short-term swap. Wherefore, once realised, the naked eye could make out nothing of the aforementioned, straggling figure. For all that, there were other matters still to behold. Directly beneath, to one side of the projecting jetty, was what appeared to be some kind of pen: one into which animals might normally be herded. Into this corral was being pushed or prodded, percase squeezed, a stramash of fed-up and fashed internees – largely barbarous but passive men – whilst the ragged pantomime was being spitefully expedited with spiked, metallic emphasis. Oddly, the careworn convicts had blankets, fibrous and rough, folded shapelessly about them. Apparently, too, the shanks of all were bare, whilst their fettered feet unshod.

'Why are those people wearing coverlets?' asked Joshua. 'Exactly where are they heading for?'

Bill blinked, rubbing the one remaining pupil.

'It'll turn cold, especially at night. They're prisoners. They're making for *Detention Farm*. Heartening, don't you think, to know that severity and command still hold sway! Should you care to descry more, affix your best blinker to yon tubular jut of tin. Alongside the railing. It's even better than this gismo here.' (Hitched now by a thin wreath of twining, it was hanging from the captain's neck.)

One upstanding pupil did as he was told.

Once more a panorama opened-up by now more inclusive as well as a deal closer than any envisioned through eye alone. The prisoners, hitherto corralled, evidently were being directed by enthusiastic minders – impatient guards each of whom had pinpointed on a detainee a long iron weapon with a bayonet. Captives were hirpling as far as an area of common, adjoining one of sphagnum morass, along which various personages, paradoxically, appeared to wander – a myriad distractedly, yet a number with manifest resolve. From these last, several were tugging hard at clumps of spiny-rush, munching said plant with nigh-frantic intensity. Not far away, a few were vigorously and viciously fighting each other, with bodies conspicuously soiled from both blood and dirt. Furthermore (who knew why?) a number near at hand stayed supine, questionably stretched-out, consistently across the ground. What's more, further away, a triad of prisoners (of uncertain gender) were engrossed in some sort of rutting procedure. Then again, nigh to the gate of the compound, there peered – already angled and broken-limbed – seven shuffling men trembling and juddering under torrents of water. Immediately abaft these were clearly-tensed and affrighted associates, queuing so as anon, forlornly, they might be beheaded; whilst the stockade's own butcher, bending with a broad blade, cut and lopped at a corpse – bashing, hammering, sundering joint and slice from the chine, from the rack of bone.

To the watcher, the whole of this was excruciating even to behold. Howbeit, he gave witness purely to give avowal to the extent and horror of these appalling deeds. Higher up, away from *Detention Farm*, two other camps came into view, both of which were entirely enclosed. Verily but with difficulty was it possible to make out the clumsily-depicted characters, laid forth considerably upon the high, weighty doors – whatever markings at this distance being, of course (and assistance notwithstanding) extremely small. The closer of the twain ostensively read, *Clone Farm*, whilst the other, farther off and more opaquely, *Mengele Farm*.

Obviously perturbed, Joshua had seen more than enough. Outraged, he immediately challenged the inquisitive and partly-sighted skipper over what he'd just witnessed. Tiresomely, the half-blinded Bill was busying himself with the oversight and unlading of additional cargo from the *White Raven*, as well as the hoisting on board of divers bulky, wooden crates. Yet, he suddenly veered leftward to his land-lubber, informing him: 'Extra supplies. Plus plentiful provision of frozen meat. Albeit, forasmuch as sourced from here, I'd resist making a feast of it. Several visitors one year opted for vegetarianism – after having bolted down a local sample – the entire group declaring it'd made each and everyone ill. The trots! And worse!'

The other struggled to make reply. His gorge hereupon wanted to heave. Still, he managed to ask, in some dread of an answer: 'Really – and those compounds? The two higher up?'

'Ah well – mayhaps the rightwing imagine – it's by and large a glib sop to the urbane (and generally those of a liberal-outlook) that all surveilled mewed-up, stabled within the primary garrison, be not cooped up the whole time, being authorised to enjoy free range in the open air. Just the same, the next encampment is non-organic – translate as you wish (*he grinned*) – to which one may but remark, that, those immured would presumably be denied any vitalising air and quotidian light of day. None thus far, even so, have been notified as to whether they are indeed regular prisoners. Possibly they're not. Anyhow, yon compound beyond is an unusual one, being entirely devoted to invalided children. I've no idea what betides therein.'

Whilst the skipper endeavoured to depart the pier, Joshua detected a thickening cloud of smoke rising from the horizon. Abruptly, he felt that he was not going to be able to stomach the image then evoked, even as the contemplation of what fortuitously had not been revealed – invisible, yet conjuring horrors from within the darkest core of his soul – made him doubt for an instant that he was of sound mind. He recalled Jacob; then withal put to himself this question: did the *Being of God* endure malaises of the terrestrial mind, in addition to corporeal suffering? And then, unable not so to conclude: must the *Core of Benignity* confront a category of darkness similarly within? Of a sudden, he retched over the starboard-side of the vessel; saw his mess unravel in the wind; smelt a tang of its stench, then tasted the slimy acridity adhering to his mouth.

As his eyes began to clear from the physical stress and sudden sweat of his vomitory action, the voyager espied something that was breathtaking to behold (if uncanny too) and, to be sure, not remotely credible. Instead of gazing down a span the compass of ten or eleven men, he was scrutinising wide-eyed a drop of starboard looming down many times more, down if not literally into a submarinal world of oceanic whale and basking shark, at any rate perceivably into the thrashings of beings abounding in the blue-and-white mayhem of waves, churning and spilling about the wake's outward rush. Furthermore, also discernible, was that the external woodwork had by now been replaced. The flanks of the ship instead were constructed of steel. Sheer swathes of unfolded metal-expanse fell and rose, coldly-defiant abutting trough and wave, even whilst each bevelled side upheld the solidity and frame of this man-made leviathan.

The recovering patient stood and shook himself in the breeze. He felt hirsute and unbarbered. Chagrined, he glanced in a porthole, combing for a cursory gander to detect how drear and grim, how tormented he'd started to appear – natheless, descrying merely the liquid field behind his inquisitorial yet invisible face. Almost afore he knew it, a soul with visage upraised sharply turned round and down, focusing upon his chapfallen self. Strikingly, this not unfamiliar form was properly attired in a bold, singularly-white uniform, and, when faced full-on, disclosed his authentic colours and, *mirabile dictu,* his regulation captain's-cap. The visage of the man was well-barbered; similarly, his person had about him a demeanour implying confidence and military training. It was solely the disc of black silk, attached with a thread across a closed eye, which implied that this was indeed *William* (elevated master of the *Corbyn Albanus*) the common appellative of whom remained that of *The Curious Conniver*. However, once he elected to give forth in words, the aforesaid did so with authority, with sobriety, with an inkling (one might have thought) of avuncular solicitude.

'One anticipates you are feeling better. Many are the things at sea that disconcert us. Mentally, your character may be a tad susceptive to them, scarcely acclimated to the motions of our world. It is yet feasible with the binoculars – over the cobalt ocean beyond the stern – to see the last of the Three Farms' Peninsula. One obtains a better sight via the tin telescope; whilst withal you may prefer to keep an eye open, nigher the vessel's prow, for the Animal Archipelago. Actually, it ought to invite a fine piece of reportage. You'll pardon me anyhow for the moment; I'm needed on the bridge.'

The assertion noted, the troubled inquirer now found himself to be alone, albeit withal prey to a bizarre sensation that a copious quantity of people be gathered around; veritably, as though he himself be located on some sort of palatial domain now floating upon the undulant, briny waters. He returned to the telescope. Evidence of smoke, now was there none. Even so, its absence remained a curious indicator of its presence earlier. The realisation then occurred to him that, for all he knew, different ocular scopes might be available nearby. Mayhaps, one of them might give out onto the Animal Archipelago.

So in sooth one did. The wildered passenger soon found his scene homed, finely-focused and centred, on the far-flung islands – a chain of a dozen enveloping into a circle, as perspective allowed. Granted the range obtainable seemed considerable, the power of the novel device was scarcely less.

Sighted through the magical lens of moulded-glass was a scene of a group of primates. Hairy and wild in one respect they were, withal, partly vested (and weirdly so) in standard khaki, comprising about two scores that sat upon chairs attending, ostensibly, to a gorilla featuring peculiarly a grey mortar-board, apparently slanted downwards across its head. The civilised brute was pointing to a canvas perched upon an easel. Then, all at once, a dozen furry paws lifted up within Joshua's gaze.

An involuntary movement of his own humerus occasioned here a further aberrant view, equally odd, pivoting, centring upon a wondrous chimpanzee, upright upon a podium, besporting itself almost erect strumming dramatically a violoncello. Descrying that an audience was nowhere to be seen, notionally, said creature might've been reprising some *capriccio* for an up-coming recital.

Standing a little way off was a further, distinctive simian, one plainly apparelled in a clinical white coat, monitoring a water-tank, right out of which there leapt into the air a golden fish, again and again and again. Diligently, this erudite, academic monkey was evidently taking notes, afterwards gesticulating to a student – a variety of hominid lacking clothing, being secured with an iron shackle looped to each foot. The servitor carried to the learned ape an item – likely a porringer of food, in view of the protuberant spoon – delivering it obsequiously to the monkey. Regardless, the pedagogue summarily dismissed him, singularly brandishing his clawed and dextrous hand.

Though evident still within the range of the telescope, the illustrious, cruising liner managed such a rate and elected course to terminate rapidly any protracted survey of the archipelago: a valedictory cameo the surveyor managed to conjure, through the enchanted circumference, manifested a bizarre, partly-pithecoid creature – owning a terrestrial crown on an ape's body – withal, likely feminal since wearing a bikini. The discoverer inherently reckoned how, were he to elicit from the captain some interpretive account, probably it'd transpire to be an analytical exploration of the links between differentiated primates: a behavioural evaluation designed to include genetic components within its overall analysis and trial. The genesis for the description wasn't obvious: the words adopted arose unconsciously, coming to his mind unbidden. Howbeit, further scientific deliberation hereupon was denied. The ponderer found himself awoken from his reverie by a triumphant call: '*Megopolis ahoy!*'

Straightaway, the beholder was cognisant of a lively assembly of people, bestrewn chaotically all about the decks and peering excitedly into the distance. Notwithstanding, Joshua spun the visual aid wholly towards the remote passage, even as a blear finger of ground magnified into an imposing headland, itself overlaid with complexes the scale and placement of which intimated quite massive proportions. Maintaining his grasp on the magnifier soon became more difficult. Several emulous passengers were muscling-in to appropriate the coveted view. Stepping to one side, Joshua descried the new outlook rising before him, larger-than-life, and growing nobler and grander by the minute. A profusion of buildings rose high as hills, towering into the sky, framing everywhere their vasty plates of glass, sheer and transpicuous within their gleaming, shining structures. A heavy sense of claustrophobia befell, whilst discerning, comprehending, these edificial giants.

Part the Sixth: *in which Joshua explores Megopolis, encounters manifold citizens until, by and by, he secures access to a captivating park.*

The wanderer's return to properly firm ground diminished his perturbation not a jot. Veritably, a nigh-enough swarm of people surrounded him. What's more, the unintelligible-babble audibly buzzing, surfeiting, disconcerted him so much that either where he was or what he was doing exceeded his proficiency to grasp.

Resolutely, he paced onward as best he might, seemingly indeed for a considerable length of time, tiresomely rubbing shoulders as well as craning his neck the easier to see, high up, the columns of this magnificent city wherein Ann-Gel (opined the itinerant) ought percase, perchance, to have felt herself at home. Here, even as he jostled and squeezed through an especially dense part of the throng, unavoidably he realised that a myriad faces within the crush of citizenry evinced an appearance more rounded than he was used to. Peculiarly, their equilibrating eyes appeared to slant; and, even more, their regular intonation sounded more sing-song (indeed, not dissimilar to a certain, importunate *Awkin*) – itself augmenting the notable impression of prattle and absurdity.

Several moments elapsed within this outlandish environment, until the newcomer observed in front of him a large placard onto which had been intricately drawn a detailed guide, denominated, '*The White Indian Quarter*'. Strolling more slowly (nervousness subsiding) said peregrinator detected how the language spoken by virtually all around him had lost its previous timbre, so close again to familiar utterance – howbeit, the listener had endeavoured not at all to converse.

Responsive to a fresh requirement for respite, here was the stage at which to pursue in earnest some suitable spot wherein he might rally and revive. Forthwith, he identified an untidy row of variously attired adults moving forward slowly through a wide doorway, above which illuminated vomitory a billboard notified the imminent showing of three films. None of these last appeared remotely to be of the genre that his earlier disputant, Othias, might – given their titles – have himself opted to watch: they were, *Pink Mist*, *Hiroshima*, and, *The Holy Cause*. Nevertheless, he could be misguided in his appraisal; considering, after all, said stipulated *mist* was denoted *pink*, whist the supporting title, *Hiroshima*, might refer to some alluring woman. Bemusingly, a fourth film, *Peaceable Mayhem*, also transpired to be 'coming out soon'.

So far, indeed, had he roamed and voyaged upon departing his former companions – notably, Jacob and Pedram and Tom – the occasion now for a spiritually-uplifting experience (indicated in the available choices) furnished him with joy and relief. Therewithal his way-in was secured without cumber or hindrance. Natheless, peculiarly, it was required of those in front that they'd need to make a payment to obtain a ticket; whereas, he'd merely himself to walk-on-in, almost as though authorised via a fable or surrealist dream.

Despite this, all was not well. Scarce had he settled down within the roomy and comfortable amphitheatre than the selfsame lighting that'd before revealed the appearance and admission of those subscribing suddenly dimmed. The visitor therefore found himself sitting in a thoroughly strange place, confined within a darkness almost entire. Albeit not for long.

An horrisonant racket started to sound-noisily from the flanks of the theatre, centring mindfulness on the frontage along which, melodramatically, two grand, hanging curtains of beige parted to reveal an imposing screen hideously depicting (on a picture of wavering monochrome) not the three words he'd anticipated so much as a triunity minus one: *The Holocaust*. There was a gasp from the audience as a wide, roughly-dug pit was shown heaped high with naked, nigh-skeletal corpses. The outsider decided that some mistake must have been made in a suitable construal of the words, potentially from one 'quarter' of the capital-city to another. His own appetency was to survey one of the alternative *movies*; to wit, even that awhile the woman to the fore essayed volubly to discuss. Howbeit, whilst he of a sudden then, in the company of others similarly-disquieted, pivoted half-round to confirm the location of two exit-doors, withal, there was to be seen standing by them a duo of muscular attendants with arms akimbo, their legs robustly stationed. Overtly, when one's choice had been made, it'd willy-nilly to be endured; mutation of sentiment, palpably then, not an option.

Images of horror fulgurated across the vasty screen. Morose citizens herded into closed wagons even as beasts from the field; weeping mothers separated from their stricken *kinder*; individuals shot in the head with a pistol or from the deadly end of a rifle; cavernous garners inside of which companies from an ethnic race were shoved and pressed before being overwhelmed by fatal fumes; straggling queues of bent inmates waiting to follow, even as a coterie of seated musicians broadcast ornate music in a bizarre configuration of incongruent sound; sombre men frighteningly attired in direful black setting about women – beating, bloodying and bruising them, whilst coercing those with a rhythm of pulse to numerous sexual assaults: in short, the effecting of such acts of humiliation that the mind could scarce conceive of such atrocities.

No less perturbing was an impromptu revision-of-scene rendering the spectacle of a stone-clad subterranean vault, over the crescent sides and ceiling of which were scored weirdly-strutting hard-edged, stygian letters, void of nicety and chiselled to terrifying effect. Added to which (deviantly) there at the centre stood a raised altar, about which twenty-seven hooded figures in shadowy robes moved deliberately, ponderous-step by ponderous-step, harshly chanting, perturbingly, in a linguistic register which made the gazer's heart thump.

Long before the flashings had terminated, and the awful blaring of discordant harmony had ceased, the itinerant (cupped hands upraised) dolorously covered his eyes. Discernibly, he'd comprehended sufficiently: veritably, a fulsome, deplorable drama impossible to forget or ignore; indeed, o'er which his gimlet-eye of conscience might not e'er nictate. Further, theorising to himself – imagining the character of *The Friendly Challenger,* his utterances reiterating in his memory – he resolved that no, indeed no, whatever be the due and proper calculus for those now dead, utterly base would it be to discern in it the apodictic word upon their existence. Each and every one of those desecrated souls, occluded deep in the golgothas of agony (degrading and evil) decidedly deserved what was just, merciful: verily, a purposeful redress. More than that. Solely the living now were able to speak-up upon their behalf; preserve an insistence in the face of the carelessness of death, of denial; of disregard, of forgetfulness: of the insatiability of the wonted moment for those who essayed to survive, keep going, continue.

As the deceived filmgoer, rid by now of the confinement of obligatory revelation, took in the air, yes, even of the lanes and byways of Megopolis, deliberating over the *Awkins'* celebration of their 300 years of life, their delicately managed compliance with absolute eradication as they apprehended it, he deemed it to be insufficient: it was not enough. He cerebrated, too, on how in sooth they had got as far as they had. Had they built their civilisation without any trampling-over, without any exploitation and annihilation of others? Or, was their history by the same token littered with the foreshortened lives of lost souls, eradicated by time and abandoned by the living? This metropolitan city, too: was it built upon the brutalism of the racially advantaged with the crushing of an original population? Had greatness been emblazoned whilst a multitude struggled unfed, not housed, mastered harmfully in an exploitative chaos?

More was required. More was demanded. He, Joshua, adjudged it to be so to the very core and fibre of his being. Verily, verily: solely God could make it so. Moreover, if he should be God – amen, he himself – crucially, should he not implement an uplifting hope: have it realised because it should – yes should (beyond quibble or cavil) come to obtain properly and fairly? A strategic marriage, withal, of cosmic synergy and ultimate being, benignly directed, inherently should evidence a force of *realisable potential*, conditioning its fruition. It could happen. It should happen. Wherefore it would happen. 'Verily, verily,' he affirmed *sotto voce* into the late-afternoon brightness that even then glanced angulate, graced and beset, smote along the cornered edges of glass, the layers and planes of an overpressing architecture.

Soon after then he observed, coming into view, a lavish inner-city vision of verdant, cultivated grass, prettily taking in a purling watercourse, wending and winding between carefully-designed lakelets attracting ducks and geese and swans. Whilst drawing closer, the itinerant smiled inwardly, set footfall instanter to its welcoming gate. Nonetheless, his progress was curiously slow.

Weirdly, the more he hastened towards this alluring reserve, the farther off it seemed to be. What's more, he realised he was sudating in a sheer tizwoz of perturbation, so irked, so pothered he'd thus far become. Wherefore, all at once, he slackened his pace. Anon then did he notice, situated in a corner between a forked right lane and an adjacent narrow-passage – toward the foot of a smart, modern, glass-filled tower-block – how an identifying sign had been placed aloft a low-but-wide bay-framed window, enunciating the four words: *Ye Olde Watering Hole*. At once to this facility Joshua now purposefully strolled.

All the same, incongruously, he did not go in. He chose instead to hover outwith, finding himself observing a table on the far side of the big, curved window, aside which were sitting two women: both attractive, young, not by any means without glamour; their hair being blonde-coloured in the one case, jet black in the other; both wearing close-fitting, designer-garments; each exhibiting a demeanour evidently poised, smiling-often, lips glossily moistened with a cosmetic balm utilised via a small stick. Opened in front of each was a luncheon-menu; and, turned ninety degrees, also beckoned a tempting supplement, signalling a special 'option of the day'. Coincidentally, this last was positioned in a style confronting the observer full-on, being propped midway between the two conversing ladies: it indicated, *Bubble and Squeak*. The cognomen of *Bubble* announced itself before the ebony-haired creature, the client divulging a tendency to throw her head back in a tee-hee at some fancy or another. The appellative of *Squeak*, by contrast, stood before the light-haired creature, a customer who'd a tendency to incline her face forward, discoursing conspiratorially, with a thinnish but ready smile.

Either through the art of lip-reading, else through a similarly enhanced capability, the observer perceived that he was able to comprehend clearly what the two confabulators were saying. Wondrously, albeit espying them beyond what amounted to a translucent fenestrated wall, they prated-away as if unaware of his presence.

Squeak: 'Only, do you not reckon at times, well, a good few of those dudes are often more of a nuisance than they're actually worth? Really, as if I should have to try to bewitch some bozo so as to *float my boat…*!'

Bubble (*Her head thrown back in affectations of giggling.*): 'Exactly, exactly. A provocative guy purred at me the other night, pleading, pleading my dear that he might *make love*. Why oh why, even so, should I want anyone to *make love* to me – with all its inexorable emotional baggage, commitment, and guilt-inducing rigmarole?'

Squeak (*Again leaning forward with sweet and mischievous grin.*): 'Darling, you are so right. I've noted the same thing, myself. I've had guys who've promised they'll adore, they'll cherish me. Huh – reckon we surmise bang-on what that'll involve! Suffocation, jealousy, boredom – overall martyrdom! No – thank – you! I'd settle for a nice leap of action between the sheets—.'

Bubble (*Interrupting.*): 'Actually, I'd prefer a duvet! If not too thick! Quintessential on a water-bed!' (*Another howl of mirth.*)

Squeak: 'A way of speaking, my dear, that's all. Who needs diddly-squat – soon as the going gets good! Afterwards, next day, nine o'clock – he's got to go. At least – unless it's my day off. Oh, and he's hands-on in the kitchen!'

Bubble: 'Absolutely. Should we add to that – entertainment? They can be good for that, or, some of them can. Would you agree?'

Squeak: 'Yeah, yeah: some of them can. Anyhow, it's dandy to enjoy a few thrills and spills and frills! Sure, I like to be treated properly.'

Bubble: 'Oh, I think you mean *im*-properly!'

The emendation declaimed, even the politic *Squeak* let her head fall back, overtly parting-wide her orifice in a refined guffaw of laughter, itself disembogued curiously and paradoxically *fortissimo*.

Whether logical or not, after the two ladies had emptied their delicate cups and proffered suitable payment, the pryer himself, seeing now how he was close to the building's own entrance, stepped forth discreetly a touch to one side, closer to its corner. And yet, and yet. A kind of inner reverie demanded he make utterance, thus betraying perforce his presence. The more so indeed as – rather to his surprise – he next beheld the women assertively pushing buggies carrying wide-awake infants. He proposed: 'Mayn't one observe about this matter as of all? Sex was made for man – not man for sex. Intimacy espoused to truth comprises the chief pearl prized.'

Oblivious or not to the aforesaid pensée, the proud mothers disregarded the comment. Resolutely, each leant into their fashionable push-chairs, insisting: *first* – 'Elmer was able to read by the age of three, having recourse to a system of synthetic phonics'; *but next* – 'Astrid didn't till five; anyhow, some say it's unwise to coerce them.' Walking on defiantly each tossed her head. One to the left. One to the right.

The woebegone visitor to Megopolis regarded again the municipal park opposite, renewing his anfractuous pursuit of an opportune approach. Irregardless, the coveted sanctuary would not surrender an opening, pothering him, befuddling him, naturally handicapping him in his striving to find a way in. Even so, perchance there was a more germane access, he told himself, a little way ahead. As a consequence, he adopted the main route, past the detour he'd just made, discovering as he did so an unusual phenomenon. There were innumerous people who were jostling, shoving, pressing, whilst exhibiting a dubious trait of behaviour that occasioned his disbelief, acclimated at last as he was to the altitude and queerness of the buildings: explicitly, how in sooth the majority of the crowd were not chiefly concentrating on where they were making for, but, on their hand-held linked-in gadgetry, into which either they spoke wantonly, else in hearing attended to, or, even listened-to music therefrom – the reverberations of which emanated as tinny, pulsing rhythms – even at which, again, unusually they were staring, given that various numbers, letters, images *et cetera* were available in tiny windows over which it was possible to make likenesses move. Surreally, the recollection of Othias – who'd evidentially inserted food and drink into his bag – permitted now a certain cold comfort, making of the atypical something tolerably normal. Or, contrariwise – possibly not.

Predictably, for all that, his complicated advance inexorably ebbed, at long last, to a standstill.

He'd ended up at a highly polished, mahogany entrance, around which newly-glossed doors had facilitatively, at each side, securely been hooked. Now, prominent and already poised upon the claret-carpeted steps was a debonair citizen exigently rallying an assemblage of people (foregathered near to the kerbside) how they needed to *sign up* to his philosophy. Seemingly abrim with the newest and finest of wares, the building itself was a most imposing shopping-mall. Not far from where the caller stood – withal wielding as he did so a large, tubular contraption, towards which he vented his address, as well as to his attentive audience – an arched banner boldly declared: 'TEMPTATION'. The burden of the speaker's rescript was as follows:

'Hearken now, listen-up! Here's the thing: this is the day to get the whole of the retail sector, right now, to *sign up* to our primary objective – allowing our economy to survive, our youngsters to obtain employment, our industries to succeed. Poised then upon the cusp of national renown, this stupendous store behind me represents one basic aim: to inspire decent folks to go over the threshold, pass through its portals, consume its products; purchase its ornaments; walk inside. Yes: walk, *walk in-side*. So, let the cry go up, let us shout it from the rooftops, with might and with main. Are you ready? I can't hear you. Are you ready?'

And the crowd roared back, 'Yes, we're ready, we're ready!'

Encouraged, the enthusiastic speaker began to brandish both arms, to the left, to the right – in a mode not entirely dissimilar to a well-evolved ape inciting a disorderly coterie of players – as one and all chorused together, yelling-out unitedly a curious, awesome cry: 'Lead us into Temptation!

Lead us into Temptation!

LEAD US INTO TEMPTATION!'

Discernible all the while, what's more, was that copious individuals were clicking away with their portable contrivances; whilst, in the melee that ensued, a critical bystander noticed an egress towards which (between the participants) he edged carefully, so that in due course he escaped to the other side. There, amen, he breathed a sigh of relief, a sigh of life, one that seemed to go on and on and on.

Anyhow, it was reassuring to him that the architecture was becoming less tall, less grandiose, betokening perhaps how he might be abandoning the centre of Megopolis, belike departing the district of the White Indians. Then, intuiting that this was so, close to the space where he'd been delayed, he espied a duplet-throng of intemperate agitators marching indomitably, carrying aloft splendidious signs, albeit evidencing such discord and defiance as to presage some mayhem, some madness afoot. Placards and posters indicated diametric points of view. Perceptibly, a certain side was protesting about a cartoon that had been made of a prophet, although another was baying for free-spoken utterance for everyone as an absolute right. For all that, in amongst the second, a covey of dissenters began differing in their view of a curious picture of a further prophet pacing upon the water, forbye handling in his right hand a tinny, carmine-coloured canister of aerated liquid. Just as queer, various irate characters from the former flock were igniting effigies of singular terrestrials. Also, within the same lines was upraised a gawdy poster with the words, 'Political correctness for all', and, 'longside, 'This is crass and offensive'; even as a triad from the other covey bore placards highlighting the words, 'Political correctness gone mad', else, 'All should have the right to offend!' A newcomer coerced his way through the multitude, realising thereby his escape.

Co-occurrently, whilst he exited, the liberated itinerant was aware of two women promenading, each in the opposite direction. Highly visible, one stalked onward upon high heels and wore a scarlet dress that hugged her body to her upper thighs, only then to disclose her slender, bronzed legs. Her modish dress was contrived to expose one shoulder and her suntanned, lightly oiled arms – yet included, too, a curious zip upon her left breast. A shining black belt emphasised her svelte figure, whilst its fulgurant hue mirrored the cascading flow of her loosened, withal luxuriant hair. Raised above her head, moreover, she bore a gaudily-painted statement across a fold of sheet: 'Respect women's bodies! Women's choices are theirs!' Contrariwise, the second female was clad in a dark, drab vestment that well-nigh enshrouded her person, enclosing all of her hair and most of her face. She bore no banner aloft her head, but, as she happed to go by, opined: 'Always, man is alike child of mother and father.' The lady walked with dignity and stillness, her poise resonating some inner self-possession. Joshua was astonished by the contrast exhibited.

A little way away a 'feminist' was demanding attention, with voice raised and slogans aplenty:

'Join the Emasculists' Campaign!'

'Five year paternity-leave compulsory!'

'Smash the glass floor!'

Joshua willingly appreciated the commitment of the campaigner, albeit was mystified as to the denotation of 'Emasculist' as withal the rationale for *smashing* a 'glass' floor. Nearby, making hearing itself difficult, an additional broadcast was being purposefully bespouted by a man:

'Citizens, look, I've always been clear. What's required is a grown-up conversation: joined-up thinking; enhanced transparency; openness and honesty. There's too much disingenuousness. Now's the time to come off the fence. Yes, to tell it how it is! Exit means exit, Horace is Horace, and hindsight's a wonderful thing. Those articles are definite and indefinite. But, to start-off, we need front and centre a stop-back to the back-stop: a serious policy for serious times. It's vital to negotiate a new narrative: a *bad deal* is a deal worse than a *good deal*; a *good deal* is a good deal better than a *bad deal*; *no deal* is neither a good deal nor a bad deal – it is no deal at all! Clarity. Openness. Veracity. Illumination. Dependability! Critically, we need breathable air, breathable air, breathable air! Pivotal, if we intend – at the end of the day – to move forward.'

A few young girls, scantily-attired, chorused their earnest approval.

Though deliberately setting out for the park, some peculiar passageway (veering to the searcher's right) surreally exerted a novel fascination; likewise did the visitant's curiosity, coupled to the presence of a man coming towards him with a firearm, plainly convert him to adopt a mad dash several metres down its caliginous vennel, even unto the darkened and dirty windows of evidently inferior premises; indeed, somewhere that'd distinctly seen better days.

Whilst the armed terrestrial strode promptly along, the obfuscated traveller hid himself from view within the external vestibule of the aforesaid poorly-lit and drab-looking shop. On the point of returning to the main thoroughfare, however, he suddenly became aware of a column of card affixed to a parallelogram of framed cork-board. Realising its details, regrettably, was not straightforward; for, by now it was neither lucid nor free of blemish. Irregardless, the opening line (being an elucidatory subject-title) was tolerably accessible, advising: *DISPOSAL OF LEAVINGS.* Lower down, however, it became more difficult to discern, supposing it appeared as though the following elaborative sentences most probably would be intelligible; withal, particularly to the interested citizen:–

Leavings. To comprise as a minimum: nuisance-people – including beggars, alcoholics, dissenters, outcasts, et cetera; those with terminal illnesses;

those with genetic aberrations; those deliberately espousing 'strangeness'; old people patently past their best. *Methods.* To include: flu-vaccinations; curative clinics; tailored holidays; laptop-emissions; smartphone-shocks; dietary supplements.

Handwritten near to this paragraph, even so, were the words: 'Meeting cancelled, alternative venue sought. Telephone *Hairless Harry.* Same number.' Maybe it was good (conjectured the philosopher) how the gathering had either not taken place or, feasibly, was not now going to occur. Alternatively, malign objectives or suspicious stratagems were here being driven *underground*, thereafter making them yet more difficult to monitor. Irrespective, the surprised itinerant divined it to be expedient to depart the venue. Actually, even the air itself seemed unpleasant, unwholesome, having about it a stench not dissimilar to urine: cogitably, a disgorgement of an untimely nature. Fitting, in the event, to return to the original road.

Surreally, the-close-to-paranoid pilgrimer detected he'd by now returned to a corner located nigh to a certain fork in the road and its adjacent sidewalk, and, besides, sensed himself to be espying a glass-encumbered high-rise edifice, the lowest level of which incorporated a chic brasserie; whilst, furthermore, the noteworthy sign over the eatery was oddly familiar, to wit, that of *Ye Olde Watering Hole.* Seeing moreover a pair of familiar women, ensconced as before, the newcomer hesitated a short distance from its notably modish front window, thereby renewing his aptitude for hearing their discourse, notwithstanding the solidity of the prodigious glass-laden pane.

Squeak (With drift of gold sweeping forward and partially screening her face.): 'Plainly, you yourself are aware of the imminent opening of *The Big Building,* the loftiest edifice within this area of the continent.'

Bubble (Adopting a haughty expression of confidence.): 'Why darling – indeed yes! One does follow the news you know! Afternoon, Friday upcoming. Yes, yes – of course! Visitors from all over will secure the chance to visit its uppermost floor, there to witness the magnificent panorama of Megopolis.'

Squeak (Reversing her head a touch.): 'Ah well, yes, it's true. Even so, indulge me if you would: one hasn't – or has one? – understood how a variety of dignitaries may obtain an introductory *viewing* of its outstanding vista? Possibly, again, one doesn't know how – beyond the already-famous and well-to-do – how a select trio (earlier drawn from a prestigious music-lottery) will also attend?'

Bubble (*Appearing momentarily shaken.*): 'Bless me, for sure, I'd no cognisance.'

Squeak (*Surfing upon a fresh comber of pride.*): 'Equally, you'll not know that my aunt's best friend is, serendipitously, one of that trio! Cool – or what! Yeah, absolutely: the bestest friend of my aunt, she'll stand among the worthies marvelling atop the nonpareil of *The Big Building* on the very, exact day it opens!' (*Her enunciation gathering pitch, exponentially.*)

Bubble (*With raven locks ablaze about her straightish figure.*): 'No! You don't say!'

Squeak: 'I do!'

Bubble: 'Literally? Your aunt's best friend has gotten a valid permit to climb to the upper, penthouse floor of *The Big Building* to attend its opening? Really?!'

Squeak (*With shrill delight.*): 'That's what I said! Affirmative! Now then, how's-about we declare this *ristretto* is on you…?'

Bubble (*Her hair all-of-a-bounce.*): 'Of course, of course. Well, well. Awesomely wicked! To mingle with the primary echelon. Enjoying that view. Yes, from the pinnacle of *The Big Building*. Oh well done her. More importantly, well done you!'

Squeak: 'Added to which – she'll maybe enjoy an auspicious encounter. All those well-off types. All those hunky men.'

Bubble: 'For sure. What a thought, eh! There'll be a proper romp or two, defo, I mean, after such a prodigious erection… Goodness, did you catch what I just said? Typical me, that! Oh, but what a shame, you and your aunt's best friend cannot – or, can they? – change places! Dear, dear, dear!'

Squeak: 'Only, do you not reckon at times, well, a good few of those dudes are often more of a nuisance than they're actually worth? Really, as if I should have to try to bewitch some bozo so as to *float my boat*…!'

Bubble (*Her head thrown back in affectations of giggling.*): 'Exactly, exactly. A provocative guy purred at me the other night, pleading, pleading my dear that he might *make love*. Why oh why, even so, should I want anyone to *make love* to me…'

Surreally odd, mused here the disquieted Joshua, taking into view how he'd already been subjected to this moiety of dialogue. Really, really, though, once was quite enough. Intently glancing about, he again strode forth, wholly minded here to re-enact his way as best he could, discerning how (inexplicably) he felt he was being directed. The mephitic whiff of a disagreeable odour bore out to him that he'd chanced upon a familiar venue.

Likewise odd, withal, he espied at this time a singularly dubious, preposterous figure; perchance, a runaway on parole from a nearby, visiting circus. A cursory glance disclosed an abnormal, not to say deviantly-tall, rara avis, ludicrously pacing (though clumsily) upon two stilts. Afore long, however, the verisimility transpired to be weirder yet, bespeaking a mainly sinister overtone, the kind applicable to the shadowy-unconscious – in place of the typical outlook of one's waking hours.

Conspicuously, the noteworthy pole – for in reality there was but one – supposed earlier in his mind to be a stilt, all of a sudden became a wooden peg-leg – a prosthesis betraying strange spillages of dust at miniscule holes hitherto-wormed into it. If truth be told, the upright was appended (remarkably so) to a creature possibly some dozen feet tall. Correspondingly, the inelegant wight progressed with a hobble, awkwardly. Howbeit, hardly less fabulous was the overall look, attire and external mien curiously he embodied. Obtrusively as an instance thereby, his one shoe was missing its toe-cap: emerging from the breach-created (the centre-digit pitifully excised) now poked forth the frontage of his foot, which itself (adding insult to injury) chanced to be swathed in an inadequately-darned, still torn, short-woollen sock. The extremity itself, noticeably, had withal bled, galvanising an unruly, yapping terrier to lick-and-lap at a viscid gob of blood not quite congealed.

Anyhow, the solitary, regular leg of trouser was of a feculent, navy colour, and had, here and there, been markedly ripped. Forbye, it transpired to be heavily stained with yellowy paint, right up to the uncovered buttons – two of which were, by the by, undone, presenting loose shreds of fibre hanging therefrom. A spiralled hank of old rope was serving as a belt. Curiously, however, a distinctive pair of damask braces further availed in checking any southward slippage beneath the considerable midriff, a noteworthy corporation that haply could've gainsaid any reference to manual labour.

Notwithstanding, just as one's eyes were raised, so did they alight upon a prospect of nobler decorum. Granted how a single side of his striated shirt lay pendent, visible over the belt, and, though it had been incorrectly buttoned lower down, the white collar was primly fastened, disclosing thereabouts a fine, black, bow-tie. Over the oddly-formed shoulders was draped, cowl-like, a khaki-cotton jacket upon the port flank of which was an ornament of sabled velvet. An arm upraised gestured, with a duo of digits (asserted symbolically) to asseverate some glory accomplished. Inside the clench of the right shoulder was a swagger-stick, including at one end a steel-ball. Perhaps the victory, thought Joshua, remained indeterminate.

The character's face was square and rugged, chiselled by indentations of passion and enterprise, albeit notably discoloured by sanguinary contusions across halse and his nether cheeks. Decidedly, in addition, his nose was aquiline, his smile liberal and comfortable, his forthright stare assuredly attached to the fore, indicatory of aspirations towards recognition, probity; theoretically, honour. Neatly-combed black hair edged visibly around left and right of his pate, nigh withal to the rim of the fine top-hat prestigiously he happened to possess. Notable to the viewer besides – emphasising the jet, satiny plush of the bold stove-shaped headpiece – stuck forth now two vocables, silvern and capitalised: a definite article, plus a triple-letter-word opening with an 'L', closing with a 'W', an initial indefinite article between.

Peculiarly perfecting this apparition was a midget monkey, committedly and stalwartly perched (forsooth upon the flat head of his hat) edaciously clawing into a mini-sliver of potato already belike cooked in fat and fried. Irregardless, in between strikingly-minute nibbles, fronting each and every descrier, the crinigerous scapegrace would bequeath its glance and mete-out feeble mewings to sundry citizens.

Solely after the off-putting vision began to retreat was it possible for the beholder to see, printed on the back of the partial jacket, the oddball's freakish title: *Lord Mighty of All-In-It.* Pursuing again his purpose, the less-tall pedestrian ignored the disquietening distraction no more than he was able.

He retained, nonetheless, a consciousness of the park's existence, albeit the amenity herefrom was environed from the public by an imposing wall, under which he forthwith promenaded briskly. Doing so, he started to enjoy what was now left of the late spring sunshine. A boy, scooting about on a set of wheels, called over to him, 'Hey, dude, dig the retro-boots! Wicked!' Discerning the phrase to comprise a type of compliment on his sandalled footware, the 'dude' grinned back.

His blithesome mood anon seemed to find reflection in a familial group of four, strolling nonchalantly towards him: a jocund couple in their thirties, accompanied by a twosome of freckle-faced children; a junior-sister with a teenage-brother. They were guffawing and joking about an escapade, patently oblivious to a perceptive Joshua descrying how the youngest of the issue visibly had one of her palms closed tight, spiritedly holding within it some precious object.

Regardful of how his erstwhile scowl was mutating into a smile, the outsider felt flummoxed when the ebullient figure of the father proclaimed: 'Cheer up, it may never happen!' Then, realising his error, added, 'Oh, I am really sorry. I shouldn't have, well, opened my mouth! On top of which, you're hardly the nadir of dejection!'

'No – discernibly happier,' chipped in the young, rather comely wife. 'Alas, somewhat typical of my husband, Clive, expressing chirpy, optimistic things, be they felicitous or not. Clearly, too, today he's even worse than usual! Amen, only just now we've quit the surreality of the Hall of Mirrors, prominent gaggle-pleaser, integral addition to the latest fairground. Markedly queer and bizarre reflections! What's more – all of them of ourselves!'

'That's right,' corroborated Clive. 'All the same, however you're feeling, possibly you too should give it a go. I mean, why not? What's to lose?'

Joshua apprehended a probable defence as to how this mightn't be a productive idea. However, his pivotal focus of interest was on the closed, diminutive fist of the child, intuiting how her right-index finger was in reality a mere stump. All at once, rather as if she'd been the whole while waiting – suspecting she was being ignored – the girl tugged at her father's sleeve, imploring his attention.

'Yes, Chelsea, what is it?' the mother quizzed, exhorting: 'Patience, dear, your Pa-pa's busy. Pothering this honourable gentleman.'

'Oh never mind me!' the gentleman protested.

The teenager, till now but listening, intervened here with a remark of his own, asserting: 'I've a hunch, Pa-pa, Chelsea's found your badge.' Wondering thus, the lad gave a look towards his sister.

'Well, well, has she indeed!' replied Clive, spiritedly. 'You realise, Frances,' he declared, turning to his wife. 'It'd be a terrific break.'

Sure enough, the excited girl unfurled her hand, offering within it – as though it be some choice and sought-after jewel – the precious badge harbouring its debossed trio of symbols (in glossy gold), the abbreviation, **DWP**.

Passing to her father the elusive item, sibling Chelsea wasn't anymore prepared to hold back from chiding her tell-tale brother: 'Spoil-sport, Rory. *Can't, can't* (almost chanting) – *can't keep a secret!*'

'Here, come on now you two,' admonished the father, 'let's not have a fuss. You see, son, your sister's point of view? Chelsea's done good to have gotten hold of it. Even better – maintained her grip. It's an agreeable surprise.

I'd say too often such surprises are not so propitious! It'd have been tricksy to have needed to own-up to the loss of my personal identification, prior to managing the latest assessments. Wouldn't you agree, sir?'

The resident was addressing Joshua with – so the latter deduced – a kind of erstwhile courtesy, withal prompting the stranger to respond. 'Absolutely. I, too, am relieved you've secured your work-identification. Notably in the wake of your sightings in the mendacious Hall of Mirrors...'

At this the whole group vented a guffaw. Clive himself extended his hand to the stranger, wishing to demonstrate a gesture of friendliness. Rory, Frances, and Chelsea followed suit, exhibiting a courtesy that issued naturally – as a group, as well as individually. Providentially, it was the girl who was the last to give her hand (deformed as it was) into the grateful and open palm of the genial traveller.

Immediately, the benevolent explorer insisted he must henceforward be upon his way, accordingly betaking himself from the members of the family resuming their schedule, themselves every bit as contented as before: even, apprehending their cries, with a contentment greater yet. Indeed, the female child was whooping with glee.

'Daddy, Daddy, Mummy, here – look, this finger! See, it's normal again – completely whole! Was it the stranger?'

'Wondrous indeed, for sure it must've been,' replied the bemused and thankful worker. 'Heavens! But, *mirabile dictu* – where has he gone?'

'Disappeared!' exclaimed Frances. 'Nowhere to be seen.'

And Joshua (for certain) had moved on, intuiting in his mien – though with a surprise scarcely other than that of the young girl – the confident surety of a contented smile. Excluded still from the elusive gardens (masked within the immured enclosure) what had just transpired – as well as certain sightings now and then of irregular, overarching trees – lifted his heart. All the while, too, mild wafts of air gifted flowerets of scarlet and white upon the remnants of the meridian's ebbing aftermath. Furthermore, invisible birds were singing in enchanting trills, warbling away in carillons of joy.

Then, at last, a viable entrance was detected. Looming in the wall came a signal opening, revealing a rectangular steel-and-glass frame across the neon-fitted abacus of which could be made out its eponymous aim (stated briefly and simply in upper case, if also gaudily) THE TRANSPORTER. Closely gazing into this he was now able to descry the many banks of colourfully-planted displays (abrim with their yellows, pinks and violets) dramatically adorning every bed in a coruscating profusion at once enchanting and uplifting. The theurgist, heartened again, wholly now relished the intoxicating scent of flora and wind-blown blossom. Thereupon, as he guided his footfall to the portal, he appreciatively and readily proclaimed: *'Blessings on the Father for the aromas ethereal of this flower-filled hour.'*

Part the Seventh: *in which Joshua deploys* THE TRANSPORTER, *enjoys a brief reunion, discourses with* The Old Soldier *and progresses to* The Pilgrim's Path.

Yet, even as the pilgrim tentatively stepped into and through the aperture, ingress to exit, he straightaway experienced a sharp blast of air, noticing withal a wide welkin visibly-alive with a wind-driven mixture of blue and poppling, rolling cloud. In addition, he was disquieted, squinnying downward, lo to discern how – although there'd been before the efflorescence of the year's awakening – there was bestrewn leafage and degradation of an autumnal decline. Even so, sufficient continued to be observable above: the manifold ochres of seasonal colouring; the variegated reds, saffrons, madders and ambers. Aloft forbye out-spread the bulked-forth limbs of tired, deciduous trees, more than a few now denuded yet divulging arresting silhouettes of bulging boughs; an anatomy of ligneous elbows and arms curiously interlocking; even in sooth, salient squirrels running amok, else mayhap a ragtag of children blootering the frangible foliage. Whimsically for sure came the prayer: '*Blessings on the Father for the piggledy-with-higgledy, katabatic gallimaufry of leaves.*' The very air, albeit chillier, betrayed a certain briskness to it, thereby kindling within Joshua a feeling of energy and enthusiasm. He marched ruggedly on, fast alighting upon a stream, stuttering and babbling as it went.

This purling course, by-and-by, it grew in width and strength of flow; anon its spate alike welled and filled: what was once a shy and humdrum gill here in truth ranged and rolled a river, now such as flanked by verdurous growth, with skirted, escarped, concreted revetment. By this juncture was descried besides a wide array of buildings: a more inclusive city-scape subsuming bridges, towers, halls and chambers; and withal – despite a modest way removed there rose up superior, strident, sharp-edged, glassy constructions – a *noble* guise of consolidation over the while, bearing the imprint of nostalgia via plenteous sculpting in stone of tradition, custom, and the worth of antiquity.

People began to come – now began to go: to merge, to mix, milling all-about upon the river's low-bevelled bank – even whilst certain students had met to listen to an old man (with full flowing beard) who, with belovèd bow was tunefully chafing a quaternary of strings on his upheld violin. The inventive soul looked to be blind, possessing opaque and glassy eyes that stared vacantly into a world beyond. Now and then, someone would drop or throw a coin into a cap deposited in front of him; whilst, belike, a follower would downward-go to wedge paper currency under the scattered silver or copper pieces.

This music after all, being perfused with patently wondrous quality, seemed to soar, dance, effect melody upon melody, crafted in a rendition distinctly up-to-date, yet consonant with the disciplines of an earlier age, affording it thereby a timeless register. Skeins of sound rose, tangled and clarified; entered new intensities – ascending, plummeting, weaving into the sharpest, most masterful of affective slurs or strikes; realising the most profound soul-searching, scoring the heart with its rapture, its doubt, then emblazoning its awakened bliss: a coda engendering its own sumptuous resolution – a spiritual *synergy* of aspiration with defiant determination.

The young listeners gradually departed, calling back to the player, 'Keep at it, Jake! We'll see you again!' Joshua stood then alone, reclining against a shallow wall hearkening to this hobo-performer furbelowed in badly creased trousers, quite shrouded under his mangy brown greatcoat. Soulful in regard, he averred inwardly, *'Blessings on the Father for the elbowing-bow along violin.'*

'Indeed, Joshua, indeed.'

The music had ceased. Wondrous to observe, it was the wizened violinist who'd asseverated this endorsement.

Abruptly, Joshua's own caliginosity departed. Full well now did he view in the old man the figure and frame, perfectly, of the whilom one – quirkily, he who'd had an irritating habit of tripping him up. Regardless, evidently he was without sight: as, considering long the blankness, judiciously he sought reassurance in the timbre and place of the other's voice. Which one, noticeably, was eager to oblige.

'Jacob, can it really be you? How is it you are here? I have been travelling – so indeed it feels – far, far across worlds: over multiple spans of our planet across an unfolding of years. Now, here in this dimension, I discover you! Delighted I am, heartily, so to have done! Assuredly, my friend, assuredly!'

'All is not as it seems,' suggested the player. 'Be aware of this. Dimensions overlap, for the place and the hour. Please here, reach down, yes, hand me that braided cloth-cap of notes, withal its coinage cast. Their currency will afford me by and by a bowl of soup. Besides, besides, I'm promised this day a porringer of stew!'

Joshua leant down and picked up the head-piece with its jumbled treasure. He was inspirited to think upon Jacob ceasing awhile his exertions, beholden contentedly towards God, relishing his much-deserved guerdon of hot food: plus company plus kindness. Howbeit, as he straightened up, no longer was he witnessing the esteemed musician to be identified as Old Jake. Not at all, Jacob was evanished from view. He noted then how his round of fabric was not in truth a cap. Now within his grasp, instead, he was holding a crinkled paper-bag full of crumbs – whilst, peculiarly, he himself was back in the leafy park with its myriad hues, curiously busy in nourishing a group of birds with the common provender he'd so wondrously acquired. In his heart and mind, regardless, he continued to be inspired by the jubilant sublimity of the empyreal violin.

Upon emptying said bag of its bits of bread, Joshua, who'd appreciated pitching such tit-bits to the finches, to his surprise felt inclined at this point to seek out a nearby bandstand, viewing present therein a forlorn terrestrial in his middle years. The pitiable man was apparelled in a soldierly uniform, revealing a cutaway limb tucked judiciously into a hung sling. When he walked, he revealed an injury to his left hip.

The bird-feeder initiated the dialogue.

'Hello, I am Joshua. You appear, should my vision be correct, to have been in the wars.'

'Good-day to you!' replied the other. 'What you observe is true. I am *The Old Soldier*. Regardless, call me Murdo – should you so wish. Besides, aged four and forty years, I'm not yet soothfully old: withal, possibly younger than yourself! Honesty, for all that, compels me to admit how at times I do feel older. Significant lesions of conflict, moreover, deprived me some twelve years ago of my erstwhile looks of roguish glamour, the undeniable allurement I once enjoyed!'

The eyes of the veteran blazed with merriment. He grinned with a self-deprecating gaiety. Barely a moment though did he defer before resuming once more. 'I promenade up here more days than not, oft-times reviewing the great mysteries of life – as also that of death. Again, it could be – well, almost, conceding the sheer extent of the park – I could be miles away, removed from the city, out in the far-off sticks – truly, should it be dreich and mist-ridden and none can espy those none-too-distant high-rise buildings!' Saying as much, he laughed. Then he prompted, 'But you? What are you up to, yourself?'

'Me?' questioned Joshua – not only to Murdo, for also to himself. 'I'm a wanderer, wandering here and there. Oftentimes I believe I'm on a journey; to be exact, a pilgrimage. Like yourself, I ruminate upon life's puzzles and predicaments. Irregardless, rarely do I garnish cognitive activity with joining-in on the battlefront!'

'Ruminating with the cows, eh! For myself, cerebral-doings, alas, make up these days close to all I can do! Sounds pretty gloomy, but, vis-à-vis the question of *terrestrial* mortality, opining personally, my mind veers towards an approach that's more philosophical: endeavouring thereby to weigh up my own demise, first and foremost, as inevitable; inexorable and final; issuing to nothing beyond, yet, in its own way, substantially acceptable. It occurs to me that, however much we brood and fret about its eventual arrival, when it comes it comes – and that's it. Necessarily, whatever particular realm we've been in, pleasurable or wretched, when death – be it sudden or anticipated – reaches near, indeed naught then of the worrying or fear or trepidation makes any sense or any difference.'

'Needless to say, just the same, it sounds pretty bleak,' answered Joshua. 'Allow me, please, to demur. Consider again – to illustrate even briefly – how, Murdo, you've been enlisted into a terrible war, where your life is full of mud and tunnelling; discernibly, of parasitic lice-infestation, of barbed-wire, of bayonet and rapid gunfire; and, close by, now you notice a fellow-soldier who has lived with you for almost four years, when, all of a sudden – just weeks before a truce is called and peace thereupon confirmed – this same sapper (let us say) is ripped in a zip of bullet-fire; at random, cut down, all his days and life ended. Decidedly, the latter's demise would not be satisfactory.'

'Satisfactory, Joshua, no. Far from it. Regardless, those who have breath in their bodies, they, but they alone are given to apprehend a meaning, to explicate the likely import of it – its sense, I mean, the sheer unsatisfactoriness of it – its tragic irony, the waste entailed, the onerous bereavement now laden in its wake. Gallingly, for the soldier, naught of such bewilderment applies, being himself dead and done. Beyond life and hope and joy: just the same, disenthralled from misery and suffering, too. Dead and gone. Out of the game. Abhorrent though it be to us. By such token, we might conceive of an engirded soul, a prisoner in solitary confinement, entombed in some dreadful hole – appalling to envision – yet, for all the meted-out cruelty, my resolution obtains. As the overpress of blackness comes to the combatant, basically, nothing else is to be said; or, verily, to be by our sapience apprehended. Joy has departed, but sorrow too.'

'Indubitably, you are most brave,' replied the other to *The Old Soldier*. 'For all that, are you able to adjust yourself, Murdo, to such a belief? Is it of an order to grant you peace of mind, whilst you draw, little by little, closer to the necessity and ultimacy of death?'

'I believe that I can, and, that it is. I profess as much discerning no justification for propounding an alternative. Verily, appreciative I should be for what (thus far) I may have, actualising my expiry equably, mindfully, with what dignity, nay withal longanimity I can muster. Even so, were you to adhere to a philosophy of an afterlife, these opinions may well perturb you.'

'The possibility of an afterlife,' answered the philosopher, 'is veritably one I maintain. Howbeit, providing a demonstration of a positive proof exceeds my proficiency: given it's dissimilar, after all, to the pell mell of leafage, observable when summer ends, a feature I can point to or reliably predict. Really, it's nigher to a steadfast hope, let's say, than it be to a dogmatic belief: withal, more intelligible to discern should we be open to a creative and benign process, analogous to a *Heavenly Father* loyally defending our corner, even if His alleviating hands are (paradoxically) in some explication restrained. The *kairos* has yet to be decided; whilst the dimension, it is different. Irregardless – marvellously, miraculously – does it remain the greatest mission involving us all, incorporating the quiddity of God working in, beside, and through us. As denizens of our world, it may be we can do little aside from adhering reliably to a potentiality of salvific process: labour to realise what power and love it represents. Solely to long for it, anticipate it – itself might be to facilitate its realisation! Just the same, I should concede how, to many these days, purely to allude to *divinity* is seen as tantamount to infantilism. Conceivably, too, I often use those words *perhaps* and *maybe*. So, I speak of hope, not certainty – albeit, I aver it to be as essentially possible as is the glory and miracle of our multi-dimensional cosmos the reality that it is.'

'I don't know,' replied then *The Old Soldier*. 'It is unquestionably a wonderful idea, besides in notion a magnificent hope. Even so, I have a requirement to know. I remain unconvinced. To jettison one's ideational life – with its cognitive integrity – on a mere whim or pathological delusion would be terrible. Basically, my way I retain a certain sureness; I am true to myself. Notwithstanding, dear friend, I thank you for your thoughts. Loftier than a glass of milk, I dare say!'

Joshua grinned. He warmed to Murdo, could see that the man was sincere: how he prized discernible integrity-of-soul. 'Ah well,' countered the former, 'should it betide finally I'm in tune with reality, never fear. Assuredly I'll be bounteous in putting in a word – or ninety-nine – on your behalf! Amen, you do the same for me, eh, what do you say? Here, shake on it.' (With guileless awe, he added interiorly: *'Blessings on the Father for the heroic, the doughtiness and daring of the dutiful.'*)

With that prayerful laudation inwardly offered, said staunch believer shook the militant's available hand good-naturedly, warmly smiled, and quietly departed the bandstand, strolling towards an area of park still awash with the lumining of the sun. How agreeable to be enthralled once more by the loveliness inherent in a dither of dusk. So much was the viewer's mind abrim with its approach, that, when he saw on his route an arbour of honeysuckle – interwoven with roseal pinks and whites – he momentarily ceased his progress and tarried to read the sign, positioned to his left, betokening the aisle for travellers to take: it read, 'The Trickster's Trod'. The mellifluent and somniferous scent of flowerage wafted all about – albeit the feasibility of the floreated exhibit escaped attention or reasoning. It was too inviting to ignore – or purely prosaically controvert.

Initially, the unconcerned devotee paced stride-after-stride across the floor of the bower, inhaling deeply the pervasive delight inspirative from its lucent, seductive colours, feeling strangely encharmed by the twisting, living plants that overarched his lazy progress. Howbeit, the way did appear interminably long. By and by threat did he perceive a degree of vexation – given he was diverting so far from his intended course. Although he maintained his pace, indication was there none of the boundary to this near-numinous grove, one that had lured and lulled him onward into a mesmeric reverie. He stopped and turned.

Lo! There opened up then, between him and his backward track, a wide and yawning chasm. Too far it was to try to jump. Forward he needed to go; verily next to jog, haply anon to run. Minutes passed. Waveringly, having eased-up to a bare (albeit fitting) 'canter', Joshua, twisting and turning, discerned at last a digressive route giving forth onto a northward-fronting metalled-road. Observable a little way ahead were buildings of an irregular nature, less stark in their horizontal and vertical alignments than hitherto observed, standing less tall and grandiose in their upward design; yet, in their own individual and valued way, featurely, unusual, character-ful.

Then, of a sudden, a rare vision presented itself to the jaded rambler. Boisterous ranks of people seemed to line the way on either side of his chosen trail, which last (correlate with a post signalling it to be so) appeared to be denominated, *The Pilgrim's Path*. Scarce-able was he to proceed so strong and full the irresistible flow of terrestrials. Yet, immediately and peculiarly, the encumbered foreigner cried out to all those around: 'Hearken! This citizenry, let it be riven in two, contriving for me a highway to follow, betiding even as walls of water, parting to my left just as to my right; occasioning a passage down which I may advance.' Assuredly, so it was. Ebullient, Joshua discovered afresh his ability to promenade and progress.

The attention of the wanderer was drawn thereupon to two edifices situated ahead of him, revealing (by the same token) a prominent disposition or gestalt: the first curvilinear – according to the feminine – possessing a dome; the other – according to the masculine – showing a spire (itself lodged upon a tower). More bizarre still was an urbane behemoth-like ogre, habited entirely in raven-black, save only for some smallish hoop of white fictile-material gathered about his thick, bulbous neck. Troublingly, he seemed to incorporate the prodigious size of several persons, if forbye dovetailing between one building and its opposite, in this wise exploiting such witchery that a being might somehow deploy even between this and that or still another. But Joshua the while stood his ground on the adopted route, observing the clerical character becoming less pythonic, diminishing by degrees, till the sombrely-beheld presbyter at length chimed in with the majority of his kind; while, as soon as this pair of figures on the highway – ringed-about by the riven companies of the multitude – met head-on, the one inexorably-petering asserted to the other:

'I know who you are. You are *The Father's Son*.'

Joshua declared of his purpose: 'I am seeking the truth.'

The one with the white collar said: 'I am *The Devil's Advocate*.'

The pilgrim replied: 'Yet, thou dost not look it.'

'Ah, have you not heard? All – all is – all is not – all is not as it seems! Rise of sun to fall of star, do I wander this world in servitude to your Master; natheless, through the tenebrific veneer of night – its furr, its shock, its start of dark – woebegone innocents surely do I abuse. Yearn they in whitest nescience, do these guileless minors for aegis or for mercy. Wherefore surely do I ensnare them – cajole, be cruel to them; compass them until they be so afeared they dare not say. For sure, the children, I adjure them to discover their sins! Avow they have none, I can (want it or not) enlighten them re the veiled vices likely they have. So they think, yes, at my behest. Withal, I humble them, command the maintenance of my shoes a brilliant, mirroring black. One and all, they be required – though hands so small – to furbish and polish my shoes.'

Joshua stood back, now fully awake to a type of toxicity emanating from this faithless, heartless creature, assuming feignedly the licence of authority; implementing misrule by the filth and frightfulness of his direful acts. There was in the air then the whiff of evil. A certain stench of something devilish and incongruent: something that should not have been.

Alert to *The Devil's Advocate* continuing, even now towards him – queerly, in an occult attempt to enter by default, personally: an uncanny form of diabolical assault – Joshua, in an instant, stood to one side. Suffering the unwholesome creature to pass on by. Also, in expediting his passage thus, his scale *nolens volens* lessened, becoming smaller (tinier and tinier) till fantastically this demoniac with the sabled footwear disappeared entirely into the black tarmac of the road. The other looked up, forthwith discerning another peculiar-tableau once more to behold.

Apprehending carefully, he heeded how, rhythmically (first now; then afterwards) there could be espied, issuing out of the dome and from the spire (here one; then the other) – like alternate tongues outjutting, impolitely, out of open mouths – weird souls from a world of fable and dogma and tradition. Proclaimed one to the other: 'We are right and you are wrong.' Similarly, yet dissimilarly, the opposite manikin proclaimed: 'You are wrong and we are right.' Backwards and forwards they went, in and out, fostering their proclamations.

Wide-eyed, Joshua here resumed his advance below the mechanical shibboleths, cognisant of how his cumbered footfall had brought him beyond the building with the dome and the building with the conical top (lodged upon a tower), even to behold, besides, two more fabrications beckoning, enticing him irresistibly to resume his momentum forward.

Alongside his right, there reared aloft an imposing creation involving a neoteric cupola, as withal, unusually, a tower upon each flank; whilst, posited opposite – though void of any tiered addition – was a functionally-oriented rectangular hall, attired in radical icons with characters painted clumsily, hither and thither, across its external walls. Vicinal to the first was a coterie of twelve men and women stomping agitatedly within a circle, upholding individual signs for everyone in the vicinity to behold. Woven upon each of these, one isolated vocable appeared highlighted in bold calligraphy.

Whilst the parade doggedly circuited, round and round, a diligent newcomer collated the specific utterances (one by one) noticeably being upraised in approaching his own indeterminate maunder: 'we', 'the', 'because', 'want', 'do', 'tholed', 'may', 'we', 'of', 'as', 'affront', 'we'. Again, edging now to the bourn, centring his focus, the scrutineer juxtaposed the morphemes and phonemes suitably so as to harmonise in meaningful averment, thereby creating some sentence (peradventure, too, indicatory of death): because–of–the–affront–we–tholed we–may–do–as–we–want.

The analyst, notwithstanding, continued his progress, curious in case he should uncover anything occurring beyond the grand, albeit peculiarly illustrated, chamber. Defiantly, an arthritic old local had put together and then set ablaze a considerable bonfire. Over and into this, one, then another – among a variety of wild-looking, agitated activists – were hurling variously books, papers, icons, manuscripts, together with ornate rolls of scored notation. As to the two closest, one repeatedly called out, 'Do away with bankers!' Even whilst the other urged, 'Get shot of law-lords!' Again, a duplet beside them bore a banner comprising the words, 'Abolish Institutions!' A further two were yelling, 'Kill the fat cats! Kill the fat cats!' Half a dozen, forbye, straddled easily their gleaming gas-driven bikes, vulgarly venting nigh-incessant, roaring reverberations: three couples they were, male and female. Stepping forward to the flames and the uproar, the pilgrimer then noticed a duo (conversing by one of the machines) urging breathlessly, laughingly: as–naught–that–matters–there–be let–us–do–whatever–we–want. A leather-clad girl, squatting on a pillion close by, giggled.

About then to avert his gaze, the explorer's interest was reawakened by one of the dissenters busy at the conflagration. A youth it was, who, in freeing a partly-burned folio of paper-sheet, ruckled it thence into a queerly-elongated shape that was pointed at one end: which forthwith he threw into the air in the onlooker's direction. Somewhat to the latter's astonishment did it then wing its way unerringly towards him, acquiring purchase beneath the poorly-fastened front-flap of his knap-sack. Excising thereupon this object, the recipient saw printed across it the following narrative:

'Once upon a year there was a politician involved in assizing benefits, who one summer's eve had had too much to drink. On his way home, staggering and hirpling along, o'er he cowped beside the verge of the road. A secreted quarter bottle cracked in his pocket, thereby setting a trail of yellowy liquid to drain onto the ground below, even whilst a dribbling of blood ran forth from the side of his head. He lay there motionless.

There chanced to come by then a wealthy banker, who, seeing the other fellow lying across his way, cast a look about him, crossed to the other side of the road, ere then disappearing. Notwithstanding, a certain while later did there hap to come by a laid-off correspondent. He, noticing the subject so awkwardly and intriguingly positioned – and, recognising withal who he was – retrieved from his pocket a camera, snapping several photographs. Realising he was unobserved, he too then went similarly upon his way.

Shortly following, a disabled worker – upright within his wheelchair – came likewise to a halt, desirous to examine this supine, incapacitated figure. He, however, impatient to empty his bladder, decidedly had to wheel on past – albeit, now mindful as to the whereabouts of the victim.

Finally, a middle-aged man (of reduced income) came upon the scene, occupying in his un-gloved nieve a flask of water but half-full. He proceeded to the politician, whence – ensuring the airway clear and bleeding staunched – he procured a polka-dotted kerchief from the other's jacket using it (with water from his flask) to deterge the wound anterior to wiping consecutively his mouth and eyes. The lavement complete, said stranger then lifted to the patient's mouth the flagon of mineral liquid. By now, the fallen-over statesman had come fully-to, covetous to ingurgitate from the water as much as he could. Thereafter, the middle-aged man (of reduced income) availed the rallying dignitary to his feet, encouraging him kindly and serenely to a nearby bench. Here he was able to sit awhile until renewing his homeward journey.'

Having narrated this anecdote, the Teacher of Renown paused, beholding sombrely all those listening, and declared: 'By the by, it was purported of the beneficent citizen – carrying out this act of care – that he didn't withdraw the drapes of his house until after midday.'

At this observation came there then an audible gasp in the company there assembled, and, in its turn, this minded the Teacher of Renown to reveal once more what he'd just observed. 'Indeed, for sure, it was asserted of the aforementioned man that he did not pull back the drapes of his house until after midday.'

Attending to this repetition several of the audience turned their backs upon the orator, walking hurriedly away, their faces downcast. One, however (a noticeably smart individual with a boyish mien) smiled – appearing immensely gratified. He, together with two burly protectors, promptly tromped off (rigid like buckram) conceitedly from those twelve who tarried yet.

To those few in the assembly who were left, the Teacher of Renown candidly inquired: 'And yourselves, will you too now depart?'

'Teacher,' replied –

Right here, however, the deckled corner of the manuscript was irretrievably charred, impeding alas all further rendition of this rare account. Vis-à-vis the recipient, the thought-provoked diviner deliberated upon how practically to dispose of his unexpected gift. Scrutinising closely the earlier indented, folded parts, soon enough the pilgrimer returned the single page to its earlier, peculiar fashioning. Now aerodynamically viable, the original pinched-and-angular creation forthwith was released by Joshua into the air. For all that, its commander tarried-not in the discovery of its subsequent destination – albeit wondered whether anyone (markedly with a strong hand) would manage to catch it.

The terrestrial moved on. Before long, he noticed a little way ahead, cross-legged in the middle of the road – sitting with each palm turned upward – a glabrous-pated worker attired in an orange-yellow garment. Perceptibly (withal audibly) he was a monk cantillating sincerely his chant of litany – or, conceivably, a section of mournful lament. Anyhow, the listener in measured fashion now made his approach.

Despite his quiet deliberateness, betided there then a sharp jolt to slacken his resolve. Displeasingly, not to say surprisingly, his right foot dashed upon an object untowardly obtruding from the ground, occasioning him to tilt, trip – almost fall over – to recover his balance. Patently, this felt odd; particularly given the road ongoing had seemed regular, not irregular – at any rate, so he'd presumed. Despite this, bending down, he now noticed how, shored fast within an unnatural split in the pitch-asphalt was an exsertile shard, not unlike pottery, several inches in length. Hurriedly, Joshua extracted this surprising fragment of clay, perceiving it to be glazed upon the outside, whilst (per contra) on the obverse as subfuscous as originally fired. Assessing it dutifully, he made out on the pure dun surface a word carefully scored into it, apparently in its entirety.

It proffered, simply and unintelligibly (at least to the one currently detained) the signal term: *Myanam*. Studying thereafter the glaze of the potsherd-piece, he forthwith descried a particularly thought-provoking assertion etched over, silvery, some feint blue ribbing: *I am at one with the entirety, striving to comprehend the whole*. For several seconds the diverted pilgrimer held this unusual affirmation in an overt act of rapt attentiveness, whilst imagining that this sole extract might be a sutra of great or long-held wisdom. Accordingly, he duly pocketed the item before resuming his gentle gait.

Even before reaching the other-worldly mendicant, now contemplating before him, the hearkener reliably heard him announce, 'I am *The Holy One*. You may call me Alberic, should you so wish.'

'Hello, Alberic. I am pleased to meet you. May I sit with you awhile? I need the stimulus of a quantum of true holiness – excusing my presumptuousness.'

'Gladly,' replied *The Holy One*, smiling. 'Nowadays, the whole world seems to have gone horribly-haywire: a mad habitation full of mayhem; crazed, chaotic, quite quit of ordering or coherence; void of direction such that it will redeem from the incongruity some radical meaning. All the same, remains there yet the typical, the wildering, insolvable posers such as *When?* and *How?* Terrestrial surely we be. Irregardless, we also need to regulate ourselves and our lives: fostering an internal appetency that we may strive (as grace and capacity permit) truly to align ourselves with *The Source of All*, who is also *The Aim of All* – which is to say, *The One* rightly divined as, *Our Heavenly Father*. Surely likewise, Joshua, you hold close a kindred aspiration, essaying to realise it as best you can.'

'As best I can –,' the other concurred. And continued: 'Even so, voyaging around *Terra Firma*, an itinerant discerns so much to bespeak sickness, torment, absurdity: there are withal so many living beings with so many differing degrees of consciousness – perceptibly, this very passage, lined as it is with its wide array of disparate characters, comprises a metaphor of such – as to divert the mind from divining how the entirety could be subsumed into an eternity of goodwill and purpose, incorporating into its fold the fullness of time, the vastness of creation, the multitudes of millions all struggling, all travailing, from the tiniest insect to the most-gigantic of the dinosauria, now extinct and gone forever. Notwithstanding, may we yet hold firm with those who suspire for amity, for answer; yearning for, and endeavouring to realise comprehensive justice; emboldened to revere *The Ultimate Life*, the elemental entity every decent life must mirror and reflect.'

'You have travelled far, oh friend and brother,' *The Holy One* concluded, before augmenting further: 'Amen, amen; it is according to our living faith that we must (one way or another) demonstrate our trust: trust in our heartfelt if defective *choices*; those choices to be made alike on behalf of others as well as of ourselves. *The Ultimate Life* would have us so do. Similarly, by way of a parallel choosing and a correlate trusting, does *The Ultimate Life* too strive to prioritise with discernment; to believe in – perchance, to depend upon – us, all who have consciousness and benign intent, to realise our quiddity in the evolution of *Life's Ultimacy*. Still, let us not forget the mundane, the modest, the minutiae of our day-to-day existence. To yield willingly to the day's imperative is similarly to embody great faith. I mean, to quieten the exalted mind, beset with its furrowed brow, its torturous and complicated contentions: and then to apportion bread; present cup of wine; remember our friends; countenance God to be God awhile, indeed a while.'

Upon the latter's averment, readily then was Joshua able to recall his comrades of the beach, Pedram and Tom: assuredly the while in which they'd conversated, strolling by the shore; their colloquy and cheer; their reciprocity, withal their farewell, afore arm-waving propitiously upon the deck of the boat. Once more did he concur, 'Of course, of course. Mayhap there be bread in this carrier of mine; with clear water (restorative as wine) to quench our thirst.'

The benefactor, reclining here upon the soles of his feet – illustrative of discipleship – forthwith put his hand into his leather knapsack, howbeit to bring forth (to his alarm) not nutritive blessing but hazard: veritably rigid, metallic, with trigger with barrel, with handle to hold. Disquieted, he exclaimed: 'Change this gun into bread, weapon into fare; instrument of malice into emblem of love!' Instantly he fell silent, shut-close his eyes. Soberly, onto the tarmacked roadway, he set down the unwanted item.

Then, wide-opening his eyes to see, the righteous philosopher espied within his gaze a clean square board, upon the stark facet of which stood modestly a roundel of white bread. Aside of the stated provender had been placed, mindfully, an old wooden goblet of sanguineous wine. *The Holy One* picked up then the small baked loaf, and, sundering it, dealt back a wedge of it to Joshua. Breaking off some of the remainder, Alberic drank from the cup a modest sup (in an act of sharing and ritual) afore companionably passing it on.

Like-minded, the men remained awhile, sitting silently in the middle of the road, eating and drinking, enjoying their break from diurnal abstinence – chosen or not. At last, *The Holy One* extended supplementary counsel to his attentive acquaintance.

'Earnestly pray lest you have need of a gun; lest you be so irate as to fire it at a fellow-terrestrial. Blessèd be thou in the happenstance of eschewing that choice, eluding that necessity, either veridical or imaginary. On the origins of war, consider: antagonisms are generated by enthusiasts who appropriate control, as well as by their ambitious cronies; withal, often by those of an elevated caste. Pivotal wars are never won; verily, only altered: further victims are abused; prejudicious treaties obtain approval. Across *Terra Firma*, outwith abundant campaigns, men and women till the fields, feed their young, derive gaiety where they may.'

Thereupon, he declared enigmatically: 'Now and then, counsel if you can not so much *inside of a box* as (neoterically) *outside* of such. Should a clever secularist offend a multitude of the pious, have the nation's premier join with spiritual leaders and devout persons for seven minutes of silence. Again, if a movie-maker wishes to lampoon an egregious dictator, have him chronicled not as some villain to be eliminated – rather, present him as the premier he'd in time become; that is, as soon as his ideas adhere to ethical principles: how, in his solicitude, likewise, he'd endeavour to nurture and safeguard his troubled people, winning their honest regard and warm admiration. Bethink you after all, feeling humiliated tends to gainsay (effectively) even charity in speech. Any nation's governor, voicing scorn apropos another, comprises an outlandish phenomenon, as well as signalling a pitiful prognosis (very like) for its populace. Again, how risible to escape the liberal mind of the leadership, that, heretofore what it was disposed to do itself is the very deficiency it aggravatingly and vigorously condemns in another.

'The best form of government is a benign dictatorship. Even so, democracy is not all bad. Still, many who are disadvantaged will vote out of need – whilst those pocketing profit will elect out of greed. Arrogating wealth be not our end, not our aim. Exhort politicians thus: within mind, heart and will, enkindle the discipline, the reality of kindness. Likewise among doctors, lawyers, vicars, peelers; the empowered wherever they be. Beware the nasty cabals, for whom politics – when the sum is said and done – is largely or mainly a game. Perceived in such a way, it is delivered (generally) to maintain tribal allegiances and familial dynasties: in fine, to diminish or sway the rolling bore of the terror-struck or justice-seeking.

'Beware, too, the intelligible violence of the trodden-down. Their voice must be heard; their deprivation addressed. This planet, forbye, is overpopulated. All the worlds within our globe require growth to be realised equitably, with thoroughgoing benevolence: no two are the same, whilst the uniqueness of all involves a common respect. Moreover, and urgently, individually and together, all must remain cognisant of the whole, our very survival upon *Terra Firma*. Wherefore, till we protect our race and our planet, journeys outwith need now to be halted. Repeating evil elsewhere conjures reprisals inimical to life itself.

'In a similar vein be forewarned: psychopathy wedded to power will translate, sooner or later, to maleficent disease. Infiltrating far and wide, it besmears our species and assumes a ruthless, systemic potency. It must be stopped. Withal, cessation achieved, it is indulgent and unwise to scape-goat a single source. Better that one and all should aspire to be kinder yet. All are implicated: more or less; those manifestly closest to the core, those marginally at a remote periphery. Ultimately, whilst a potentate brandishes a mighty stick, domineering innocent and evil alike, a variety dragooned will conjure a similar cudgel to utilise themselves. Failure to grasp this is tantamount to espousing a paradigm of imbecility.

'Be bold and beneficent in dealing with terrorists. Insurgents *neutralised* will neither convey information nor attain integration. Numerous are the individuals more or less disordered. Wherefore, arraign if you must, albeit condemn not. Remember, not one abides who hast not tholed the heft of fate. Should four men and women, within an epoch of world-wide media, be guilty of dispatching and maiming in the name of their faith, be assured, co-believers will be blamed and undergo brutality through association alone – be they innocent or implicated. Wherefore, have not the country that has suffered abuse, itself react similarly. Rather, be it inspirited to consign a premier-quartet of skilled facilitators to an area wherein co-religionists of the assassins struggle to exist amid difficulty and disease: surely though slowly, have those same volunteers garner their renown plainly for benign conduct, itself emblazoned far and wide. Have, withal, resources spared by non-violent action targeted then towards benignant creativity. Bear in mind, forbye, the valiant Arjuna, renounced by his helpmate and co-workers on the day he resigned (cherishing for sure his ideal) from the Sorcerer's Manufactory of *Streamline Missiles* and *No-Risk Deadly-Drones*.

'And remember: optimal freedom is guaranteed not by an arsenal of the most potent weapons, but, by an heroic preparedness to forsake everything rather than annihilate others or violate principle. He who attains this freedom reveals the actuality and nearness of God. Think creatively and with kindness. Surprise those listening, that they may discern with clemency and wisdom.'

Joshua was pondering these uncommon ideas even as Alberic imparted his last utterance. 'Behold, at last a way is open for you into our glorious park. Time it is for you to leave. Fare forward. Yet, ere you go, there is one last thing. The distinctive shard you acquired (before we discoursed) let me have it please. Copious surely are those aptly advantaged from its wisdom, amen, more than yourself. Your requirement is less, your wisdom greater.'

Slowly succumbing, the disciple manqué withdrew from the inside-wrap of his mantle the diminutive oracle, previously purloined (it might be opined) in a similitude of innocent theft. Thus implementing Alberic's charge, ventured he then to his soul this provocative inquiry: *Ought I to do, do more than simply fathom the whole? Realise risk, endeavour further? Natheless, in humility always.*

Barely stirring, the sometime-master (and donee of the precious fragment) did with the apophthegm something now to engender wonderment to any who were near; withal assuredly to his erstwhile associate. He raised the shard in his right hand, and – with an *uber*-like, consummate ease – pitched it into the air in such a particular trajectory that it landed (in sooth) precisely into the identical chink of tarmacked road out of which it had been deracinated by the inquisitive pilgrim.

Joshua arose at this, betaking himself from Alberic the monk – denominated appositely as, *The Holy One* – forthwith ascertaining his whereabouts marched positively ahead; nigher now to a single tall, aisle of trees, ostensively tapering: visibly here an arbour of which he perceived fronting the leafage of russet and ochre and etiolated magenta. Deep into and through this corridor he went, striding step upon step, only heading now not to *The Pilgrim Path*, but towards the intended park where (in another place) Murdo, *The Old Soldier*, had been.

Part the Eighth: *in which Joshua becomes involved in creating pictures and in a prayer-recital; alights upon curiosities, then discourses with both* The Man Who Watches *and, surreally,* The Good Mother.

Although finding himself once more in the park, the thinker noticed things differently. The whole area seemed to have been shaken, unfolded, cast forth anew in a broader, more expansive levelling-of-landscape, setting forth a chequering of variegated grasses and manifold crops far o'er-flung into the milky distance. There remained nonetheless trees aplenty, a plethora of which comprised the deciduous type in seasonal colouring. Others there were that were evergreen – standing tall, elegant, rhythmically listing in the ruffling breeze. Over to the viewer's right, apart and by itself, a small chapel nestled, built of mortar and stone, round-about which several roses and fuchsias were growing; just as, very like to augment the whole, spectacularly stood a great towering pine. Joshua decided post-haste to explore the aforesaid place-of-the-pious.

However, already assembled evidently lay, between himself and the oratory, a surprising ensemble of thespians and related crew, sprawled or draped upon woollen tassel-edged rugs, enjoying a magnolious picnic. Then, too, a dozen more were promenading and conversing with enthusiasm – arms gesticulating, here, there (who knew why?) – even as two or three on the periphery concentrated on poking and prying through pointed cameras attached to tripodal stands. One such fellow, drooling and chewing upon a cigar – occasioning its smoke to go puff-puff into the air – promptly stepped rearward, plonked-down within an isolated canvas-chair, whereupon enouncing his complaint to one and to all: 'We can't do anything more without a script! Bring me, anybody, Joshua's lines!'

At the mention of his name, the inquisitive saunterer felt somewhat discombobulated, albeit (naturally) he appreciated the summons just as likely might apply to a body specified similarly. Hoping quietly such was the case, anon the witness saw the sedentary fellow rise, thereby disclosing a red fivesome of words proudly stitched athwart the coarse material reverse of the chair, denoting – *The Man Who Makes Pictures*. Hereupon, whilst the newcomer was comprehending said title, the irascible director turned to him, barking out loud: 'Joshua! So there you are! Man, already we've delayed for nearly an hour! We've to turn right away to the scene in the chapel; execute the shoot on *The Recitation of Prayer*. Where are the lines?'

The mystified pilgrim was, yet again, further-dumbfounded, noticing how already within the grasp of his hand, observably, was a sizeable wad of paper folded in two; although, anxiously riffling through the pages, he discovered everyone of them betided to be blank! Wholly abashed, he lifted from the singular bundle, arbitrarily, a solitary sheet, afore bearding the questioner with a query-and-another of his own.

'Anyone here own an implement to write with?'

'What are you like!' exclaimed *The Man Who Makes Pictures*. 'Go on – other question?'

How this secondary intention came into the grasp of the director's mind conjured a degree of mystery, albeit it insinuated (peradventure) a characteristic of *Awkin* intelligence.

'What's the name of the film?' implored the one embarrassed. 'Will you tell me what it's called?'

'Request denied,' came back the reply; while Rafael – verily, such was the supervisor's name – tossed him a finely sharpened, wooden pencil, removing himself forthwith and walking towards a circle of imbibers in the picnic-area.

Joshua was nonplussed. Did Rafael mean to imply that the *request* – that he be told the title of the film – was *denied*? Or, did he mean of the overall production that the title was, *Request Denied*? Feasibly, following said response, he'd promptly need to conjure requisite material for a postponed 'shoot' (so-called) made up of a prayer-recital. Just the same (even in an oratory) earnest petitions were liable to be refused if judged to be alien to divine intent. Equivalently, his outlook would need to reveal the aforesaid, imposed *realism* – or, if one preferred, *scepticism* – were it to do justice to the most likely thesis of the film. The scrivener (manqué) pondered hereat over content congruent with the perspective of his former companion, Tom. Only, would it amount to hindrance or abetment for a paradoxical dialogue such as this? For all that, *The Cautious One* (needless to say) was removed from the current locale, wherefore as scenarist at hand it'd need to be none other than himself who'd to conjure duly credible material.

He sat down in the grass (albeit with a hint of wariness) discovering it was (mercifully) quite dry, but, ah no, actually not wholly dry: warily, warily then did he stretch upon the earthen floor situated neath the shade of an arbour, set tall within a myriadfold of fallen, minuscule, needle-pointed leaves, amassed, at times bestrewn, closer to those more recently dropped and deckled cones. Breathing in the resinous smell of the pine, withal, having licked the lead tip of the pencil – though ignorant as to why – he forthwith started to score the following lines, surfacing (as in truth they had to) with undeniable haste.

The Prayer-Recital.

The faithful process into the chapel down two columns. They divide to the left and to the right, procuring their places in opposing stalls, lowering misericords and taking their seats in readiness for the service from The Man Who Might Be Me. *The celebrant enters, paces-forth slowly but intentionally onward, as far as the lectern at the front of the aisle. Anon, his bearing upright, calmly does he place his trusted hands upon the closed holy book, beforehand placed upon the unfurled wings of a bent-brazen keen-eyed eagle, the very emblematical raptor upholding the inviolable scriptum for the hallowed exaltation.*

From inside the bible-volume, The Man Who Might Be Me *extricates a solitary, olden, membranous page. Then – dumb for what seems a dire amount of time – he of a sudden coughs, opens his mouth, commences the ensuing, devotional imploration.*

The Chosen: Blessed be God for ever.

The Congregation: Blessings and Thanks to God.

The Chosen: May the Being of God in me be Well. Let God in me Become.

The Congregation: And in us all, and in us all.

The Chosen: And in those who shall sin else starved decline.

The Congregation: May God be Well, let God Become.

The Chosen: In those who must moulder in gaol, be punitively treated.

The Congregation: May God be Well, let God Become.

The Chosen: In those bedevilled, ignored, from family estranged.

The Congregation: May God be Well, let God Become.

The Chosen: In all who mourn, who themselves death await.

The Congregation: In us all, let God Become.

The Chosen: In those owning doubt, a loss of faith, cessation of hope.

The Congregation: May God be Well, let God Become.

The Chosen: Withal in souls benign; endeavouring, furnishing our world with wonder.

The Congregation: In us all, in us all.

The Chosen and The Congregation: May God be Blest, let God Become.

The Chosen: Blessed be our God, unto whom, for aye, do we render our thanks and praise.

The Congregation: Amen, amen.

The Man Who Might Be Me *replaces the borrowed vellum within the pages of the sacred tome, posited upon the untaken wings; directs eyes down humbly for a sustained while; next, upraises his eyes to those without, ere stepping ceremonially through the flagged nave, guiding the recession – all hymning of thought in abeyance, all radiant-lumining now in abundance with its blue, maroon, magenta through and through the polished, tinted glass. Welcomed he is to the tambour by a flood of colourless white. Into and through this dazzlement, continues he now to the finish.*

Such brilliance seemed then to diffuse far and wide, else lost within the splendorous aura here surrounding *The Man Who Makes Pictures*, whilst the scribe, upright once more, imparted thereupon the desired manuscript with its pencilled lines to Rafael, who remarked, perfunctorily: 'Thank you, my friend – a fine rendition. You did not disappoint. Endeavour to be more punctual henceforth. Here, this is your payment.'

The purveyor of prayer found in his hand a small knot of paper bills, though, upon looking upward, strangely, the granter of the guerdon had somehow departed. The character conducting the drama had vanished from view.

Came there then to the recipient's earnest notice another structure, standing beside and somewhat behind the chapel proper – always there, albeit in the here and now more evident: a bare, functional building it was, a bit like a warehouse, possessing great depth and breadth, and, once discerned, noteworthy alone by dint of its size. Nine or ten strides should take the searcher directly to its huge barn-like doors.

Evident on the way to this compelling diversion was a tiny tablet of material exsertile from the ground, largely disguised by a welter of fallen foliage. Suitably curious to have its purpose revealed, the inquirer bent over to descry a miniature gravestone, propinquitous to which was an inscription, framed and covered by glass. Niftily fastened to this in its turn was a large lens. Joshua procured the latter, and, lying down on the autumnal leafy floor noticed a paragraph of beautifully-penned handwriting, paradoxically advising: 'Here lies the *corpus* of *The Nameless Child*, who was inhumed below, within this precise place, inearthed within terra firma whilst still alive, with tears and cuts to his skin and organs, the soil all-littered breathed into his nostrils, gasped into his lungs, envisioned into the lenses of his wide, wide eyes, and who had been most shockingly abused.'

Joshua felt his heart pounding; experienced a kind of faint descend upon him. Once he'd posited carefully the magnifier back on the ground, then he stood on his feet, shaken and greatly perturbed. Respiring heavily, rubbing his eyes, he stepped hastily beyond the oratory and thus to its side. Beheld he then, looking upward, a dominant article preparatory to three words, all in upper case, adorning the entrance and indicating: THE LIBRARY OF RELIGION. He pushed at the doors. At first, nothing happened. Thereupon, he employed the whole weight of his body to one of the duplex wooden masses – and slowly, very slowly, it groaned, then withal, edged. After yet more heavings (leadenly proffered) it bit by bit turned and nudged, angling open – a dark slit thereby ceding to the visitor a far from hospitable admission.

Instantly, said visitant was struck by the frowsty air, here prompting him to sneeze and to splutter. Taking in his whereabouts, he perceived himself to be in a vast area, a plenteous space comprising an abundance of stacked shelves, several storeys high and receding far into the distance. He pulled out a conspicuous volume, a considerable publication marbled arrestingly across its reinforced cover, thereby inviting the learner's gaze. Pulling front and back apart, gingerly he began a delicate riffle through its disposition of crisp and yellowing pages, albeit must and mouldiness wafting towards him, inclining him with a rapidity to slew his head to elude the dust.

Even so, he now saw, eyed rivetingly, a portrait painted bold, sombrely cast in brown, feculent gold and inky, bluish black: a thin face aghast with horror, lined and wrinkled, exhibiting pinched cheeks horribly framed by flowing-white hair; even as with its elongated-mouth the thin, frangible lips were made to open into a wide venting of utter frenzy. Nigh-to the foot of the page, the disquieted student could discern the words, 'Anon Fearest Thou Death.' Presented in such a dismal manner, the perturbing trope unsurprisingly alarmed him. Heeded he, *nolens volens*, the title as he shut the book: 'The Black Curtain: the Finality of the Last Gasp.'

Stuffing the macabre *opus* back in its place, the anxious inquirer started to search along the aisle (ecclesial it could've been) by now straitening it appeared between the dyad-sets of shelves. He paced and paced and paced. There seemed to be no end. The interior got darker and darker. Soothfully, it escaped comprehension how light of any kind could infiltrate such gloom. Little by more, the intimidated novitiate endured a sense severally of negation, of loss; of profound emptiness. Upon turning round moreover there was to be seen no sigil of any exit or entrance. In thrall for a trice to the breath-choking intimation of panic, said reader persuaded himself how it would be possible – simply by veering round and walking back the way he had come – to behold again the high and hefty door, disinterring himself thereafter from death's doom and ruin. It'd surely make little difference to the outcome – bar celerity, or economy of hour – he then supposed, should he promenade rather earnestly. To avouch naught of starting to run. Really, of beginning to flee.

Wherefore, in only a little while, the very person denominated *The Man Who Might Be* experienced himself confronting a near-pleroma of white, fulgorous light cheerily resonant of air, of wholeness, wellbeing, plenitude – freed hereby from the powder and cobwebbery: moribund resource of wise or less than wise words; onwards to the light of life drawing him back to the arboreal reserve. Where (roundabout combing) he could see nothing anymore of those picnicking, or making movies – amen, even the single, folding, canvas chair. All had gone. What's more, the park itself, familiar by its previous appearance, visibly had changed, suddenly transformed, now less open, less accessible – containing as it did a loftier compassing, a heavier proximity of trees.

Even so, there existed a singular and broad exception, almost circular, a near-lucent green-glade, itself bestrewn with grass, with at its heart an ancient oak with sizeable pond beside. Sited beneath the aforementioned tree was a plain, wooden form, gifted with at one end a gentleman of indeterminate age. To that circle and tree, and to that bench and man, Joshua now forged his faltering advance.

Even before the runagate had reached the circular clearing, this other person (hitherto resting) forthwith got to his feet so as to near, openly to welcome, serendipitously the genial newcomer proffering him his outstretched hand: 'Hello, Joshua, I am *The Man Who Watches*. Howbeit – should you not mind – then as lief call me Hank! Please, shift the weight from your feet; parley with me the while upon this rugged but backless pew!'

Joshua did as he was invited, although tempted, too, to ask *The Man Who Watches* how indeed he knew his name; albeit, purely knowing he did surreally now felt more important. Besides, he was ready to share with him his beliefs and opinions.

'Readily I'm willing, Hank, to join you beneath this nut-bearing oak. Seemingly, the exercise of watching must be something in which you take particular pride.'

'Absolutely I do,' came back the reply. 'People identify me according to just such a task. Even today, barely an hour ago, a neighbourly boy came loping out of that company of larch so as to disclose information he discerned I should know. He'd sighted a singular notice advertising a talk on *Other Modes of Experiencing* – some creative presentation to do with the whole of our present knowledge and philosophy being based incompletely on a model of reality perceived through mental processes; when, actually, there might be other and alien filters for apprehending the truth that could make all current surmises and proposals intrinsically redundant. Definitely, a colossal subject: conceivably, evidencing this overturning of the terrestrial intellect – away from its ascendency as primary mode for comprehending reality – would, *per se*, make of theology a balderdash and ideas of an afterlife irrelevant and misplaced. Anyhow, odd to aver, none of that accounted for the youth having invited my opinion; for, he wasn't disquieted at what was being advertised, purely by a coincidental detail – to wit, how the bulletin in question had been malleted and pegged against a living tree.'

Iterating with emphasis, *The Man Who Watches* momentarily halted his report, smiling genially, as though his dogged companion might interject or register surprise. However, no such interjection or consternation occurred – inclining the former to resume his story.

'Amen, amen, it's commonplace nowadays to find those uncomfortable at what appears to be a discounting of the spatial separateness, uniqueness of identity, and manifold years – centuries in this case – every individual tree must represent. Unsurprisingly, sticking things into else along the enfolding bark could be perceived to savour of a certain impertinence. Furthermore, occurring in this case was a queer, additional attribute: for, the advisory had been affixed across an already executed act of vandalism. Somebody (by now) had carved, deeply and heftily, into the broad and knotted trunk – discernibly cutting into the tree's skin with a blade – indicating thereby (and to a few not without irony) a shameless disclosure of love: recognisably, a heart bearing a primitive arrow going through it, withal a sentiment offered beside that a named individual doth *love* another. On the face of it, such had taken place here, the corollary of which was that the previous disclosure was nigh occluded by the latest notice – an arrow-head, alone, extruding from one side; whilst, observable at an angle clearly stood the letters 'R' and 'a', and, diagonally opposite, the symbols 'u' and 'a'. Irregardless, the teenager and I concurred, that, whoever had arrived to promote it in such a way, the selfsame person had visibly assayed not to disfigure the trunk across a heretofore-unviolated area. Moreover, the advertisement would, as likely as not, come to be detached by the promoter, else, corrupt in time owing to the weathering of wind, sun and eventual rain. The youth and I believed then there to be no additional need for action.'

The wanderer, attending to this anecdote most carefully, realised he was intrigued to ascertain a comparison of the poster with the overall placement of the chiselled lettering, thusly determining the denominated identities divulged of the lovers. Added to which, proper scrutiny was fuelled further by the import of the note – his intuiting in the rationale manifested the likelihood of something fallacious. Compounding his bafflement, besides, was the perception that a notable function of his brain contravened another hallmark of his self; or, just as disturbing, the trivial appeared to be weighing with something profound for priority of attention. Accordingly – preferring not to select either way – he endeavoured to give a rather perfunctory reply.

'In apprehending certain phenomena, I'd reckon you'd need to alight upon true interpretation and (if duly required) as a corollary react.'

'Exactly so,' returned the lauded watcher. 'It won't suffice merely to behold: evidence has to be assessed, considered, probed, recorded, acted upon. Hearken well, Joshua. Across the years I've observed more and more citizens espouse what they believe to be the principle of tolerance, viewed as a cardinal aspect of contemporary culture. Even so, notwithstanding this growing acceptance of difference in category and behaviour, outlook and singularity – *passing over any examples of intolerance plainly confounding the general rule* – one perceives a growing casualness vis-à-vis opinions and actions taken as a whole: what is spoken of as tolerance is nothing these days but indifference, millions practising whatever they choose – perturbed not at all, one way or another. An erstwhile laudable virtue, nowadays it denotes little more than inanity of mind or apathy of soul. If a person hears of a tradition soon to be broken – ignoring whatever penetrative reasons may've precipitated the precise rupture – usually what supplants it is mere *insouciance* vis-à-vis the determination earlier in place. Just the same, a particular consuetude or principle or habit of behaviour may have been embodied for centuries by men and women of passion and responsibility; themselves – who knows? – having forfeited their lives championing such robust thought or intelligible action: and now, upon a whim, their descendants or disciples required to witness it being countermanded by others reckoning any notion of gallantry, or tradition, or morality to be befitting not at all to their preferred way of thinking. Better to declare, *Know what? Anything goes!* – surely than to have a citizen one day remark to another: *Excuse me, only I disagree. I object. I don't want you to do that.* Laudable it might be for those of liberal inclinations not needlessly to cavil over worthless matters. Only, conversely, it's bad – accepting I can offer a suitable (so called!) *value-judgement* – likewise to treat all rivalries as being equally slight: zilch but havering and junketry!'

Joshua, thoroughly cognisant re the argument, felt pleased to assert as a reply: 'Myself, I'd outline the argument a little differently, not quite as dire as you've depicted: more *paradoxical*, deserving of more subtle nuancing. Nevertheless, I think I've got the gist of your last word! Withal, I concede you do have a point!'

'*Mirabile dictu*! Not quite a disaster!' bellowed a delighted-looking Hank. 'Likewise – so does he. Have a point – in my view!' Pronouncing thus, he signalled to a sinewy and scantily-attired masculine-figure bearing on his back a shirt-like banner, professing in print the solitary assertion being iterated, *fortissimo*, over and over again:

We are all damaged goods!
We are all damaged goods!
We are all damaged goods!

Indeed, on and on and on.

The Man Who Watches agreed: 'The notion is neatly and aptly phrased. Think besides: ours is such a consumer and commodity-oriented society that any mention of *sin* – whatever that was! – or, then again, moral toxicity, only repels – as possibly it should! – albeit, the concept of an imperfect *purchase* pertains nicely!'

'Even so,' said sentiment may apply to ourselves,' observed The-Man-Who-Listens, 'never mind the single-minded herald courting simplicity.'

'Of course! Of course! Honesty demands I recognise my link alike to the spoiled and soiled – realising I be of uncertain *shelf*-life: conceivably, beyond my sell-by date! Discernibly – should I be free to comment – you're not looking too good yourself!'

Joshua smiled. Candidness applied to the terrestrial condition was gratifying. No less, the attribute of humility heartening. Acquiring a more pedagogical approach, the commentator continued to provide further observations from his analysis of their shared kind.

'Predictably, seated here beneath this tree, many a time and oft I get to descry a good deal to incline me to hesitate; to pause and reflect. To illustrate: I discovered a girl, many years ago, examining butterflies; painted ladies, red admirals, cabbage-whites, tortoise-shells, withal others too, that have now flit – amen, fled the memory. Examiner of the natural world, an aurelian furthermore, studiously she wrote down notes, collating all she'd monitored prior to creating some preliminary findings. Thereupon – to improve and accompany her thesis – she started to include detailed pen-and-ink portrayals of whatever was worthy of remark; taking time, much time, in implementing her indagation and rendition. Naturally, I identified within her routine a desirable template for the classically hard-working, aspiring scholar. Verily, then it occurred to me how all the theories of things – be they of nature, essence or kinship – e'er devised, drafted, drawn up, and taken to an apposite conclusion, could thence prosper and do well following an expenditure of appreciable effort plus due enterprise, by individuals both alone and in tandem with others: basically, how all the iotas and scantlings of industry would, by and by, come to comprise a contribution to the broader picture. Absolutely! Even whilst particular findings may've appeared not typical, or misleading, or in some other way false – accepting that the fallacious also needs to be uncovered, discerned with care, afore being discounted, qualified or corrected. Veritably, the entirety of this necessitates enormous output, built up over years and years and years: in order that, in the fullness of time, our conclusions can finally – else, ought I to say, more-or-less provisionally? – be deemed reliable; be held consensual.'

Audible indeed was the sigh that came forth, heartfelt and well-earned. Hank upraised from his head the chapeau of felt he was wearing, thereafter sliding it rearward, allowing the knotted strap along his chin to fall back below the apple of his throat. Riffling the fingers of his right hand into the flood of his almost blonde if-greying hair, he asserted: 'That's purely the start of it! Think of it, Joshua: amen, this hat here, my favourite denims; your worn-out sandals, the knapsack over your shoulder; the bread you eat, the wine I drink – *someone* has had to contrive, to render all of these! Withal, to be precise, whilst I suggest *someone*, really I'm guessing a goodly gang of folk: for sure, those artists and fabricators inspired in the initial act of imagining; those in producing and manufacturing; those in marketing and advertising; all those in vendition, distribution – and so forth. A largish deal of this withal many are disposed to rely upon automatically – possibly all of the time! – careless as to how much of it is rooted in hard graft! Again, it's mainly a question of who's carrying out what, as well as the calculus of how much. Furthermore – should I iterate freely – this one, solitary reality is a Plato-of-an-apt reminder that each and every one of us, all of us, patently needs to play our part, pull our weight – get good-and-all stuck in!'

Hank paused. Hardly at all: 'Likewise, within the great chain of continuity – clichéd or no – the smallest nexus is absolutely essential. Accordingly, the beggarman, pin-pricking at the guilt-denying or vacuous superegos of busy purchasers, is perchance *doing his bit* for the rest of humanity; the unhappy *babushka*, belatedly lugging her rubbish from yard to dustcart, evidences her quotidian hardiness; the sightless citizen who permits the proud benefactor to assist him, arm-in-elbow, across the road – albeit, he'd already managed to cross it! – favours the possibility of kindness. Ineluctably, when our allotted span reaches its end, then we'll readily defer to a *Preponderant Authority* to adjudicate as to the outcome: obsecrate, of course, lest we ourselves be condemned; we who, similarly, could have been overwhelmed by a laziness of will – a crassness of mind; some torpor of indifference – this way or that, exhausted with travail.'

Hank, sighing once more, a second paused – before vigorously resuming: 'Now, now, I'm smart, you know! Oh yes, Joshua, I'm smart! Give me the nod to start and there'll be no stopping me! Reliable old windbag – eh?' Laughing with confidence, he slapped a mighty slap between the blades of his bench-sharer's back. Withal, then exclaiming: 'Oh! goodness gracious, what have we here! Look! It's *The Good Mother* – coming up out of the water!'

Joshua gaped disbelievingly. From the little lake beyond (as well as to one side) there emerged from the rippling liquid a tall and handsomely-built woman. Following her, there traipsed obediently three children – of whom the early-teenagers were girls, whilst the brother (to judge by hair and by height) bordering on adulthood. In the maternal forearms an infant guggled and chuckled – the epitome of dimpled delight.

She stepped towards the watchers with not a drop of water spilling from her body or clothes or riotous curls, advancing to them (surreally) as dry as they were dry, sitting there relaxing and talking under the mighty oak, as she came closer and closer. Except: analyst first, thereupon pilgrim, up-standing politely strode forth towards her, beckoning her cordially into their midst.

'Good day, good day, *The Good Mother*! We are pleased to see you.' The benevolent beholder spoke for the two of them.

'Likewise. And thank you. I perceive once more, Hank, you are watching carefully as ever. Appreciative I am to behold the apostle, *Joshua*. Prior to certain weird women having to spin, measure – one day to cut. Afore he travels outwith our range.'

'Indeed, indeed. The troika of *Fates*, it must have its way. Anyhow, is it not wondrous to see him?'

Joshua listened silently, as if a dreamer in a dream. Improbably bizarre (he mused interiorly) this unusual knowledge of complete strangers regarding his name – credibly his selfhood, too. Only, shouldn't he, for sure, by now be used to it? Nothing is as it seems. Said axiom, enigmatic at times, was wholly applicable to a happenstance such as this. Anon, he summoned his voice to assert: 'I'm fortunate, good mother, to meet you, albeit in a continent of many mysteries.'

'Assuredly. Even if not all of them – haply as *The Man Who Watches* has intimated – not all of them timely or desirable.'

'No, decidedly,' corroborated Hank. 'Irregardless, one's minded now to elucidate upon the subject of motherhood. Vis-à-vis yourself, methinks I'm surely on the mark when I declare, although you love your children with a devotion no earnest soul would dare to question – scarce try to follow, certainly not excel – howbeit, you'd reprehend them on their going awry, either in action or intent? Virtues you adhere to, you advise them fully to grasp, as indeed to realise – as far as they are capable. Your sobriquet, *The Good Mother*, it does not bespeak privileging the wrong or actions that are bad or immoral, else – analogous to what we've already noted – *damaging*: comparable (let's say) to some bit of trivia or some paltry issue supposing even if stated or enacted by your nearest and dearest. Verily, you care; congruent with which you endeavour most diligently to make your children care, too. Assuredly, I am correct, am I not?'

'The question, Hank, is rhetorical. Even so, in my reification as *Mother*, dearly do I desire – for the majority of my progeny – absolutely as much felicity as a proper balancing of *Life* and *Cherishment* will allow. Seriously, it grieves me to find the wearers of the mask of *agápē* concealing sometimes a coldness of heart – desiderating for the poor and aggrieved that their gain be limited to shelter, food, water, habiliment. Critical as these indisputably are, they should be accompanied by creativity and purpose, by delight – by rapture withal.'

'In an ideal world,' abruptly added the opinionative other, inspirited to advance the tide of the argument. 'Which is why we need politicians and campaigners—'

'What I'm professing,' interrupted *The Good Mother*, lest her flow of meditation should eddy awry, 'is that the agony and the ecstasy need to be shared in respectful measure: notably, among those who eschew the regular calm of compromise and contentment. For all that, Hank, I'm emboldened to discern you've lost not a whit of your keenness for pontificating and moralising! Have you taken our friend here through what I waggishly refer to as *The Eight Pontifications*? No? All right, then; let's see if I can call them to mind.

Since I wear fine clothes, I feel superior.
Since I live in a handsome property, I feel superior.
Since I travel in style, I feel superior.
Since I proclaim with an eloquent voice, I feel superior.
Since I'm illustriously educated, I feel superior.
Since I palaver with an elitist kind, I feel superior.
Since the rare feel superior, so the rare are selected.
Since the rare feel superior, myriads must shoulder the brunt.'

Here, *The Good Mother* smiled affectionately, concurring with the maximist in *The Man Who Watches*. Directly addressing the newcomer, she genially added her confirmation.

'First (if as well to be frank) I'm agreeing with Hank's disapproval, delivered and positively-enriched with irony and perception. What's more, it's markedly the case that he has a talent for cataloguing. Forbye, then and now, folk still tease him for having contrived – on a swelteringly hot day, during the election of a new Prime Functionary – incredibly to go so far as to recite 23 of such *Pontifications*! Notable as it was, one could still ask: *Crumbs! Whatever's the point in watching* (here a pause, likely for effect) *should you not then be able to enjoy a good old beef about this – else that, else – maybe the other!'*

All three laughed. Decidedly, Hank had a reputation. Unequivocally did he err towards venturing his mind afore alien advice or excess-discrimination could curb his resolve, inclining memory to fail. Abruptly (her levity notwithstanding) *The Good Mother* demonstrated next a certain severity, narrating now a narrative of a pitiable phenomenon evidenced in a far-off land – beyond, far beyond the womb-like mere whence her offspring and herself had but lately stepped forth.

'Distressful to communicate, I've latterly encountered an additional syndrome tearing apart the lives of numerous children in an erstwhile, faraway colony. I conveyed to you last time what I'd had to witness during a famine: how I'd beheld countless children with prominent bones starkly visible; abdomens bloated and distended, with cheeks hollowed through hunger; eyes manifesting a helpless stare whilst countless flies all but crawled over those poor emaciated figures, withal vacant pitiable expressions. (*Joshua strove hard not to interject, appalled at the account here summarised, but cognisant too that an update from* The Good Mother *was about to emerge.*) Today, the distress I lay bare is denominated *the nodding disease*. It debilitates the innocent child, necessitating it to jounce its limbs, to nod its head, to coil or twist its torso in fits and spasms. Instances spoken of include those of certain young ones, unbeknowingly having gone off into some afforested area, anterior then to having bits of their convulsed and blighted corses dragged-back by dogs into the family-hut. Existing in that environment, a child so-afflicted needs perennially to be monitored, attentively held safe and secure within the confines of home and steading. One mother said of her son, upsettingly – fighting back the tears – how minding and caring for him was like *tending to a plant*: the boy himself would conspicuously neither be able to *become* nor be able to *perform* anything of use.'

'That,' asserted *The Man Who Watches*, 'is an assuredly dispiriting account. Even so, tragically, what can any of us do?'

'Possibly, my friend, nothing at all. For all that, I'm deducing you yourself might be able to ascertain – recalling how you enjoy access to the eyes and ears of the influential and informed – some potent medication theoretically to be made available; plus, importantly, any recompense that the nation involved might adjudge to be passable and judicious. Naturally I come to you, Hank, believing you to be a citizen who watches wisely this troubled world, assaying such terrible quandaries. As do I, realising my particular role as *bona fide* mother.'

Joshua watched then as both *Man* and *Mother* awhile embraced. Thereafter, the empathetic lady gathered about her her four beloved, corralling them down to the sun-bedizened oval of water, all around which now a light zephyr drove numerous ripplets over and along its precious shadow-patterned surface. Into it the five visitors dipped, dipped slowly – each disappearing as evenly and as elegantly as first they had emerged.

The cogitators as a corollary were left sitting again, the two alone upon their bench, soberly there to dwell upon what they had seen and what they had heard: even if in brief beheld, still weighted with burden of import and attenuated bereavement. A silence enfolded them under the tremulous whisperings of leaves, brittle and decayed, whilst they gazed disconsolately at the ground below. In due course, the one blessed with a Stetson placed it upon his head, squarely, ere tucking the strap beneath his chin – likely sensing the draughts about his pate. Assuredly, it did seem then as if the air was bereft of calm, bestirring itself to a stronger purchase: even, forbye, as to inspire further *The Man Who Watches* to recount a former visit by *The Good Mother*, one that had disquieted similarly – furthermore, profoundly so.

'Conceivably, I'll unsettle us yet more,' he began, 'should I here lay bare the narrative she divulged earlier, involving occurrences (again contemporary) bearing upon her distant cousins in the Defiant Sisterhood, inhabitants of the Vast Territory. The narrative she reported chanced to be that of ravening cruelty; of barbarism perpetrated upon hapless mothers; of brutal, armed warriors, empowered by lust and contempt, who stole dignity and enforced harm, having recourse to sharp weaponry to prolong the lingering ordeal. Equally, said afflicted, sadistically misused wives later were ordered to verify that their menfolk had also been dispatched, their hearts withal torn-out: just as, buried in their blood-riddled cavities obtained the pitiful remains of expired infants; and, not far off, the attendant corpses of ridded-toddlers more or less equally mutilated. Child soldiers would watch and keep guard at the height of these atrocities.'

Then it was that Joshua remembered the words of Alberic, *The Holy One*:

'Earnestly pray lest you have need of a gun; lest you be so irate as to fire it at a fellow-terrestrial. Blessèd be thou in the happenstance of eschewing that choice, eluding that necessity, either veridical or imaginary.'

Had he been a witness to such barbarity, possessing lethal force besides, then, what would he have done? In the awful contest between cowardice and killing, amen, what choice should he have made? Assuredly, grateful he was that he had not been called upon to answer that dilemma, required to effectuate a response.

Now, as though to steer the discourse away from such stark realities, a convivial question entered the listener's colloquy: 'Tell me, *The Good Mother*, what's her proper name?'

Merely turning his head a little to one side, the other grinned and shrugged: 'Well, I've never, I confess – never known. Discombobulatingly, it was never divulged, not once proffered! Conceivably, it is strange how I presume she and I are friends! Irregardless, I've been instructed privately that it be a wondrous, indeed beauteous name; forbye, that a sea-lubber, plying the waves under the *Shimmering Stars*, has denominated his vessel after the very same. Naught there be that I can aver beyond!'

The reply seemed odd – though stranger still what followed. 'Remarkably, you could well appreciate the unsatisfactoriness of this; for, you do not know, not for sure, the chosen name of *The Lady With The Long Neck*, merely conjecturing at what, theoretically, it *might be* from the clue of a single letter. Howbeit, dear friend, worry not if we be beholden to endure lives inexplicably seeming to taunt, teasing us to the tether's end. This species' *Empyrean Father* does not, one dares to believe, in truth *play games* with our hearts and souls. Whence, conclude not that each instance of frustration is imbued with inherent, pertinent significance; *envision rather*, that the very complexity of evolution – of time, space, the randomness engendered by their entanglement – necessitates the existence of these maddening unknowns: even the sorrows we must assimilate, verily thereby to realise our peace. As best we can. As best we can.'

Staring serenely ahead, he went on to observe: 'Oh dear – a tad too much breeze for your comrade to light up his briar! As a corollary, he'll relish a goodish pinch-or-two of snuff! Thereafter, upon your departure, I'll be exchanging my head-piece for one more conducive – forsooth, my thinking-cap! Identify whether I can effectuate *The Good Mother's* request – even if it'll call for wings with orisons-galore to deliver! All that averred, amen, there's a lady I have in mind, ample, a formidable speaker in the House, even if – well, apropos really of nothing at all – she prompts me to laugh whenever she doth dance...'

The Man Who Watches trailed off, but then suddenly picked up: 'What's more, I know of a surgeon that'll as like as not aim to travel there to assist. Evidently, it be his recreation. Other staff commonly enjoy a vacation so as to relax. He himself re-creates in the world's hotspots and repairs lives, instructing indigenous personnel thereafter to operate similarly.'

'Goodness!' exclaimed the listener, in humbled admiration. 'What, may I ask, is his name?'

'Disappointingly, I do not recall,' the other observed. 'However, he slingshots at Death and Disfigurement. A myriad times they'll yield to him in response. Mind, even so – not always, not always. And yet, even then – mayhaps, especially then – his epitome of giving enshrines and extends the power and purpose of cosmic expanse; its divine ordinance.'

Joshua noticed then that the lines on his ally's countenance were taught and stressed; how visibly his eyes watered; his voice, too, it sounded almost as if it should crack. Such benignity perceptibly bore a price. Even in the telling. And then, instanter, he became calm, smiled and sighed, confiding to his companion a recollection dear to his heart.

'Eight years ago,' said Hank, 'I heard a piece of music, identified as a *Requiem*. It uplifted, even if it challenged, too. For, though it depicted the awfulness of death, it bespoke the wondrousness as well of life. It not only raised the possibility of something beyond our demise, for, in its defiant grandeur it evoked that aspiration as though it were a demand. It was paradoxical, outrageous and utterly splendid. When my time comes, that would do nicely as a farewell anthem!' He grinned, ceasing his narrative.

Composure regained, the descrier produced from a lining in his trousers a branded softish packet, from which sundered end he derived – in-between digit and thumb – a modest pinch of reddish powder. Dropping it onto his other cupped palm, the calm espier upraised now said compound to his nose, where, squeezing one nostril, he insufflated quickly into the other, ahead of doing it again the alternate way. Hereupon, he shook his head (a mite-ludicrously) from side to side, making a whinnying sound between his cheeks – before beaming effusively.

'Oooh, that's better, Joshua! You should try some. It'll pick you up; give a fillip to your mind and spirit. Here!'

The initiate took the packet thus offered – discerning (albeit warily) the tell-tale calling-card of ruddled-brown noticeably peppering the front of Hank's half-secured gilet – essaying his level-best to repeat what he had just observed. At first, all seemed well. Whilst the especial envelope itself fortuitously made contact again with its affable owner. Even so, all at once a reaction set in, of a type that the luck-less novice appreciated he'd *sneezed* (a great and tearful sneeze besides) which, to his chagrin, made him shut tight his eyes, as he coveted openly a person's handkerchief; only, before such could be found, another nose-tensing guffaw of a sneeze was emitted, and then, in a trice, a further rendition did spoil once more the allurement of the earlier, now-lost reverie.

Part the Ninth: *in which Joshua deliberates with the* The Artsman Of The Croft.

The patient opened his eyes, blinking fitfully, roughly dighting them dry with his knuckles, the clearer and more vividly to apprehend, hearing a lilting voice next to him proclaim, encouragingly, 'Bless you!' Only, this voice was different to that of Hank, The Man Who Watches; whilst, as Joshua's gaze attached more steadily on the distance ahead, he discerned that he was incumbent not upon a wooden bench under a colossal oak set in a glade, or, for such matter, beside a womb-like mere of surprising beneficence.

Instead, he discovered himself to be sitting afresh, dismally, upon an oblong slab set end-to-end over two inchoate boulders, each asquat below the skirt of a cliffside-ascent, aside a thin and winding path below which fell like rolling riprap, slantwise, a broad mass of rubble down to the sea. To his fore, mounting upon an intervening sleeve of tide, there lay an island-strip of terrain that upheld hills on an arresting horizon – some of them fiercely delineated, almost jagged; others milder, more roundly contoured – yet also, striking to the starboard was out-jutting an airt, a mull of land comprising further elevated angles and raised features: knolls and lochans and ridges, here and there enticing the distracted eye, luring it to dwell awhile afore beholding anew. Silhouetted on a protuberance of stone reared proud a mighty stag, flourishing monarch-like its tined knot, before, with sudden raising-up of throat, clarioning its far-reaching stentorian roar.

The light, too, was noteworthy. The sea itself, where an open loch issued then into its lane, strikingly was coloured a milky blue; whereas, elsewhere was lain dully in a shadowy grey. Likewise, an elbow of the foreground had put on a deepening pitch, even as, prominent on the higher ground, the gloam-laved bevels shelved, being bathed in an almost numinous glow of yellowy and lustrous green. Equally, here and there, the backdrop presented an occasional black-tipped gannet: winging, wafting – thence of a sudden dropping in a dive *full-fletched* oceanward, and so therein to the silvern deep.

Next to Joshua sat an approachable-looking, able-bodied *bodach*, attired in the plain garb of someone born and bred within the cincture of high places: a crofter it was, occupied variously with availing cattle or with herding the wild flocculent sheep; else, at the lower end of the tardy burn, leaning with delving spade, stabbing with lustreless, triple-pronged fork; or, later in some steep and covert inlet with fishing-net flung, line cast, or kelp garnered. His huge hands had about them the suggestion of power, a characteristic which the rest of his sturdy, ample frame also demonstrated. A cap sat firmly tucked upon whitening hair (by the array of it the whole mop) which hung higgledy-piggledy to the curling mess of his unruly beard, forbye along wiry brows and hefty sideburns. Visible too, his suit was weathered and torn, biggish boots black and cumbersome, whilst the stick which lay across his knees had about it a makeshift quality – although it was craftily and pragmatically furbelowed, being embellished with a ram's horn at the top end, itself now closer to the interloper.

The latter then uttered, tentatively, the following words: 'Perhaps you know who I am?'

'No. I cannot say that I do, or, if we've happ'd upon each other before. As for me, I am the *The Artsman Of The Croft*. I should be glad, however, if you would call me by my name, which, as happenstance would have it, is Peter Anthony. Of course, in another time, or another dimension, who can say? Even so, I walk forward as best I can within our current domain: our planet, *Terra Firma*, with all its milieus for us to weather and endure, else, should it be so ordained, to culture and to tend – and then, at times, to celebrate; so here, even here, this wild and gale-girdled upland of the bald mountain and the flood-washed lochans below; this rugged, roughish terrain wherein the beasts of slope and summit awhile exist and yet abide.'

'Please excuse my seeming-presumption,' replied the pilgrim of old. 'For, so long have I peregrinated and seen so many strange sights, conversing with so many strange persons – myself among them – that I know not quite whence I come nor whither I go. My name is Joshua. I am rather a well-trod wanderer, a mindful student now and then of the mysteries of life. Direct me now, please: is that a roll of canvas perched amongst the stones?'

Notable here, along with all the gritty shingle and myriadfold rocks (partly comprising the pathway) stood there a tubular artefact of material (bound round by a twist of frayed ribbon) wherewith four brushes pointed upward.

'Why yes!' *The Artsman Of The Croft* confirmed, with a look of pleasant surprise. 'Let me show you.'

Offering warmly, the newly-encountered and sanguine painter-labourer bent forwards, grasped the cloth cylinder, un-furled it warily against his own open lap, before raising it high for the sharer of the stone-seat.

'See!' he declared.

What was to be seen was the very sight that lay extended before them, depicted nocturnally however in multitudinous blues – of indigoes, cobalts and sapphires: pluriform tints and hues contrasting in depth and texture, edged or bound by their sable rims and ebony curves, all fangled-anew in an astonishingly luminous light. Athwart too the immensity of the heavens there burnished white the celestial stars; withal, welkin-ward again, full upon the dark skies across a furling of hills was there drawn, in intricate filters, the precipitous shafts and beams of silver that flickered and glistened, quickened with an electric intensity, veritably a vibrancy to make the temples pound and heart race – rob the beholder virtually of breath. Creator and observer were awe-struck alike.

A noteworthy pause at last having passed – the remarkable canvas reliably rolled, ere restored into its sanctuary of broken ground – said-quester hereupon queried the creative painter: 'Even though the rendering relates to the witching hour, noticeably one or two brushes have not yet dried.'

'Ah, yes. Still, the singular occurrent, memorably witnessed, it arose at least a week ago. What's more, the weather then was exceptionally cold, a deal colder than for a long, long while. Maundering along this old, excavated track, your hirsute highlander began to enjoy a truly wondrous sight – in truth, not for the first time – which is generally referred to as *The Northern Lights*, or again, the *Aurora Borealis*. Regardless of the fall in temperature (severe as it felt) I dallied fitfully and distractedly, the entire while gazing up and all around. I strove hard to take in the aggregate adequately, apprehending reliably the fulgurating intensities the stars themselves seemed to enshrine and extol. By and by, in the days to come – when I'd finished tidying up around the potato-plot, conducted a tally of occasional stray-sheep along by the shore, perhaps stowed now and then any snatches of wet and fibrous dulse, torn from specific rocks – well, then it was I'd stroll up here and begin. Critically, I've been struggling to conjure the wild wonder disclosed to the fore, forbye adjusting, altering it in my mind's eye, withal mirroring the particular hour, abrogating the diurnal template to parallel that scene, the nonpareil it bestowed. I'd only today, finally, to place but minor touches not dilatory in the drying. Now, like as not, I should surely step-back – let it alone, leave it by itself, its essence undisturbed. An act of faith, if you will. Present and past – dimensions of day and night – they interlock and overlap; dimensions of memory and actuality, over each other they ebb and they flow.'

'Peter Anthony, thank you, I appreciate your explanation.'

Uttering thus, the visitant noticed he was looking towards (there in the closer quarter of the promontory) a glistening speckle of yellowy light, cynosural upon the dark periphery of the loch's edge. 'Does someone live over there?' he asked.

'Very like you be meaning in-a-wee-bittie from the headland's end, identified geographically as, *The Point Of Rachel*. Absolutely, a person does. Oh yes: a young man, very bright, very intelligent, very modern. Should you and he hap, one upon the other, well – who knows? – you'd perchance get on. Regarding his name, however, I'm unsure. About him, too, there's something rather unusual, whimsical, perhaps quirky. Abides by himself – same as myself!'

'Go on,' prompted the other. 'Maybe there's a tale to be shared.'

Came there now, perplexingly, over the inquisitive traveller a tiresome, unwanted mood. Consequently, afore Peter Anthony was able to begin his account, the other rose to his feet, temporarily taking himself out of the narrator's vision, veering about a coign of splintered rock located from him surely but feet away. Thereupon, wholly eclipsed from the sight of the *Artsman*, encompassing his self within his arms in a paradox of self-embrace, Joshua bent forward, then back, distress palpable upon his mien, anguish scored across his brow.

'Rachel, dear Rachel!' dolefully he exclaimed. 'Oh where, alack, where are you now? How be it, belovèd, we are parted thus? Open my eyes – how have I done wrong? Could I but recall! Here, suddenly, does it seem you were the point of my life!'

Hereupon, the supplicant looked up, 'Pardon your servant, oh *Heavenly Father*. Amen, how can I give to her presence in my life some rhyme, some reason? Moreover, a terrestrial I am, alone, alone this while: albeit, I've happened upon the alien, Ann-Gel, or forever-elusive, beauteous, peculiarly-remembered *Lady With The Long Neck*. To be sure, the appanage in this gifting I acknowledge. Helpmate, however, have I none.'

Securing his place afresh, upon the solid trestle – an ersatz-altar, diminutive of stone – the pilgrim then beheld of Peter Anthony how he remained entirely calm, notwithstanding the man's torso being angled-about so as to remark, questioningly:

'Better?'

'Decidedly. Thank you. Please do continue.'

Thereupon, heartsore and with his soul at odds, the disquieted listener attempted to apprehend the *Artsman*'s tale.

'Well, like I was conveying, with respect to his name I'm at a loss. Howbeit, the young man settled-in overby around seven years ago, renovating the ancient chapel, updating it to a habitable dwelling, fully fitted with *à la mode* conveniences, all the latest appliances – of which many I doubt I'd be able to fathom! What's more, the locals down our way discerned that he'd acquired a powerful generator, now operating at the back of his premises – as well as two windmills, just identifiable a shade to the right. He's able moreover to utilise powerful signalling emanating from a mast atop yon island opposite, situated as it is away from the actual headland of the peninsula. Really, this is indispensable, bearing in mind that the primary area of the work-room – inside of which erstwhile parishioners congregated for worship or again to hearken – well, these days it has around it a number of different screens, along with various intricate declivitous tables, many comprising keyboards and dials, with levers plus goodness knows what! Long associated with the region – daily he is beheld stravaiging our hills or befriending crofters at the *clachan*-bar – maintain he does yet a curiosity for contemporary affairs round and about the entire world, monitoring what is going on in far-off countries, states and continents. Likewise, I'm given to understand that he communicates with planets outwith our own – wandering the heavens on courses unknown to ourselves – forbye, connecting with different, even *alien* life-forms already having settled upon the very same. Should such indigenes in reality exist!'

A clear wobble noticeable in his voice, Joshua commented while his companion halted to take breath: 'Theoretically, anyhow, I opine that they do. Consonant with your earlier assertion, potentially there are many dimensions; even too, an overlapping of many realms, including outlying beings, beyond. Do go on.'

'Well, by and large, that's the gist of it. He'll conjecture upon a myriad strange notions – or, more faithfully, strange to myself! To quote you an example: the sea itself rising alarmingly, with terrestrial defences being utterly inadequate. Again, real corruption being rife all about, albeit underhandedly hidden in nations of privilege and power. The fragility of civilisation – that any lack of water or oil, else accelerated population-growth, or breakdown of supplies would initiate uproar or anarchy, or (heaven forfend) terrorist government. Or, verily, clandestine interchange with beings – as we were just saying – of an extraterrestrial kind – or, quite as likely, hell-hurling wayward meteors. How everyday-antibiotics, moreover, have proved defective and how, at the very same time, shocking deadly viruses are waiting to emerge. Withal, maybe the latest – how we've mortgaged ourselves to a communist empire in a fashion to wreak havoc, given in time the indenture could turn out to be unmerited. Nonetheless, he exclaimed in a greeting to me seven nights ago – hands upheld in the air, proclaiming wildly: *Human cloning is a metaphor of the life to come! And the cumulus repository – that of the embryonic divine mind!* Truth to tell, I find I'm more and more overwhelmed by it: its signification, what it might portend!'

'Truly, I divine your dilemma,' replied the visitor. 'It spins the head. Greatly! What more can one say? Time itself uncovers my ignorance: the more I strive to know, paradoxically, the less I realise I genuinely do!'

'Be of no doubt,' concurred the other, 'I'm just the same.' Hereby sympathising, *The Artsman Of The Croft* proceeded eagerly to pull out of his inside-jacket's lengthy fold, a coiled, gnarled-looking pipe: which briar he next pushed between his parted lips; evidently (howbeit bizarrely) not so as to smoke the tobacco in the bowl, so much as to gnaw, even then drool upon its mouthpiece; once having chewed withal its dented stem for but a moment, he spat heartily, popping the article (queerly) inside an alternative lining, prior to venturing his own, well-appraised spiritual, or existential, view of life.

'All in all, courtesy of hindsight, principally what I've *achieved* – for my life, as well as for the world – has been to stay true to the chosen objective my temperament has inclined me to pursue: honouring and staying true to its course. Essentially: to attend to my ewes with wethers and offspring besides; employ a favoured ram ferried from the Isles, besides herding sundry-kine o'erseen with the postie nearby; peradventure to shove forth the dinghy on a clement morn, haul up the fish from the most promising bay, go-garnering lumber-and-log at the drift of the tide; be loyal to those sharing the communal township, its diligent community of *crofters*; then as well, carrying out makeshift repairs all about upbye the *lorn* byre, and, ere summer arrives, the shieling too. Just now and then, extended benignly time and mind, only then do I admix oils and colours, awaken upon hessian the semblance of my environment, reaffirmed afresh, aye, in a new and particular way. A life lived for myself, yet lived for the world. Consent to others, I must, to follow their path, lay down a track for themselves. Little more in truth may any man do.

Aye, and woman too. Beholden I am to find myself here. Anyhow, that is how I feel. Well – most of the time!'

He grinned, amenably. Joshua, feeling decidedly grateful for the old man's words, thoroughly at home with them albeit novel to the ear, smiled too, gazing out at this scene, ruminating with this person. Even so, henceforward did he discern that he'd need to pioneer for himself a specific path, one envisaged singularly, uniquely, should he be able to accomplish progress beyond: supposing of this idea he felt a degree of demur, a certain trepidation. Just the same, be it for retreat or advance, the valour of the endeavour must be re-engaged, readily and with resilience besides. Stoically, he sighed: realising the mesmerising pull of the nominated headland's end; the almost direful attraction of the purpose and *The Point Of Rachel*.

* * * * * *

Someplace further down the track (around a mile, maybe more), opening a wooden gate – fastened with its loop of twisting, turquoise string – the aforesaid Peter Anthony entered, descended then the concave steps afore trudging to the door of a middling abode, thereat boldly rapping his fingers at its pushed-aside door, continuing thus to a congenial space: halting then within the spacious lounge, with its coke-fire ablaze and its folk unfolded in chairs and conversing (adults with glasses of *uisge-beatha*, drawing-in on fag-ends again) where conspicuous, unstudied laughter echoed happily on a reliable basis. The visitor sat down. Here was a place hospitality was guaranteed.

'Hello, Peter Anthony. Dare say you'll be, aye, well your usual?' Even so inquired the generous mother, holding forth unto her guest a sizeable saucer of jam-lined sandwiches, plus appreciable cup of amber-looking piping-hot tea. 'There you are, now.'

The Artsman Of The Croft gave reply. 'Really, there was no need. Ach, thank you, thank you. Were you seeing a passer-by? A bag on his back, no from these parts; no very young an' all – who knows how old? *On the side of the angels*, it appeared. Well, d'ye' know this? He was clinging to his soul – aye his soul – by just a thread. You'd to adopt due discretion apropos matters discussed. A rare pilgrimage it is that he essays. Conscious I became of a void, an absence, a real loss eating away within. Closed in by a darkness, he was. Hanging-on by just a thread; just a thread.'

* * * * * *

The darkness wherein Joshua clung to a life that was wondrously his – albeit with tides of despair – did hap here a rattling and shaking to be, barrelling with speed and with noise, with whistling and shrieking and massing of tenebrous, malodorous, sulphurous smoke.

Abruptly from tunnelling a fresh light out-spread and did shine. Forbye, Joshua descried he be resting among a myriad passengers: lounging, sleeping, conversing, reading, snacking, watching – all sorts and ages they were, all on a journey going somewhere, somewhere; and so into more darkness, then back into light, then the dimming again till the star-ridded firmament, the depth of tenebrosity, into which he must fall, fall – sink heavily and far, wearily into a slumbersome repose.

Daystar and consciousness. Another day broke.

Part the Tenth: *in which Joshua promenades again, obtains directions from* The Helpful Verger, *comforts Tobias,* then formulates his conviction of hope for The Twelve *curiously gathered.*

Joshua noticed he was drinking from a mug of hot coffee, as well as (between sips) munching hungrily on an ambrosial hexagon of sugary shortbread. Surveying watchfully, he perceived sitting in front of him a child aged eight; perhaps nine. She was examining images and figures in a hard-bound volume, which, splayed apart, made them seem unusually large. The pictures were of giant lizards, of massive reptilian-creatures of variegated kind: vast, winged, scaly-beasts heavily rearing, ponderously uplifting (heft upon heft) high and higher into the cerulean skies.

Fretful not at all, the girl almost mesmerically beheld one-after-another multiple drawings illustrative of terrestrial prehistory. Strikingly, evidence was there none of a drawing of her particular kind. Her mother looked on. 'Splendorous monsters they were,' she asserted, 'existing over 200 million years ago. Let's ascertain if you're able properly to pencil that number on your verso of paper. Another occasion, I'll require you to execute the number of the celestial stars – one hundred trillion, rounded up or down! Thrillingly, that's what I'm informed the proverbial-*they* say! Huh, and whoever counted! Meantime, 200 million definitely will be enough!'

Obedient to her mother, the girl forthwith added to the two, zero on zero in simple succession, till she had drawn eight round noughts.

'Excellent, my dear,' the parent encouraged. 'Even so, picture now all the animals on the land with birds flying in the air, together with a myriad of fish swimming in swarms. What a cornucopia of life! Howbeit, each single life sooner or later must come to an end, yes, come to an end! Presumably, naught but a whole tome – entirely of circles! – would be able to get at all close to the totality of creatures. Albeit, still it ignores the plethora of our terrestrial race! Added to which, what about the innumerous as yet unborn? How sad! How sad!'

Realising the import of such a sentiment, the daughter queried precociously: 'Mustn't we then ask God to create enough room for them in The Home of Goodness? I mean, all of them, Mummy, all of them!'

'Dearest' – quipped the other, rhetorically – 'wouldn't that involve rather a crowd?'

'Which creature,' interrogated the daughter, 'don't you think is precious? Is not each important to God?' Discernibly unquiet, the girl was sincerely dismayed.

'Remember, they had their day, dear; yes, they had their day. Never mind. Goodness me! – not far now, supposing this watch of mine functions as it should. Pick up your belongings, put down that paper.'

The aforesaid, sweet-toothed pilgrim, if dissecting his mind for a comment, continued to be tongue-tied. Somewhat bemused, he spotted then that the decelerating train had come to a stop.

Up spoke the mother again. 'Alas, no. We're not yet there. A matter awry down-track, an issue on the line. Even, tragically, a crackbrained person desirous of an exit. Oh dear, how tiresome. Regardless, where, where can we be?'

Watchfully, Joshua got up. He found his way to a door evincing a dingy-window partly-lowered. Here, he observed how they were plainly within open country; how the conveyance withal was no longer bombing noisily through a constructed defile. He noticed besides an accessible, convenient set of steps reaching up to a concreted over-span, below which howbeit could be heard the dashing, hurtling and hurrying of abundant vehicles. Deliberately, he stretched out his hand over the sliding, already depressed window to depress further, thereupon putting weight upon an evident lever, noticing then how the door swung-forth, allowing him next to plant each foot onto a single metal step, and, from there – jump to the ground.

Regaining then his balance, Joshua witnessed forthwith his fellow-passengers being swept away in a commotion of clamour and smoke, running, snaking its way along a ferric track bedizened and aglitter with the present sun – aside from where, sporadically, it yielded to the slow sullying and blemishing of rust. Tranches of timber had been arranged across the narrow course, testimony to endeavours of mind and limb realised hitherto in creating this line – a singular iron avenue wherewith mother and child surely were impressively conveyed; veritably propelled to the dwindling petered-out point, to whatever must lie, mysteriously, beyond.

The itinerant paced hurriedly to the rungs, spotted but minutes ago, then, soon enough to the bridge – an exit issuing forth onto an idyllic and rarely-used road, this being exposed, audibly, to the chaos and imbroglio of vehicles intruding from afar.

He came forth ere long upon an arresting contrast of quiet, continuing as he did so along fertile grazing and partly-ploughed, open fields, and onward then towards modest, thatch-topped cottages along with (now and then) an established farmhouse or busy steading. Occasionally, through gaps in the hedgerows, he detected a river, one notably impeded by grassy or sand-banked corners in its meandering, unfurling motion, swirling and rippling as it went. He continued at a manageable pace, easily and assuredly, now and then descrying an odd spillage, else puddle towards which, for a second, he would throw a glance; even though of an image of himself there was not a sign – simply colourless clouds in an azure sky.

Continuing uphill, the curious Joshua discerned ahead a straggling trail of homes, hosting rooflines and ridges and gables, as well as, uplifting from the horizon, a narrowing, metalled lane. Rising up from the buildings, again, stood tall an old-stone tower, proud and sure, discernibly as if it could solidify a specific watershed in the ephemera of history.

Hereupon, ascending now the very slope he himself was going down, tardily advanced a senior terrestrial possessing the diminished height of a so-called dwarf. The newcomer gave out a salutation, at which amiable greeting the unassuming wight replied, amicably:

'Good day to you. I am Ebenezer, *The Helpful Verger*. 'Tis a pleasant afternoon for sauntering, for enjoying the sights. You're not, I think, a local. You are near the village of Silninch, a place you may be assured – like other towns situated equivalently in our realm – betides to be *twinned* with a settlement to be found in the confederation of R.O.U.N.'

'*Roun*?' questioned Joshua. 'I don't believe I've heard of that, any more than I have of Silninch.'

'Ah,' confessed the other, 'I fear it is, on my part, a modest mischief. It is – after all's said and done – not so much a confederation as an acronym. It represents – Repository Of Unpronounceable Names!' With that explanation given, Ebenezer broadly smirked – a thin-lipped grin.

Joshua, even so, failed to divine the implications behind this apparent witticism, albeit acquiescing in showing a smile by way of empathetic exchange. He was basically interested in the high stone tower. 'I don't suppose you could advise me as to that lofty edifice, castellated at the top.'

'Why of course I can. Seeing as I am *The Helpful Verger*! Five centuries old, it goes by the name of *Our Lady of Honesty*. It serves as a social hub and is withal the prime centre of liturgy for the devout of our village.'

'*Our Lady of Honesty*,' echoed the visitant. 'It's a strange title, is it not?'

'Well, it magnifies the virtue of honesty in women. It is easy for us men to dismiss such a possibility. Just the same, women can be honest as well as men. Oh yes. And, no less for sure, the converse can be true. Men may be dishonest as well as women. Oh indeed.'

The thinker was uncertain about this, intuiting it might conceal a different, not to say ambiguous, sentiment. Accordingly, he queried: 'Are you not unsettled that to emblazon the virtue of honesty in a single woman is to posit that most women are dis-honest?'

'Hard to say,' answered *The Helpful Verger*. 'Equally, to elucidate beyond this, I've to declare that although the masonry is ancient, the revered designation is relatively new. Customarily, the church went by the title of *The Wandering Judaean*.'

'Say more,' pressed the interested wayfarer.

'Lamentable to avouch, I'm not able any more to call to mind the legend or its associated history. Near to the central aisle, however, the visitor may purchase a leaflet, comprising popular historical facts-and-figures. Ordinary guidance that I myself provide is more functional. Wherefore, permit me to advise you the simplest way. Pursue awhile your present course. Thereupon, first turn left, afterwards right. Behold! – it rears-up to the fore. Impossible to miss! Even so, perchance you've timed your hour unwisely, seeing as a spiritual service is about to begin. Someone's funeral, I seem to recall.'

With this advice delivered, the not-very-tall Ebenezer partly walked partly waddled his way awkwardly to the brow of the knap.

But minutes later, the solitary itinerant espied outside the ecclesial *sleeping-place* a sculpted, wooden, sheltering architrave, accompanied below by an ingeniously-constructed wide, rectangular gate. Peculiarly, said barrier could be pushed well and hard-about, thereby fostering the impression that the *lychgate* could *swing-to* for an entire circle, if manhandled sufficiently. Readily coping with the unusual entrance, whilst also surreally-unaware as to how, Joshua drew nearer to his goal.

From a location within the edifice emanated there now the muted sound of singing. Afterwards, briefly, a weighty silence befell, ere yielding to the stentorious report of unexpected good news. Thereafter multiple voices iterated a joint response.

Discernible within the broad cemetery, complementing and surrounding the church as a whole, ranged there now a beautifully mown, richly-verdurous lawn. Observable in addition were two straight-rows of conspicuous yew-trees, along with a mélange of headstones and a grave freshly-dug. Close to several tombstones, moreover, modest posies of flowers visibly lay, together with votive-notelets incorporating remembrances, not to say expectations entertained (here and there) for a future reunion. Nigh unto a spotless headstone, arrestingly betided a disquietingly-pacing solitary, tall, angular man of mature years, evidencing a spine stooped plus shoulders bent. Said notable desolate soul was weeping and sobbing.

Beholding him distraught, the dutiful Joshua became discomfited, scared lest he himself be regarded as an intruder, given his proximity to one so palpably riven by woe, in truth stricken by grief. Even so, bowing thoughtfully to honour the sacred burial-place, he then laid his opened hand across the mourner's inclined frame, afore asserting with candour: 'My name is Joshua. Granted that, prior to now, we have never met, greatly mindful I am of your distress, hoping in truth to attend to what pierces your heart, agitates your soul. Perceive here this pew, here neath the ancient tree. Verily, here we may rest: withal openly you may talk to me of your loss, your suffering besides.'

Though temporarily taken aback, the obviously disconsolate, sorrowful soul counted it not amiss that a stranger had thus gatecrashed his occluded world, accepting wholeheartedly instead his earnest compassion. 'All right, then. My name is Tobias. Only, Joshua, call me Toby – please. Actually, doing as you say, it may assist; likewise, divulging the essentials pertaining to my grief. Although, patient be, should I but get, only so far. Doleful I feel, and guilty withal. Aught that may befall may be well deserved.'

'Wholly in your own time,' urged Joshua, heedfully and quietly.

Unhurriedly, seated upon the bench, once more the man began.

'Notwithstanding I chose to marry,' acknowledged Tobias, 'I did not truly divine my own mind. Even though eclectically intelligent, I was by no means conversant with the ways of the world – principally, with the role of sexuality in human affairs. I was the offspring of a familial upbringing, fundamentally linked thereby to a decisive-ancestral, genetic-legacy. Between heart and will, emotion and intent, there lay a disconnect. Again, time itself, abjuring nearness, presented apartness, proffering a proclivity for seclusion. Yet, sombrous cloud engaged one day with plenteous rays of aureate sun: a beauteous arc of myriadfold colours bent and blazed in the sepulchral but brightening sky. A child was born. Withal, I remained ruminative, habitually unsure apropos my character and calling: full-hearted feelings time after time went astray, actuating beyond preference or command. Barrenness of soul grew within. Ironically, I felt so alone, so unknown: so unloved. Outwardly, just the same, it seemed I was not alone, and certainly I was (howbeit not fully) known; yes, and categorically loved. Indeed; indeed. Neuroses though of hollowness persisted, delving within, bewildering sorely: whence, fifteen years later, I separated from the precious woman, even who had mothered my child – so often who'd been undeniably tolerant and forbearing. Try I did then, but all too ineptly, to find love elsewhere. Abandoned, my erstwhile wife likewise sought to normalise her neoteric state of affairs, experiencing limited success. Unhappily, after a period of time, alas she suffered a malaise, becoming seriously unwell. Nonetheless, she appeared to rally in a reassuring reprieve; yet, by and by anew she succumbed to the dire malady that'd previously imperilled her failing health. Tholing the conflict of needful surrender of soul with the body's striving for very breath – and in the end this conflict lost and done – she fatefully, of necessity, died…'

Protesting this finality – offered as though it be a voluntary, formal confession, the penitent being implicated in her premature demise, if unintended in his mind – Tobias mournfully stared at Joshua. Patent in the hyaloid stare of his eyes, umbraging vision and judgement, was the myopic, faraway look of misery – guilt, sorrow – bleakness; an awful regret. 'She died,' he repeated.

The listener glanced to the ground and sighed soulfully; then, once more, took the other's lonely regard of grief into his own vulnerable self.

'Nonetheless, Joshua,' continued Tobias, 'I (woeful to relate) was not there, not as she passed away, howbeit, mere minutes there-after I gazed down upon her now-lifeless frame; her figure fully vested; her familiar face – oftentimes radiant with smile, else elevated notion, intrinsic optimism, or, simple spirited-determination – conspicuously now drained of life, pale, worn with effort: most assuredly hers, if devoid of quickening, veritably, of any kind – be it of spirit or soul. She had departed. Whatever place she inhabited, no more within her corpse did she dwell; no more her ceded supine-frame lay bare that an hour before was identity, role, a mission in life. The corporeal presence was there, yet her being had gone. Humbled certainly, I leant over, venerating her forehead with a kiss, perceiving the observable shades of suffering below her once keen and hopeful eyes. But, assuredly, she had gone. There was no denial. Forbye, she was a good woman; a kind woman; really, a woman who, in the espousal of her beloved man, hazarded percase her terrestrial journey; still, fain yes, fain for sure, begetting for him his child, e'er, besides, pursuing energetically her days with endeavour and honour, with valiant, persevering love. Categorically I would not, not indeed have her thus – without life; not so young, unfulfilled, innocent before the derision of life's chaos and randomness, man's rudeness and cruelty; my own poor and selfish giving. She, ah well! – was worth, worth so much more than that. Wherefore now do I grieve: fathoming my relation to the destiny she had – and passing betimes – discerning the while that even now I cannot feel, soothfully, that I should've done, done other than what I did. Peculiarly, what had to be *had to be*. Never, though, never would I have had her dead. I would have her alive, Joshua. Alive!'

Then Tobias fell forward, lowered-head fixedly gripped in shaking hands – sorrowing most copiously. Joshua consoled him, placing an arm about his shoulder, pronouncing quietly this sentiment: 'Listen, dear friend – parted awhile, yes, she be, albeit withal alive she be. Alive. In the day ahead. In rapprochement and innovative relatedness. Undeniably in order and nature different, in dimension and dynamic fashioned anew: the sublimest relation of all; created above and outwith the flickering veil of our fractured vision – and its forever un-knowing; a relation blessed, benign, born of the will and mind, heart and salving of God. Steadfast, espouse such hope; champion the possibility; yield unto this, commending your spirit.'

Joshua hereupon fell silent, conscious scarcely at all of how or from where his words had emanated; just that they'd arisen, not-bidden, yet asseverative; puzzlingly, of the spirit of grace. His new companion looked up, appreciatively. 'Grateful I am for your vision. I will aspire to uphold it within my heart. Strengthen my negligible hope.'

Surreally, upon the resolve of Tobias, drew close now a propitious selection of pilgrimers (in ones and twos and threes) towards them. Descrying them collectively, the emissary of hope beheld a duodecimal sum inclusive of the sorrowful Tobias: a dozen souls disfellowshipped in spirit from the regular and ecclesial sanctuary, their guise overall appearing unsteady and unsure – albeit whose feet (guarded or discalced) did rise as did sink, deservedly, upon the consecrated ground of verdured terrain, the sods and turves which, lain fast, swirled about the cemetery with its unearthed soil and flowers, with its stone orison that pointed obliquely, mystically heavenward.

A little afterwards, moreover, a vigilant Joshua espied that the motley coterie had convened intentionally before him. Upon the sward, a grouping of five rested at his feet. Spouseless, albeit with two young children, a mother;

nigh to them, a heartsore youth upholding his arm within a sling; anent as well, one radiant in her third trimester. Forbye, reclining upon a meshwork (interwoven and tangled) of weighty and torn-off branches were four more: a seasoned workman and his trainee or apprentice, and, adjacent to them, twin adolescent girls. Outwith the latter was a transsexual woman. And, finally, a fragile-seeming fellow 'twixt twenty and thirty.

Came there then into view as well – hurrying, ranging and stomping – a wide-legged lubber-of-an-individual, who, wielding a wide, iron spade, in haste arose above the rear of the mound across the long hollowed-out void, up-shovelled for the forthcoming burial. Nevertheless, the aforementioned – roughish and coarse though he be – uncannily (on being beheld) was straightaway outwith the frame. Natheless, happened there then in the intended-one a singular, avowal in prayer: *through the grace of God shall a spring lamb gambol by that grave.*

Benevolently, Joshua greeted now those few within his view – even if at first taken, quite, quite aback – wondering what to do or to say. Regardless, the one transgendered, possessor of the name of Morwenna, spoke up: 'You are *The Man Who Might Be*. What can you tell us to inspire cheer or hope? After quotidian diversions fade or fail, too soon our lives may feel wildering, unfair, at times cruel beyond our ken. Is there not more, more than this at last to satisfy our souls?'

The lover of *The Modern Feminist*, Rachel; admirer of the *Awkin*, Anne-Gel; beholder of *The Lady With The Long Neck* – signalled within a scatter of sand by the letter 'L' – himself seemed a while to be stunned. Surveying the heavens, Joshua now quested therein – craving for some beatific, empyrean-avail: some configuration of words to convey. Hereupon did he once more behold the company around; whilst in his being did he suitably *centre* himself, the better then to commend the equitableness of providential purpose, the desideration too (at odyssey's end) of abundant glad tidings for all. To those who might discern with the mind, let him venture to purvey apposite refinement of intellection; whilst, for any apprehending with the heart, equivalently reassure via the subliminal percipience of his composure and calm.

'Privileged I feel this day to be here. You honour me with a question sincere and incisive (*which utterance was given expressly to the transsexual*) which assuredly I'll essay to resolve as best I can. We are all equal in this sense: though we are diverse (each being unique) we are born (all of us) of a specialised, kindred race, living participantly in its genetic code, its evolution, and withal its destiny. In that shared vocation we must discern our purpose. So, somewhere within all of us is a child longing to play; a young person wanting to make their mark upon the world; a person ready to parent others in whatever capacity; a handicapped person bravely making good; a vulnerable person transmuting fear to trust; a person experiencing sexual confusion or longing for intimacy, searching for happiness; an elderly person full of years if also foreboding; and yet a figure, too, who (woefully) would wield a sharp-bladed spade and bury forever all hope and goodness and truth. Each of us *aspects* these persons to one another, whilst we strive to discriminate and balance them, and grow towards a consequential fulfilment.'

The one giving utterance paused, drew breath, evoked power from within. Through the hiatus, Morwenna and Sebastian – he was the youth whose arm was in a sling – advanced closer to Martha and Mary, the teenage girls, to recline at their feet. Silence tremulated afresh with words and thoughts issuing therefrom.

'We abide upon a planet, a most beautiful world; albeit, it transpires at times to seem sinister and unkind. Whilst the life it enshrines, it may arrest us in death at any time. Thus do we die. Withal, so do we forfeit our lives, necessarily, to the *Source Of All*. Equally, because life is given to us, why all at once should it be robbed, snatched, taken from us? Since the *Source Of All* may bestow life, then, assuredly, the *Source Of All* may rekindle it; may cast it anew.

'Let us not minimise the power of the cosmos. Even we, upon *Terra Firma*, comprehend it limitedly. All knowledge, moreover, issues from our predilection to observe. Evidentially, we ourselves did not foreknow it, else purpose its operational being. Throughout its own coming we receive it. We relate to it, we participate in it; ever and anon we seek alike to alter, to modify it, strain hard indeed to remedy and co-create – albeit, as well, wantonly to pulverise and obliterate. Added to which, wherever good perdures, then, such good is benedictory, since therein grace is incarnate. Fitting and opportune it be, therefore, that we should demonstrate gratitude to the *Great Giver*. Amen, betoil ourselves to emblazon the *Great Giver* within our lives.'

Here with this avowal occurred a signal from Joseph, the master workman, silently angling his head a little to the left, whilst one eyebrow he raised. Withal, gesturing thus, he upraised his right finger – peradventure, in a gestural nod of agreement or approval towards his apprentice, Stephen.

Instanter, the aforesaid gave a grin, prior to renewing his focus on the crafter of meaning.

'Therefore,' resumed Joshua, 'how should we view this *Great Giver*; this *Source Of All*? Innately, we are dwellers and citizens of *Terra Firma*. It coheres then with who-we-are, our natural identity, to see this *Being Beyond All* as having aspects like our own; not so as to limit this *Being Beyond All* – but, to be inspirited to relate in, and through, soothfully, our terrestrial conditioning; from our special, if indeed also troubled becoming. To facilitate this overview, men and women avail themselves of revered signs and mementoes; sacred symbolic veils – conduits, albeit fallible, for the power of the *Transcending Reality* – membranes of truth via which we may draw closer to the *Source*, which is kindred in creating, yet also in creating other. May our surrender to the *Great Source* and *Giver* be wherefore as to one who shows forth the attributes of (so to aver) our *Motherly Father*: even the *Being* who parents with love, shows principled love to be a reality; *is* love's definition, the supernal definer of, fundamentally, that which is benignly possible. Dare to trust in that love. More: persevere in questioning – what chiefly do we desire for ourselves, those truly whom we treasure and respect, whom largely we have meant – however imperfectly – to love? (*The speaker cast a hurried look towards Tobias.*) Really, should such be our desire for those dear to our hearts – their full promise realised, lastingly, in truth and belonging; being lifted up into the realm of the Divine – then, be assured, the *Heavenly Father* wishes as much and more besides.'

Discernibly, the reiteration of the significant *verbum*, 'love', actuated the maternal Morag devotedly to embrace her two young children, the boy Clifford with his sibling Elspeth.

Continuing, the gospeller forewarned: 'Should you become concerned that there be no life beyond death, open to sense and heart this question: were I myself, miraculously, possessed of the power of God, precisely what should I prefer to have happen – Life or Death? And, strive not withal to become discomfited by hope-denying indices, about which in pitiless reckoning your souls may despair, your hearts reel and stutter. Rather, adhere to the one or two or three: overall, on their departure, verily what would you wish? Believe me now when I declare to you that that which ought to happen – averring how it can happen – assuredly *will* happen. Equally, not in fact because I say it – withal it be the tale I tell – only, rather because the *Fabric* and *Being* of the *Cosmos* empowers it to be so in its capacity and awesome majesty: beyond our knowing, forbye creativity; outwith our negativity and sinfulness. As a result, men and women may be buried in the earth; even so, in the passage of Spring and becoming of souls God's presence is as a plethora of nestlings – a flourishing of flowers – a positive gambol going amongst the graves.'

The faces of Sophie and Gerard – the former pregnant with child, the male with prodigious thought – appeared enraptured with wide-eyed astonishment. Though separated by several feet, the two appeared uncannily at one.

'Lastly,' entreated Joshua, 'labour always to adhere to and celebrate your hope: even if you be unable to prove beyond doubt the realities empowering its triumph. Continue resolute: your beneficent hope is legitimate; pertains indeed to the proud of soul, loving of heart, courageous of spirit; assigning conscience-driven direction to existence. Wherefore, let hope be a star in a night of disillusion; in very bleakness the immortal diamond; withal, in a season of loneliness the beloved's kiss generously blown; as too, in the conflict of the ephemeral, a stirring in the quietude, or quietness among the stir. Decidedly, our power, our sharing. My blessing I bequeath, now unto you.'

The Man Who Might Be stopped, hearkening to the hush wherein he had poured his soul, as if wine into a chalice; a potation for which the provenance must brook no dispute – forbye himself feeling glad, perchance relieved, for the pouring was over – listeners reassured, their selves uplifted, less sundered thereby.

Forthwith, there occurred two incidents wholly at variance with the mood of the gathering. Immediately, beyond and through the southern vestibule, a fervid congregation churned forth: though, not automatically towards the gravel path, ideally leading parishioners to their exit – thereby, too, towards the village of Silninch – but, suspiciously, alongside the area of sward towards and as far as the gathered dozen; also, ineluctably, closer to the declaimer. Strikingly, as the fierce throng fanned outward and forward, its spirited and resolute members soon seemed to identify their objective to be precisely him – Joshua. More than that, rather worse than that, a noticeable proportion of them showed fists brandishing upon to-and-fro upheld arms, generating a commotion *mirabile dictu* to awaken the dead. 'There he is!' together they shouted – to a woman, to a man, veritably a child. 'There he is!'

The other incident to render apart the happy *reverie* of the thirteen chanced to be a further sighting of the hidden creature. Terrestrial though he be, even so he assumed a thickened and fearsome shape appearing from aside the pile of earth – withal flourishing his oblong spade, perturbingly, as a gesturing intended for a dire and terrible enactment, to which a singular finale would lie in the yawning pit so assiduously unearthed. Heatedly then, as the giant and unkempt encloser strode forth towards the broken, wrought-away branches, he called out, 'I know who you are, Joshua, the *Man Who Might Be*! Forbye, your time has come!'

Instanter, as crowd and digger all began to converge – detached by some yard alone – the object of his disfavour descried a disturbingly familiar look upon the face of the wide-pacing, goliathised foe: older certainly; more ravaged, angry, wild; yet, behind the dolour (in part concealed) now glared everywhere the once-loved countenance of Pedram, plougher of waves by a distant shore and born of a far-off time – bethought him, the startled Joshua, disoriented by the immense scope pertaining to his decisive though dreamlike journey. Still, the careworn pilgrim – though feeling riveted by the pain apprehended in that afore-blundering friend – willed not to allow that his terrestrial end had come. At once then did he turn, full-sharply about: succeeding at the very moment that his pursuer was tripped (fortuitously by the tangle, or, peradventure by a scallywag child) in essaying his escape: successfully, behind the ewe trees; speedily, over the wall; impatiently, eschewing the circular gate – festinately, hurriedly – till fled and gone; whereupon, with surprising rapidity, alighted he by the bourn of Silninch – propelled onwards, still onwards even to the awkward gradient out of the village concourse; there slowing his rate as (slewing about) he saw no-one on his tail, only somehow an ever-growing distance from that sinister disownment, with muddle of malcontents determined to conceal him in its bone-littered void.

By and by, then, the village fell away. A calm descended. By grace alone refuge had awhile been found. Amen, and all again made well.

Part the Eleventh: *in which Joshua, retiring, is led away to an asylum for the dying.*

It was late in the afternoon. Joshua was walking along a lane adorned intermittently with wisps of green. It had led him to the ridge of a hill, extensive and broad. Along its height he beheld an open vale, distant and wide, as well as a greyish sea-scape from where disembogued a sleeve of estuary, elbowing in-land; while, from the curving ridge he noted too, outwith the populated valley, a dulcetly-embowed topography rising benignly; although hardly magnolious or grandiose – no, but picturesque, panoramic, calmly beautiful – yet also revealing elements of wildness and wilderness.

He'd promenaded, he surmised, a distance of several furlongs: forbye, with minimal society affording him company, other than the occasional cry of a curlew, the sight of a kestrel hovering in the air, or – winging in a tumult – clacking pheasant scuttling-in-a-whirr o'er field-gate to meadowland above road or hedge. The fugitive sensed how his rhythm now was more slow, indicatory of a consistent amble, allowing progress wholly through extended time and heightened effort. Howbeit – experiencing strain as he was – his heart felt good. The glorious expanse of the view uplifted his spirits, with a stirring zephyr serving as a tonic to his stiffly framed and aching figure. Well had he done forbye to fabricate a wooden stick, the worn stem of which, since split at the top, yielded suitable space for his thumb in the V-shape thus coined – an availment making his advance feel less toilsome, albeit neither vigorous nor decisive.

Just the same, predictably before long there came a stage to pause, enough properly to recover. Joshua, apprehending he was faltering, propitiously alighted upon a rickety, makeshift seat (located at the foot of a great and burly beech) granting him the available heat of the still-glowing sun, supposing its ever-petering crept imminent and near. Indubitably, his soul could enjoy a while the star's dwindling-blaze, his body moreover the mild mellifluously-wafting breeze. Indeed, an almost almond-like aroma of yellowish, setaceous gorse enabled him to relax, virtually to a drowsiness – if without the tempered *quietus* illustrative of actual sleep. Thought he awhile in his soul how pleasant this rich, verdant pasturage did seem, bearing its marginal moors with meadows aplenty everywhere to hand. Desultory, inquisitive sheep came grazing in sloping fields; forbye, nigher now piebald, placid cows – hithering, thithering – were toilsomely tearing the grass with their tongues uncurled. Inclined he felt now to wonder what *The Modern Feminist* would herself have made of it – irregardless of the others.

Undeniably, as long moments maundered by o'ertaking his mind, Joshua discerned within his soul how this agrestic locale was a very paradise; that it was – what with the gardens he'd noticed as he'd passed before Silninch, and the wide walls all draped with pink and purple pods bursting forth, and the lilac flora spreading out across the sprawling espaliers, and all the many flowers and shrubs so full of colour and aroma – veritably a domain; a realm, a locale within which a man might live out his days in contentment and calm. If only. Naturally, if only there had not happened what had happened. Miles anterior. The churchyard, the crowd, the condemnation and calling-out, the character with the cudgel-of-a-spade, the precipitate dash away from them all.

If only. Amen: neither had he been blind – on the mounting trek to this forgiving, this modest summit – to nature's ambiguous mysteries. He'd seen the torn ear of the rabbit; the badger lying dead in a ditch; the weary nag with a blanket to fend off the chill; the raven picking, then ravaging the raw carrion – the cadaver of some once-animate creature; the lamb having one of its limbs permanently raised; the cow that sneezed between forage and puddle; the blight that blanched the olive-green foliage and the yellowy-virent leaves of some oak struggling in the hedge; even, too, the lumps of growth on bulging trees, or else the parasitic ivy that wound here, scrambled there, all about the arboreal life, striven the while, yet stretching ever upward.

As long, however, as the sinking sun retained its mellowing warmth – the earlier heat yet pervading his body with a delicious and nourishing glow – the milieu seemed secure, safe, veritably fit for lids to droop and eyes to close, for slumber to come in time, in time; at last. Only, with suddenness then to be roused – woken again! Discomfitingly, to suffer an alien *touch* aspread and around his arms, two manoeuvring strangers steering him forward – as he, admittedly, doddered with pardonable bafflement; anon, his eyes apart, steadily if slowly focusing to find, perturbing to relate, the panorama had gone! – gone the far flung sea, gone the flow of the river and the sprawl of the grassy meads, gone the lovely warmth of its delicious glow.

His eyes truly, at last were open.

Immediately in front of him there rose up the massive porticoed entrance of a stately-looking building, towards which across tiny chips of stone he was being guided relentlessly, now bereft of escape. After a while, too, he noted the name of the place, emblazoned on a brass plate, to one side of a columned ingress of classical design: it read, 'Nadir House'. Two women of means, in their late-middle years and neatly attired, were speaking volubly about their mutual view of life.

'Well look,' asserted the taller, 'the whole of life is simply a game! It's survival of the fittest. The more games one learns to play, the greater some capacity to exploit another person in favour of oneself – and, of course, everyone we prefer. Which same stance underpins international affairs and successful politics.'

'I know, I know,' responded the other. 'Obvious, surely. Only, one has a problem with Rodders. After all, how would you feel should your own son want to become a vicar?'

'Amused, I suppose. Not worried, certainly. Consider: vicars nowadays espouse all sorts of games! Perhaps always did. Besides, I've observed many a civilised vicarage!'

Promptly, the comfortable ladies now began to walk away. Now too, Joshua beheld here – opposite the portal and on the gravelled frontage bordering – patently a badly-parked highly-polished metallic-red van. Over its side-panels were painted, in startling saffron, the words: LEFT OVERS; while, etched in italics beneath, appeared the proclamation of husbandry: *Do Right With Still-Fresh Food.*

A voice called out: 'Shift that flaming van to the rear entrance!'

The cry emanated from a powerful woman, robust and matronal, who had her victim's dextral arm gripped in the vice-like grasp of her closed fingers, who charged the junior colleague (gripping the sinistral limb equally tight), 'Put this one in the spare room at the front, below that noisy old tramp, Blind Jack.'

The not-entirely-willing newcomer to 'Nadir House' noted in due course how he'd ascended a handful of steps to an asylum – in this case, a dignified mansion for the aged – being nudged thereupon through a hallway towards a circular flight of low stairs, quite near to which there appeared a vaulted chamber – referred to as, *The Chapel Of Quiet* – through the wide doors of which Joshua was next able, briefly, to see an emaciated figure in a wheelchair reading out loud from a collection of ancient, once-famous scriptures: 'In the beginning was the earth a formless void.' *In the beginning*, whispered Joshua to himself, *in the beginning*. Yet, as he departed the primary, parqueted level, echoes of merriment were sounding from a flock-papered salon, where, gazing about, he detected therein a circle of elderly folk, all attending to a boxed screen of images, broadcast in black and white in relentless motion. Several onlookers were stuttering and cackling at some source of mirth or apparent hilarity. A personable young man, who'd replaced the stout warden of the institution, chuckled similarly, then knowingly confided: 'Fear not, I've viewed this programme before. The painstaking initiate at an adult literary-class is trying to complete his composition of exactly 200 words. He manages 198, only then, alas, dries up, being properly flummoxed. An idea, however, suddenly occurs to him. Picking up his pen, he appends beneath, waggishly, the two words: *The – End*. Even now it brings a smile to my face!'

Notwithstanding, Joshua was in a mood more philosophical than comedic. Across just seconds of footfall he'd been encouraged to move from *beginning* to *end*; directed to wonder whether this virtual-juxtaposition did retain some covert or occult meaning – synchronicity potentially of recognisable gravity.

A new floor of the premises materialised at last. In some other previous mental mode or reach of time, this upheld climber belike would've owned more critical cognisance of his atypical milieu; he'd surely have protested at being commanded by strangers to enact their bidding without let or hindrance. Instead, unusually, he was more attentive to the unabashed dissonance sounding from another room with its door ajar: a melody it was that indicated some sort of resonating echo, albeit one he was, alas, unable to trace in memory or moment. He entertained a discomfiting sensation – even whilst being taken to his unfamiliar home by those not familial – how this particular *tune* might have been played and heard over and over again, across years and years, decades even, as folk aged and withered and died, and some withal, ere long, likewise to grow old and wither and die; ad nauseam, this same brassy refrain played without remorse, mockingly, as real life sped by according to its own lesser span and sooner ending.

A further door then opened, slowly and screakily, permitting its own especial quartet of restricted views: to the barred window opposite – via which, admittedly, the sky could be detected, tops of trees be glimpsed; also, under the formidable fenestration, towards a solitary bed; again, to a mantelpiece over which was secured an ancient, ornately-decorated mirror; last, towards the tassel-edged armchair posited to the doorway's larboard-side. Nothing beyond though seized the attention of the resident-to-be.

'Now, come along, love,' urged the female nurse (unrelentingly) who'd been accompanying him from the time of his arrival. 'Come along.'

'For sure, it's a nice room you've been given,' encouraged the younger attendant, whilst helping Joshua to disrobe.

His colleague pulled back the blanket and white coverlet, inviting the unwilling guest to take to his bed, exhorting him: 'We'll get you comfy, love, oh yes, in no time. You're a lucky man to get this place.'

'My name is Joshua,' protested the infirm wanderer of endless days and weird locales foregone. 'Do stop calling me *love!*'

'All right, dear. Okay okay, okay. There's no reason to get your thermals in a twist. Call me Thora, if you like. This is young Rodney. Only been with us a month. Try to be considerate. Try to be patient. Not like, for example, the one upstairs. No, no, no love – not like him. Oh, but the racket that man makes!'

Rodney swung the patient's legs round and onto the bed; pulled the sheet and covers of blanketing up to somewhere near half-way up his arms and chest. 'Don't worry, you'll settle in soon enough. Myself, you – both of us, we need to get the hang of this place. Don't worry, Josh, don't worry. Ignore Blind Jack, should you hear him shouting. Guess he'll not be with us much longer. Thora will hand you your supper later. Just relax. Have a nap if you want.'

Two members of the species separated and parted from the third. The latter fell to weighing up the diametric words received, whilst he'd been offhandedly ushered towards his cell of restraint: *beginning* and *end*. Undeniably, he'd acquired several ideas during his existence to suggest that any genesis took place a long while before either his natural species or its planet, *Terra Firma* – to say naught of its solar-system – had come into being. In fact, billions of years ago. Usually, souls nowadays strove with scepticism to conceive of any deity in existence around an historical beginning. Who knew exactly what God was and when God began? Should there be a God at all. Verily, to the wanderer on his theological sojourn, pertinently his co-terrestrials found it problematic to conceive of God as if *out there; up there*: watching aloof, participating in an exercise belike devoid of point within a world laden with woes, copious sundering, plus ubiquitous wailing.

Furthermore, ought the *Word* and *Reality* of God be used not to denote a phenomenon at the dawn of time, but, conversely, a miracle coming at time's coda, time's end? Again, mightn't the Universe (conceivably, Multiverse) verily be apprehended as waxing into and towards God. Cogitably, God was the Omega-point over one denominated Alpha. Even, possibly, Alpha and

Omega were juxtaposed on the coin's rim: interconnected or overlapping. Comparably, time and karmic law might be viewed as circular, theoretically, spherical. Wherefore, God might be the core of life – from which and to which the cosmos emanated then returned.

Words – words – words. Ah, too many, the man reflected: even indeed as prayer-books, likewise, could be too full of words – requiring any intimate rapport to be inhibited by the cold of intellectual effort and mental complexity. Should God exist, whilst *The Man Who Might Be* naturally comprise an aspect, an energy, an outpouring of that reality; well, as terrestrial, it behoved him to accommodate the 'flow' of his *actualisation*; albeit, augment it besides with what openness he be able to summon or suffer for the beingness of the whole; its *Source*; its *End*: its *Core*. Again, obviously alert to the present moment, he was likewise spiritually bidden to trust that his voice asserted the truth, even whilst it tried to clarion what its blazoner considered, candidly, to be elemental: unto which his soul aspired at its best and bravest; in other words, purposeful fulfilment – the resolution of deficient love and the rendering complete of ephemeral justice.

Joshua, adhering to the matter as best he could, plainly now became distracted. Spotting on the floor beside his bed – where Rodney had been standing – both a remnant of paper and a broken pencil, he succeeded in picking up both. Along the latter he read the letters 'R–o–d', whilst across the almost white paper a creative title: 'Uplift of Wonder'. Straightaway, Joshua brought to mind an image in the cemetery of Morag's daughter, Elspeth, who'd been held spellbound by a blue-tit upon the wall greedily feasting off some crumbs – in truth, rather more than by Joshua's words! The pilgrim smiled. He was mindful, just the same, of the report narrated briefly by *The Good Mother*, dealing with some deadly famine. Pausing only a short while, he lifted the pencil and wrote down the following.

The blue-tit's head darting side to side, bib of black, probes and peeps where the bread crumbs gather. Avine precision-worker in miniature coat of colour, fine blaze of yellow, tiny huddle of detail that garners the vast galaxies within the startle of its breast. Before winging away. Into the stripped limbs of bushes interlocking. Hidden again. Sheer shock of it gone. Spell gifted – heaven's wonder – beheld within seconds of history. Howbeit scant hours away, flies crawl about a child's hollowed face, each fly another child finding its end must come; end endured.

Somehow. Over it e'en thought may not be borne: yet ought. Must. Must. To force the choice. Between the find of the unbelieving scientific mind: that such power as ranges out of nothing – through rolling maelstroms of stars and systems, and all the synergies they declare – be yet insufficient to deal with the troubled fate of one child. Or, the hope and salve of the believing scientific mind: that an ultimate energy of cosmic expanse – in unison with the love that beats best in man – could, should and will resolve the thwarted outcome of the one child. And therefore of every child. And therefore of every soul lost to evil, malady, injury, the incompleteness of its just condition. The choice. That mean and heartless spirit, trapped in the pride of its un-imagination. Or, notably, that stout-hearted spirit, humble in its recognition of the great power without, modest in allowing for a love more potent than its own. Here then the child looks-up and sees. There! The yellow bell of the blue-tit ringing in its feathered belfry, the bird bright before its half-hurtle into an elsewhere of air – an infinity of yonder. An innovative realm of mercy and miracle.

The writer sighed. He felt drained. Nonetheless, he returned Rodney's property to the floor, being careful to slide both items beneath the bed. Thereafter, he found himself asserting, interiorly: *Aim to be benign unto others. Show humility. Talk truthfully. Live sincerely. Whatever religion does or does not aspire to be, a genuinely spiritual life is assuredly not a game; rather, it is the application of conscious creativity to an engagement with all persons on a mutual footing: the other is not a mere object to be exploited for personal gain. Naught else is required than the eschatological elevation of the other as no less inherently valuable than oneself.* He thought then again of the dissident missionary, declaring under his breath: *He would not play the game. He loved benignity. He told the truth, so his arms were outstretched.*

Whilst musing upon these matters, again Joshua was awoken to the tedium of his predicament: not merely by the ineluctable shouting from the floor above, but indeed (and gratingly) by the fingered tattoo at his door, along with the presence thereafter of the unflinching Thora – actively fielding her tray, as she dealt her observation (cast as an enquiry): 'Not asleep, then, love? Good. Look here now, enjoy a warmish mug of tea with slivers of toast; yes, the nice and colourless sort. Notice, too, your solid-dollop of purply conserve on the edge of the plate. Sit up properly, dear. That's right. Goodness, let's give those squashed pillows a shake. There – that's better. Be careful now. Don't spill the tea. 'Fraid I've no teaspoon – still, you can whisk and stir in the sugar with your plastic knife – see. There we go.'

The recipient of this attention gestured as best he could that he chose neither to eat nor to drink, essaying to articulate words to convey his message. Reassuringly, this time he succeeded.

'All right, love, all right. I'll take it away. Hardly surprising you've no appetite – considering upstairs Blind Jack night and day is yelling his head off. You'd suppose we were nudging the *bodach* to an early death! Truth is, any resort to putting-down a resident within *Nadir House* is *verboten*; forbidden. Even so, maximum medication is allowed and given to him by our trained staff. Regardless, at times I'm curious as to whether he's doing his damnedest to elicit extra sympathy; maybe being outright provocative: absolutely vexing and bad-mannered, not at all mindful of the average inmate – apologies, I mean average *patient* – a joke our nurses repeat if overworked! Of course, you'd concur that I never said that and you never heard it! Eh, love? That's right, that's right. You have yourself a nice long snooze. That's it. Catch up tomorrow. To start, however, it'll be a trainee. Morning guard! Sweet dreams, love, sweet dreams.'

Fruitlessly, as the brusque and brawny Thora swept out of the room, the exhausted inmate strove to press home his complaint at the continued usage of the term 'love'; the lamentable, vacuous failure to engage with him as a real person, bred with an individual moniker – overwhelmed by a welter of emotion, withal being imprisoned in a dubious place among quirky and eccentric people, managing a precarious end. 'Don't – don't you *dare* refer to me as *love!*' in truth was what he tried to scream. No words emanated, however, from his opened mouth, as his momentarily upraised frame forthwith slumped-back, full into the pillows where he found himself wheezing and respiring with effort and frustration. Intermittently, withal, the terrestrial-upstairs did audibly moan and groan: decidedly, not without volume or sundering, full heart-rending cry.

Part the Twelfth: *in which Joshua, perforce, bids farewell to* The Faithful Fighter, *ere long resolutely setting forth.*

Joshua was alone. He had a sense, a strong sense, that the unpopular sufferer, living in the room directly above his own, wasn't merely some dubious occupant gallingly bereft of sight, duly creating a rumpus and for whatever reason (discernibly several) but, if history be known, likewise his whilom acquaintance, the now elderly terrestrial whom he took to be his friend, the erstwhile virtuoso who bore the appellation, old Jake: in spirit, conceivably, the one-time combatant who'd wrestled till dawn the agent of the Beyond, refusing to let go despite infirmity or cataract; despite incommodity in being alive itself. Indeed, indeed – Jacob! Evidently did the present-day arrival to Nadir's number now judge – albeit again unsettled, agitated, struggling hard to summon nerve and sinew, reaching up his hands imploringly: 'License me now, one more time, oh Heavenly Father! One more time! Yet purely to reach, climb those stairs, hence be at his side; withal, avail a valiant hero in his dire distress; aye, this rueful servant, similarly, in his own. Openly, though, do I submit this request; it may be denied. Howbeit, I ask with longing, passion, sincerity.'

Amen, so it was, if more some miracle in the creating, surreally, suddenly, that the disciple intuited himself aloft from the mattress, borne beyond the uppermost stair, and, incongruously, facing the formidable door patently flung open to the sightless man's room. He declaimed with a smile: 'I supposed I might trip you up, you helpless old fiddler!'

'Nice to see you, too – *old* Joshua!' Somehow the words took shape. After all, albeit the man's *spiritus* quickened, clearly it was with singular effort that the worn figure struggled to continue. Yet continue he did. And, to be sure, with remarkable coherence.

'Assuredly, should I counsel with candour, dear brother – you'll perceive here a dearth of mind or zest, of fine fettle or face preferred. For all that, I'm consoled to find you here, *deo volente*, shortly to witness my life's end. Yes, Joshua, you – *The Man Who Might Be.*'

Visibly exhausted by the endeavour of speech, the pertinacious communicator ceased, yet straightaway added: 'Ere I should forget, some local journal, take a glance – over at the dresser. Rodney was summarising. Some reassurance, your mind at rest.'

Flummoxed, for sure, the additional and apparently not-altogether-beguiling incumbent of 'Nadir House' compliantly detected to his right a modest chest. Here – upon the studiously-polished surface indicated – a narrow stock of printed papers patently lay, the principal item of which was bannered with the headline: 'Gravedigger Arrested For Impersonating Fisherman!'

Even so, the newly informed resident appeared now more sober than sanguine, musing enigmatically: 'To echo an old friend – percipient boatman named Tom; withal, if I recall fairly – *If it's to be believed; if it's to be believed.* Just the same, I defer in judgement to an omniscient Father. Ere long, anyhow, Jacob, I too must depart. Wherefore does it matter to me that I testify: fellow pilgrim, I am indebted to you; to the vitality of your example. So much have you endured, stalwartly embracing your faith in the *One Beyond*, who yet dwells among us. Wilderingly, the blight of your faded, stolen sight, has gifted you with a notable discrimination and singular humility: never have you abandoned God's grace and purpose. Honoured I feel to have met you; inspired to celebrate – however briefly and brokenly – your presence and legacy.'

The ghost in the blind man flickered; but blazed again.

'Adherence to what is right must be prioritised. Again, maintain in conscience that God alone is the final arbiter. There be none more meet, more noble to whom we should forego the gift of our being than the *Ultimate Mystery*, of whom you and I alike have been vouchsafed a beholding – a gift of knowing; some moiety in the co-creating, for thus were we created, yes for sure, so to do. Let it be in justice; aye, but more, in loving-kindness.'

'So I strive, Jacob, so I strive.'

'Here, now,' replied the other. 'I am in pain. Grant me your hand.'

Forthwith, straining to conjure a voice, Joshua lent to the blind combatant's white and clammy palm the warmth (similarly diminishing) of his own, venturing: 'Our *Beloved Father's* is the victory, amen, now and for aye. With humility, I look forward to our meeting within the pleroma: at the Serenity of Realisation. Here, you have my love, even as you enact – as destiny dictates – your corporeal leave. Farewell, oh Jacob – quintessentially *The Faithful Fighter*! Fare well!'

There and then did it feel to the utterer that he of a sudden could hear the uplifting clarion of a trumpet-blare, heroically rippling its aria of future envisioning. Whereupon pathos did with triumph blend. Sorrow, too, with steadfast hope.

Feeling then most highly esteemed, Joshua, albeit his fingers sclerotic, reverently closed-shut each eye of his wilderness-companion, fellow traveller in the weft and warp of time. And turned. Turned to the open door – thereupon to tread-soft the flight of stairs well-nigh absurdly as far as his room. Though not, veritably, to his actual bed.

Instead, whilst being bereaved (though not wholly bereft) spiritedly he began to seize, then pull at the two blankets, cumbrously doubling them, twice, thrice, into presentable squares. Likewise thereafter pillow-slips with topmost-sheet, all were passably folded. Little by little, stiffly were these then dropped upon the embowed arm of the winged chair. Lumberingly, achingly he yanked, then tore at his clothes, situating them – even as he relucted at his etiolated condition – adjacent to the pile already made. Staggering, he managed (somehow, somehow) up from the mattress to haul fully its separate sheet; withal – before wrapping it about his enfeebled, now-withered form – to upraise the whole bundle and put it at the foot of his bed. Nakedness unnoticeable, he dodderingly flumped into the vacant chair. Whereupon had he then to wait: wait for vision, dream, morning star – peculiar, mystical fate. Nevertheless, day's star rose upon the asylum soon enough.

An unfamiliar attendant entered Joshua's room close to the echo of six. Pushing aside the door, she detected the noticeably vacant bed along with the folded clothes plus bedding redundant. Discernible, too, was the long framed-mirror, fastened above the mantelpiece, its mirrored-image visible within, incorporating the only bolstered-chair neath a swathe of linen – as of a winding shroud – lying rolled upon it. The scenario wasn't as anticipated. Possibly an employee had made a mistake. Else, the occupant of this room, similar to the one above, may've precipitately exited his life at a moment during the course of the night, notwithstanding she'd not (surprisingly) been informed. Conceivably, he'd had assigned to him the other man's cell; one, that being higher, permitted a more extended prospect. Now, having brought a greenish tumbler of water, plus an orange-thimble of tablets, she instanter banged-to-a-close the open door, hieing-off to seek and enlighten her several colleagues.

Joshua stirred. Might he even now be alive? He rose to his feet, letting fall in doing so the winding-cloth, which, all too briefly, he'd tried to doze within. He drew closer to the mirror, staring into it. Doing so, something very curious happened. There slowly began to issue a substantiating apparition, impossible initially to identify: a ghost-like presence nonetheless in the chamber's weird, fluid reflection. Across a trice, no whit more, the seer panicked. Then he knew what he must do. And, singularly, summoned the wherewithal to do it.

Immediately below the mantle, by the foot of the long-disused fireplace, a copper scuttle happened to reside, about which had been perfunctorily deposited a run-of-the-mill circlet of crisp and wizened flowers. Now, in little more than an instant, *The Man Who Might Be* had hoisted high the emptied pewter-hod nearly an arm's length into the air – next, onto the mirror brought it down hard, shattering the wondrous glass into so many awkward fragments; divers pieces to puzzle and confuse those that might seek a true replication, albeit now who must confront only a cluttered icon.

* * * * * *

Wildering to relate, even as the glass broke and fissured, the pilgrim – nigh to the uplift of the morn – commenced wakefulness, disquieted and be-numbed in the aridity of a remote though recollected land, visibly translated in time and place from the domicile and country into which he had stumbled. He was shivering, involuntarily. Of a fire, vestige-embers had almost died.

The revenant roused himself. With eyes wide-open, anon he spotted beside his feet a bottle (now tilted-over) providing a modest quantum of liquid slopping in the end lying in the sand. Committedly, Joshua stirred the dying embers with a nearby stick – blew at the rekindling of the violet and vermilion – until, once more, a half-workable flame firmed, then wavered. Thereupon, he upheld the bottle to the small and lambent tongue, ill-descrying its watery libation to be dyed a most unusual and brilliant, luminous blue. Plainly bemused, Joshua deliberated in his mind over what might constitute its source. Envisioning him, just the same, as being tempted to drink of its remains would decidedly be ill-judged. Also, now alert, the philosopher was unsure apropos the probable outcome. Unbeknownst, he'd already utilised time, dreamily, in a state of languorous somnolence. Upraising, thence, the glassed flagon in his hand, Joshua poured forth the remaining blue onto the tremulous blaze. Nevertheless, naught occurred save a whimsy of fire ceasing, its charred detritus spluttering and sizzling, traces of colour utterly extinguished. No anticipated, ascending column of rainbow-combustion did pitch unto the heavens, percase betokening the strangeness of his unconscious peregrination. Even the thought – illustrative of some random, vagary of the mind – became here an idea at war with necessity; with essential, felicitous, mundane-exigency appertainable to the hour. Discernibly, here was the juncture, the hour, the second – not to cerebrate, but to act!

Bundling his blanket, flattened and rolled, deep into his bag, the conscious itinerant descried to his relief a sizeable, uneaten orange. This, hereupon, adroitly he cleft with his bodkin halving the flavorous edible. Plunging his teeth therein, voraciously he sucked the fruit dry. It was deliciously, reassuringly lush and sweet!

Close to the recommencement of his journey, the lone walker here uplifted his gaze, espying serenely the heavens, surveying leisurely the silvern, shining stars within the vaulted ebony-blue, above. Raising his hands open-palmed, he petitioned thus:

'Heavenly Father, our Source and Trusted End, may you be revered above all that is. May what you desire attain its fruition; assuredly in times to come, as well as in this era besides. Have mercy upon us in our neediness, meeting our weakness and wrongdoing with compassion and forbearance. Assess us in truth as we strive to become. Help us to decry the unkind: endeavouring neither to call forth evil upon others, nor to be troubled by the allure of its dominion.'

Trustingly, assuming silence once more, Joshua lowered his arms. Shepherding felicitous words unto and into the open-pen of prayer required dedication and poetic endeavour. In time, an easier, forthright, more familial style might occur. For now, his imploration would suffice. Now the time had come to implement its intent.

Joshua beheld again the shaping of the fires in the sky, discerning how the existing breeze directed the final flourishing of faltering smoke. The diurnal renewal was close at hand. Darkness conjured would soon dispel. The philosopher set his pace straightway to the task – but only then of a sudden to stop. He fancied, but fleetingly, that he'd heard a noise, a rustle?

Silence.

There was no-one.

Wherefore he began resolutely to stride forth.

Then again, the man knew that in this season, every now and then, a brine-battling barque, starting out from the nearest port, must take in on its passage an island denominated, Patmos. Further, he'd been told of a young poet living there garnering even now authentic renown. Journeying resumed, the predicant knew now that he needed to meet him. With hope, let the future bring what it would – both in this life and in the life to come. Amen to that, he said out loud. Amen to that.